The Dog Across the Lake

❖ 🐾 ❖ 🐾 ❖ 🐾 ❖

Krista Davis

BERKLEY PRIME CRIME
New York

BERKLEY PRIME CRIME
Published by Berkley
An imprint of Penguin Random House LLC
penguinrandomhouse.com

ISBN: 9780593436974

First Edition: January 2024

Printed in the United States of America
1   3   5   7   9   10   8   6   4   2

*To all my readers who wish
they lived in Wagtail.*

The poor dog, in life the firmest friend.
The first to welcome, foremost to defend.

—Lord Byron

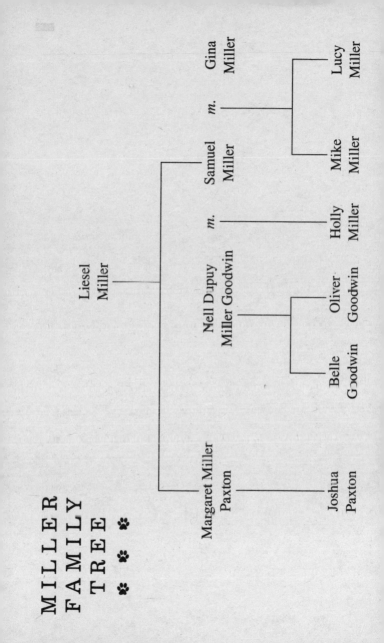

MILLER
FAMILY
TREE
🐾 🐾
🐾 🐾

Liesel
Miller

Margaret Miller
Paxton

Nell Dupuy
Miller Goodwin

Samuel
Miller

m.

Gina
Miller

Joshua
Paxton

Belle
Goodwin

Oliver
Goodwin

m.

Holly
Miller

Mike
Miller

Lucy
Miller

CAST OF CHARACTERS

Holly Miller
   Trixie—Holly's Jack Russell terrier
   Twinkletoes—Holly's calico cat
Nell DuPuy Miller Goodwin—Holly's mother
Holmes Richardson—Holly's boyfriend
Ben Hathaway—Holly's former boyfriend
Oma (Liesel Miller)—Holly's grandmother
   Gingersnap—Oma's golden retriever
Sam Miller—Oma's son and Holly's father
   Lucy and Mike—Sam's children
Margaret Miller Paxton—Oma's daughter
   Joshua Paxton—Margaret's son
   Radar—Joshua's dog
   Dana Carrington—Joshua's girlfriend
Mr. Huckle—Inn employee
Zelda York—Inn employee
Shelley Dixon—Inn employee
Sergeant Dave Quinlan (Officer Dave)
Sergeant Hayward
Nate—flower delivery guy

GUESTS OF THE SUGAR MAPLE INN

Carole Hobson
Frank Burton
Judy Davis
Brendan Hayward
Paul and Ted Mellor

One

Few people in Wagtail were surprised by the news that sleeping with a pet in your bed has health benefits for the human and the animal. It reduces stress and increases REM sleep in humans. The animals feel better, too, because it emulates sleeping with their packs.

When I rolled over in the middle of the night and Trixie snuggled up to me, that thought drifted across my mind. So it came as no big surprise when I woke in the morning and stared straight into the eyes of a dog.

But it wasn't Trixie! The dog had one of those smiling mouths that turn up at the corners. He looked genuinely happy to see me awake. He reminded me of a border collie, but I suspected he was a mix. His fur was long, mostly a reddish-gold color. But it was white on his chest and paws, and a white blaze traveled up the center of his face. His tail swished across the down comforter in a joyous rhythm.

He was probably less pleased when I sat up and asked, "Who are you?"

I stroked his head. Oddly, neither my Jack Russell terrier, Trixie, nor my nosy calico kitty, Twinkletoes, seemed upset by his presence. *They must know him*, I thought.

He looked vaguely familiar. I checked his collar. It had no tags. I scowled at the thought of an irresponsible owner. Maybe he'd had two collars and one of them slipped off?

I lived in an apartment on the top floor of the Sugar Maple Inn on Wagtail Mountain. There was a dog door discreetly hidden under a shelf in my dining room. It led to a little-used hidden back staircase that ended two floors down in the private family kitchen, which had a dog door that led to the main lobby of the inn. So it was possible that he belonged to a guest of the inn and had wandered his way to my apartment. Or maybe he'd tracked Trixie's or Twinkletoes's scent. Someone was probably worried sick about this friendly fellow.

I patted Trixie and Twinkletoes before calling the front desk. It was early enough for our night clerk to answer. But there had been no reports of a lost dog. I checked the Wagtail neighborhood group online. No new mentions of missing dogs there, either.

I was in the shower before it dawned on me that he looked a lot like the dog across the lake. Of course, I hadn't seen that dog up close. There were loads of dogs with similar coloring. And this one wasn't wet, so I doubted that he'd swum across the lake.

I dressed in comfortable khakis the color of sand and a periwinkle shirt, glad that I could wear sneakers instead of boots now that it was officially spring.

The new dog watched my every move with intelligent eyes. His ears flopped over and were fluffier than the rest of his fur, except for his tail.

The three of them followed along behind me as I walked to my terrace.

Mr. Huckle, the inn butler, and I had taken to sneaking up to my terrace for teatime in the afternoons while we had a lull in business. Each of us had a set of binoculars. The terrace overlooked the lake and was blissfully out of sight of guests unless they were out on the back lawn. Mr. Huckle always brought a tea cart with a three-tier server of the same goodies being served downstairs in the dining area. Finger sandwiches, chocolate-covered éclairs, miniature cupcakes, and a changing assortment of pastries.

We watched a bald eagle couple, long-legged herons, and a host of Canada geese each day. Not that we would ever spy on anyone, of course, but our binoculars drifted daily to the homes on the opposite side of the lake. Soft green new leaves were coming in, closing the spots in between evergreens and slowly occluding the homes, but we had noticed a few tents being erected and the occasional RV parked near the shore. And recently we had seen a dog romping along the shoreline by himself. A dog who fit the description of the one who now placed his front paws on the railing and looked out at the lake.

He could be that dog. The one across the lake wasn't there now. Or maybe that dog's people simply hadn't awakened yet to let him out.

I went back inside and opened the door that led to the grand staircase. The two dogs and Twinkletoes raced down, with me lagging behind them.

The Sugar Maple Inn was home to me. I loved everything about it, from the quirky guests to the sumptuous breakfasts and the beauty of the mountains as the seasons changed. But living where you work can also wear a person out. So I welcomed the rare periods when there weren't any major events going on in the little town of Wagtail.

The only big thing happening that week was my grand-mother's birthday, and she had already put a damper on all suggestions of a big celebration. My father's mother, Liesel Miller, whom I called Oma, German for *Grandma*, was having a major birthday but she didn't want a party. Even though she was the mayor of Wagtail, she insisted that she wasn't more special than anyone else, a notion that I admired. It probably lay at the root of her popularity. Even though she had a lot of clout, there wasn't a resident of Wagtail who couldn't approach her personally about some issue or problem.

We coaxed her by making threats like "You know we're going to do something to celebrate. Would you prefer a surprise party?" She finally agreed to dinner at her favor-ite restaurant, The Blue Boar, but insisted it be limited to family and close friends.

I'd been informed by the staff that Cook—whose name was actually Cook, so calling him that wasn't at all rude although it probably sounded that way to outsiders—planned to bake a Dobos torte, Oma's favorite, and serve an ele-gant tea for all the employees on Sunday. It was a surprise for Oma, though. I wasn't to breathe a word.

In spite of her reluctance to celebrate, I knew Oma would enjoy that. Especially if it didn't involve gifts. Oma liked to say that she didn't need anything except the pleasure of someone's company. That was a gift to her.

In the main lobby of the inn, I turned left and walked along the hallway to the reception desk, where I retrieved one of the GPS collars that we offered guests for their dogs during their stay. Well-behaved dogs could run off-leash in Wagtail, but adventurous dogs sometimes took off on their own. We didn't want them to get lost on the mountain. It happened most often with young energetic dogs and breeds that followed their noses without regard to their whereabouts.

I buckled one onto our new friend, then let the dogs out to use the doggy potty. The newcomer followed Trixie and quickly understood what to do there.

The sun shone, but the air was still crisp and not at all humid. Azaleas bloomed in bright pinks and reds, with an occasional yellow or purple one in between. White and pink dogwoods were also in bloom. Wagtail was at its prettiest.

Wagtail was originally known for its underground springs. People had traveled here for their health and to get away from the heat at lower elevations during the summer. Wealthy folk had built magnificent summer homes, and the less wealthy had built darling cottages. But as the popularity of fresh springs waned, the town recognized a need to bring tourists back. They had decided to go to cats and dogs. Now the small town of Wagtail, on Wagtail Mountain in southwest Virginia, had become the premier location for those who wanted to vacation with their pets.

Wagtail catered to every whim and need of dogs, cats, and an assortment of other animal pets, like birds. It had attracted a top-notch animal hospital with expert veterinarians who focused on surgeries and difficult animal illnesses, as well as a number of additional veterinary clinics, and stores that offered beds, clothing, toys, and everything else a spoiled cat or dog might want. Of course, there were plenty of animal-themed items for people, too, including pajamas that matched their dog's pajamas. Wagtail was booming again.

The dogs followed me inside, where Twinkletoes had chosen to wait. She knew the routine and led the way to the dining area on the left side of the grand staircase.

I joined Oma and Mr. Huckle, who were already eating breakfast.

Oma's golden retriever, Gingersnap, politely sniffed the newcomer. Fortunately, all tails wagged. They soon settled down, except for Trixie, who drummed her paws, waiting impatiently for Shelley.

She appeared in minutes, bringing me a mug of tea. "Good morning! I see you have a guest."

Next to Oma and me, Shelley was Trixie's most favorite person because she served food. Trixie danced around her legs.

"It's the craziest thing. He was in my bed this morning!"

Oma and Mr. Huckle leaned over to take a better look at him.

"Where did he come from?" asked Oma in the German accent she wished she could lose but I found charming.

"I'm not sure. None of the guests have reported a missing dog." I looked at Mr. Huckle. "Do you think he could be the dog across the lake?"

For decades, Mr. Huckle had been a professional butler for a wealthy family. When they went broke, Oma had worried about him and given him a job. He was a wizened elderly gentleman who insisted on wearing the traditional butler's waistcoat. He had quickly become a guest favorite, because their every need became his personal quest.

He studied the dog. "His fur is the correct colors, but it's hard to say. My eyes aren't what they used to be."

Oma patted the dog. "He seems familiar to me."

"I bet he's hungry," said Shelley, "but he doesn't look malnourished." She spoke directly to him. "Today's specials are ham and spinach omelet, banana pancakes, and just for dogs and cats, we have scrambled eggs with ground beef and a touch of grated Havarti cheese."

He paid attention to her every word, and when she described the scrambled egg dish, he yelped. It must have been a coincidence, but it was very cute and prompted laughter among us.

"Trixie will have the same. Twinkletoes would probably prefer something fishy. Trout, if you have it. And I think I'll go for the omelet."

Shelley ambled away as Oma said to the dog, "Where have I seen you?"

She tapped her finger against the table. "It will come to me. In the meantime, perhaps you should check with the Wagtail Animal Guardians. Sometimes a dog escapes from them or from a foster home."

"Good idea. I'll do that right after breakfast, Oma."

Oma excused herself.

When she was out of sight, Mr. Huckle whispered, "We're all set for Sunday afternoon. I spoke with Cook this morning. He's planning to bake the cake on Saturday. We need to keep Liesel out of the commercial kitchen that day."

"We'll be at dinner on Saturday evening, but it could be tough during the day."

Shelley arrived with our breakfasts. She placed Trixie's on the floor first because she was known to want to eat everyone else's food in addition to her own. Then a bowl for the mystery dog, and only then did she serve Twinkletoes's preferred breakfast of trout and my omelet.

"You've got this down to a science," said Mr. Huckle.

Shelley chuckled. "It's the rare cat who is interested in a dog's food. It happens, but cats are more likely to be picky eaters. Dogs will stick their noses in a cat's bowl immediately, and we don't want anyone getting scratched."

My savory omelet distracted me. The aroma was heavenly.

I hadn't had time to take a bite before Oma came running to our table. Her face was completely flushed, and she waved her phone in the air. "He is Radar!"

Two

Oma breathed heavily as she plunked her phone on the table and sat down in the chair she had vacated. "I knew he looked familiar! Here, you see? He is in many of the pictures."

Mr. Huckle and I leaned toward each other, and Shelley looked over our shoulders.

Mr. Huckle scrolled through a Facebook account. Oma was right, the dog in the pictures looked exactly like our mystery dog. He was certainly well traveled. In various pictures he posed before the Eiffel Tower and Buckingham Palace. He rode in a gondola in Venice and stood atop a Swiss mountain.

"Who is Joshua Paxton?" asked Mr. Huckle.

"Josh! It's our Josh!" I cried. It never occurred to me to follow my cousin on Facebook. Small wonder since I hadn't seen him in over a decade.

"Joshua is my grandson," said Oma. "The son of my

daughter. He has been traveling for quite a long time. He runs a dog rescue called Fly Me Home. I think it is the same dog. No?"

The mystery dog had finished his breakfast and now lay on the floor smiling at us. I compared him to the dog in the photos. It certainly looked like he was the same dog.

"I don't want to disappoint you," said Mr. Huckle, "but this one in front of the Louvre was posted yesterday. It seems unlikely that Josh's dog could be in the photo yesterday and here today."

"He could have posted an old picture," said Oma.

"Or he could have doctored it. I've done that," said Shelley. "Just for fun. It's pretty easy to do."

As they spoke, it dawned on me that Josh might have posted pictures of his dog in Europe so Oma wouldn't know he had come to Wagtail for her birthday. Why ruin a fun surprise? "I don't know. They don't look doctored." I winked at Shelley.

Oma's broad smile had melted away, which made me feel awful. It had been a very long time since I'd seen him, but I knew Josh quite well. He had been the third person who made up Oma's summertime trio. Josh, my beau Holmes Richardson, and I had worked and played at the inn together every summer when we were children. Doctoring photos to trick people was exactly the kind of thing Josh would do.

In fact, now that I thought about it, I suspected Josh might be staying in one of the tents across the lake. Or in a cabin or RV, for that matter.

While Oma went on about how adorable Josh, Holmes, and I were as children, I was scheming. I would do my regular duties around the inn with Twinkletoes and both dogs. Radar had been pretty good about following Trixie and me so far. I bet he wouldn't mind taking a walk through the inn. Then I would nab the inn skiff and zip across the lake to find Josh and return Radar.

Finished with breakfast, we all went to work, taking care of various tasks. When I returned to the registration desk, a Brendan Hayward was checking in.

Our desk clerk, Zelda, turned toward me and mouthed, *Wow!*

It wasn't hard to figure out what she meant. Brendan could have been a movie star. His pecan-colored hair fluffed up at the top of his head. He had a trendy barely there mustache and beard.

"Have you been to Wagtail before?" asked Zelda.

"Sure have. I grew up in Snowball. I'm just back for a visit." He smiled, and tiny crinkles formed around the edges of his brown eyes.

"Welcome home!" I said as Shadow, our handyman, picked up his bag and showed him to the elevator. Shadow's bloodhound, Elvis, ambled along behind them. Then I fibbed a little when I told Zelda that I would be seeing to some errands in town.

From our office, Oma shouted, "No gifts!"

Zelda and I laughed at the refrain we had heard so often lately. I peeked into the office to be sure Oma was absorbed in something and wouldn't notice us scampering down to the dock, since her office overlooked the path that led to the lake.

Fortunately, her phone rang, and I heard her discussing a trash pickup problem. As the mayor of Wagtail, she constantly dealt with issues that arose around town. Gingersnap snoozed on the floor.

I called Trixie and Radar and left in a hurry.

We dashed toward the dock. I was the slowest. To my surprise, even Twinkletoes sprinted along with the dogs. I nabbed life vests for the dogs and me but wasn't sure about Twinkletoes. Cats had sailed the seas hundreds of years ago, so some cats must like boats, I reasoned. I took a small vest out of the storage shed and gave her an opportunity to look around while I suited up the rest of us.

The dogs happily jumped into the boat. "Twinks?" I called as I stepped in.

Twinkletoes was a calico, mostly white with a fluffy black tail that she often wrapped around her white paws. At the top of her head between her ears, she had one chocolate square and one butterscotch square that looked like she had shoved mismatched sunglasses up on her head. Her glowing green eyes studied me.

"It's okay. You don't have to come." I turned on the motor.

Twinkletoes walked toward the boat, sniffed it, and then hopped inside. I fastened the life jacket on her, which elicited an annoyed yowl. But I wasn't taking chances. She might decide to jump in the water once we were under way. She had to wear it.

I untied the boat and started moving forward slowly to let them get used to the motion. I was fairly sure I knew where we were going, although the shoreline on the other side looked a little different from a boat than it did from three stories up.

We made it to the other side without anyone jumping overboard. I secured the boat next to another one at the pier, and the three of them leaped out. After removing all the life jackets, I tossed them into the boat.

Radar took off as if he knew where he was going. We followed him to a tent that had been pitched along the shoreline. It was a simple green A-frame tent near a fire pit arranged out of rough stones. Someone had created a cairn of colorful stacked rocks, topping it with a pyramid-shaped piece of milky-white quartz. The pretty stones beneath it had been carefully selected for their shapes and colors.

I heard Josh's voice before I saw him. "Radar! Where have you been? I've been looking all over for you! Ahh. Is this your girlfriend? You've been hanging with a cat, too?"

I was laughing by the time a bearded man carrying wood emerged from the evergreens and I could see him. I stopped cold and stared. Was that really Josh?

He was the right height, a couple of inches short of six feet. And his hair was the same brown shade as mine. But a huge beard hid most of his face. If I had met him on the street, I never would have guessed he was my cousin.

His eyes met mine, and I sighed with relief. Those blue eyes would never change, even with age. "Josh!"

He dumped the wood and reached his arms out to me. "Holly! I heard you were living in Wagtail." He folded me into a big bear hug.

"Josh?" A woman's wistful voice came from behind him.

He let go of me. "Dana, this is my cousin, Holly."

Her dark hair was tied back in a messy bun. She wore short lace-up boots with a miniskirt and an oversize plaid flannel shirt that looked as though it probably belonged to Josh. She eyed me critically.

"Hi!" I held out my hand to her to shake, and she took it.

I almost snatched my hand back. Her skin was freezing. "It's still kind of cool to camp, isn't it? Why don't you come and stay at the inn?"

She looked at Josh.

He ran a hand through his overgrown hair. "I want to surprise Oma."

"I could sneak you in through the private kitchen," I offered.

Dana slid her arm under Josh's elbow and hung on to him. "We couldn't. We love being one with nature."

"But you are coming to Oma's birthday dinner on Saturday?"

"Absolutely! Wouldn't miss it!" said Josh.

I wondered how long it had been since they'd showered, but it was probably way too impolite to inquire about that subject. "She will be thrilled."

"Uh, Holly, how did you find us?" asked Josh.

"Radar came to the inn. I think he might not like sleeping outside in a tent."

Josh ruffled Radar's fur. "You went to the inn? What a smart boy. How did you get there?" Radar wagged his tail joyously but didn't give up any of his secrets.

"I found him in my bed when I woke up this morning! I just can't figure out how he got across the lake. He wasn't wet," I said.

Josh shrugged. "He loves to swim. How did you know where to find us?"

It was the second time he'd asked that. "Why? What's going on?" I was a little miffed that they hadn't been more concerned about Radar.

"We're just chilling. It's nice to be away from a big city. Radar was with us yesterday. When we woke this morning, I assumed he was around here somewhere."

There were so many things I wanted to say. That they should put a tag on his collar. That they should have been looking for him. That one or both of them must have been in Wagtail, because I didn't think Radar swam all the way over by himself. But they seemed sensitive about something. I didn't want to aggravate them. It was important that they stick around long enough to make Oma's birthday special. "I put a GPS collar on him. Do you have my phone number? I can help you locate him. Can I bring you anything? Food or blankets?"

"Thanks, Holly. I don't think we need anything. We brought supplies." Josh gave me his phone number. I texted mine to him so he would have my number.

If they had supplies, why was Dana the temperature of

a corpse? There wasn't much I could do. It was their choice to camp. I decided that if they didn't come to the inn, I would return with some goodies and blankets.

I gave Radar a big smooch on his head.

When I was about to say goodbye to Josh and Dana, a wave of compassion overwhelmed me. Something was wrong. They looked shabby and uneasy. "I could get you a room at the Wagtail Springs Hotel. You won't believe how lovely it is now that the new owner has renovated it."

Dana's fingers tightened on Josh's arm like the talons of a hawk.

Josh didn't flinch. "I've been telling Dana how beautiful Wagtail Mountain is. After apartments and big cities, it's sort of cleansing to get back to nature. It's been a long time since I camped like this."

"If you need anything—" I pointed toward the inn, which was silly because it was clearly visible "—I'm not far away."

"Thanks, Holly. And please don't tell anyone you saw us. You know how fast news travels in Wagtail," said Josh.

"Right." I waved and headed for the pier, with Trixie and Twinkletoes leading the way. Radar followed along, but Josh called him back.

My little encounter with Josh and Dana left me feeling perturbed. As much as I loved nature and a nice walk in the woods, I didn't understand why they would camp when they could stay at the inn for free. Sleeping with a rock in my back and waking cold and damp had never appealed to me. But there were loads of people who loved it. Maybe I was projecting my feelings onto them, which wasn't fair.

A balding man waited on the dock when we returned to the inn. He caught a line and helped tie up the boat.

"You're Holly, right?"

"Yes," I said cautiously. "I'm sorry. We have so many guests. I'm afraid your name has slipped my mind." In reality, I didn't think I had seen him before. Zelda probably checked him in.

Trixie and Twinkletoes jumped onto the dock.

He held out his hand for me to shake. "Frank Burton. I don't believe we've met. I recognized you from a photo of you and your grandmother on the inn website."

Duh. I mentally smacked myself. Of course.

"I saw the boat down here yesterday. Can guests take it out? I'd like to do some night fishing."

"I could arrange that for you. We have terrific guides who know all the best fishing holes on the lake."

"I was hoping I might go alone. That's what I did when I was younger, and I have fond memories of seeing lights twinkling onshore and floating through the early-morning mist. It was magical."

"I'll see what I can do for you."

I hung up the life jackets and we returned to the inn, where there was a commotion in the registration lobby. Had I forgotten about a tour group? The glass doors slid open, and I heard multiple people shout "Holly!"

Appalled, Twinkletoes leaped onto the desk and wrapped her tail around her feet. She watched everyone in alarm.

Arms reached out to me. Kisses landed on my cheeks. Everyone spoke at once.

"It's been so long!"

"I love Wagtail. Can I move in with you?"

"Oma, you look wonderful!"

"Is this Trixie?"

Part of me wanted to jump on the desk with Twinkletoes. But then I saw my father.

"Hollypop!" he said, embracing me.

I could see Oma out of the corner of my eye. I knew that smile. She was deliriously happy. And why wouldn't she be? Her son had come to celebrate her birthday.

It had been quite a while since I had seen Dad, and it

had been even longer for Oma. His visit was the best gift Oma could possibly receive.

I hugged my half siblings, who were nearly college age now. I glanced around for my father's second wife but didn't see her.

A woman who grinned broadly poked her head out of our little gift shop. Bleached blond hair rippled past her shoulders. The skin on her face was so tight it looked sculpted. While Wagtail was a fun vacation destination, we seldom saw people wearing sundresses with skin-revealing cutouts, and certainly not in the springtime. She must have been cold.

And she had picked the worst possible moment to check into the inn. I hurried over to her. "I'm so sorry. We're having a little family reunion. If you'll come to the reception desk, I can check you in. I apologize for the delay."

"I'm already checked in!" she squealed. "I would have known you anywhere. You're exactly like your father described. I just know we're going to be best friends."

"Oh! Hello." Who on earth was this? I looked to my dad.

"Carole? What are you doing here?" he blurted.

"Surprise!" Carole sang as she danced toward my dad.

Behind her, I could see my half siblings, Lucy and Mike, making faces and rolling their eyes.

"It's nice to meet you," I said. Who was this woman and where was Dad's wife?

Three

❧　❧　❧　❧

"Your father can't stop talking about his Holly-pop," Carole blathered. "I think that's such an adorable nickname! Let's see. You own half the inn. You have a boyfriend, and your father hopes you'll get married soon, but not to that guy. Your dog is Trixie, and your cat is Twinkletoes. Your Oma built an apartment on the top floor of the inn just for you. Did I get it right?"

I didn't have a clue how to respond, so I choked out a "Yes." *Who are you* would have been my preferred choice, but that would be rude. She had clearly heard about me.

Thankfully, Zelda piped up at that moment. "Hah! We tricked them, Sam. Neither your mom nor Holly had a clue! I have you booked as the Andersons."

So this had been planned for a long time. I wondered if Josh's mom would also be surprising us.

I sidled up to Dad in time to hear him whisper, "Carole, what are you doing here?"

She wrapped her arms around him and planted a giant smooch on his lips. "You told me so much about Wagtail that I had to come see it for myself."

Zelda leaned toward him. "Would you like to share a room?" she whispered.

Dad blanched and untangled himself from Carole's grip. In a low tone he responded, "Preferably not. I didn't know she was coming."

I glanced back at Carole, who was now far too busy chattering at Oma to hear us.

Oma escaped Carole by heading behind the reception desk to stand near Zelda. "Is there a problem?" She reached across the counter for Sam's hand and squeezed it in hers. "You stay in my guest room. Ja?"

"That would be great!" He was so enthusiastic that I wondered what the deal was between Dad and Carole. And where was Dad's wife?

Zelda smiled at him.

"I'll get Shadow to take your bags upstairs." While I texted Shadow, I could hear Oma suggesting they go to Hot Hog for dinner.

That prompted a series of happy yelps from Trixie.

"What's wrong with your dog?" asked Dad.

"Hot Hog is her favorite restaurant. She knows the name," said Oma.

"Aww, you're pullin' our legs!" Carole winked at me.

"Our Trixie is a very smart girl," Oma persisted. "Once we thought she was lost, but she went to Hot Hog with another dog, and they had dinner by themselves."

Dad, Lucy, and Mike cracked up, but Carole looked doubtful. She studied Oma as if she thought Oma had lost her marbles.

I grabbed their room keys and ushered them all upstairs to their quarters.

We stopped by Oma's apartment first. Located on the

back side of the inn, the guest room featured a balcony that overlooked the lake. There was a fireplace for chilly nights and charming European country décor.

Carole dropped an expensive-looking purse on the bed and opened the balcony doors. "Oh, what a wonderful view," she said. "This is be-u-tee-ful!"

"Since you haven't been here in a while, Dad, the menu for limited room service is on the desk. We serve breakfast and lunch downstairs but not dinner, because Oma wants people to get out and about in Wagtail to try some of the restaurants. The pet parade is every afternoon at five. The front porch is the best location to watch from. Unless we're expecting someone to check in, we lock the registration entrance at six, but the front door facing town stays open until midnight. After that, you have to buzz the night clerk to get in."

Dad tilted his head as he watched me. "It sure has changed since I was a kid growing up here. Never in my wildest dreams did I imagine you living here, Holly."

"You're staying here, Sam?" Carole peered into the living room. "This looks like an entire apartment."

"I hope it's okay." Dad sounded appropriately apologetic, even though he didn't want to be with Carole. "Mom would like me to stay with her. We haven't had any private time together in years."

Carole's dismay showed immediately. "Not with me? I'll be all alone?" She ran her hand down his arm.

Dad shook her off. "Let's see where Lucy and Mike will be."

"Follow me." I led them to two connecting rooms just around the corner. Shadow had unlocked the door and left their bags inside.

Lucy immediately unlocked the connecting door and came through to her brother's room. I could hear Carole talking to Dad in the corridor.

After giving Lucy and Mike the rundown on the inn and meals, I asked quietly, "Who is that woman?"

"Carole Hobson," said Mike.

Lucy looked like she might cry. "Mom decided Dad was an old bore and she moved in with her yoga instructor."

I held my arms out to them and hugged them both at the same time. "I'm so sorry. Why didn't you tell us?"

"We were hoping Mom would change her mind and come home." Lucy's voice was muffled against the folds of my clothes.

Mike let go of me. "Holly, you should see this guy. He has a man bun and slicks back his hair with some kind of gel."

"And he puts goop in his eyebrows, like wax or something," Lucy added.

I didn't think that meant much about his character. But when a guy split up your parents' marriage, that alone was good reason to dislike everything about him. "So now Dad is dating Carole?"

"Not really. But she's chasing him! We hate her," Lucy said, grimacing. "I can't believe she came to Wagtail. I thought we were getting away from her."

"She's always pretending to be super happy, but when she thinks no one is watching, she stares at us with an expression like someone's holding a dead rat in front of her," said Mike.

I tried not to laugh. "Well, you're here now, and you don't have to spend time with her. There will be lots of other people around. So cheer up and have some fun!"

I left them to settle in and decide what they wanted to do first. Oma and Zelda nabbed me in the registration lobby and propelled me into the office, where Oma closed the door.

"Who is this woman with Sam?" demanded Oma.

"Carole Hobson. I'm sorry, Oma, but the kids told me that Sam's wife left her family and ran off with her yoga instructor."

"No! My poor Sam." Oma placed her hands on the sides of her face. "He must be devastated. Why did he not tell me about this? Why would she do such a thing? And the children! How are they taking it?"

"They're very upset about it," I said. "She deserted them, too."

"Why didn't Sam tell me? Carole Hobson," mused Oma. "I'm not sure I like this woman."

The keys on the computer clicked as Zelda typed on the keyboard.

"You're not alone, Oma. Mike and Lucy detest her," I said.

"She is so stiff," Oma said. "Like—"

"—a snob!" said Zelda. "Oh, gosh. There are loads of Carole Hobsons in Florida."

Oma's mouth pulled into a bitter line.

The only good thing about Carole's appearance so far was that Oma had forgotten about Radar and Josh. I hoped it would slip her mind so I wouldn't have to lie about Josh's whereabouts.

I felt sorry for Carole. She'd come all the way from Florida and her surprise had bombed. "Don't forget that she's outnumbered. She's probably stiff because she's the outsider. Any of us would be cautious and overwhelmed on meeting a whole battalion of strangers."

"You are correct, of course," said Oma. "What was I thinking? She is a friend to Sam in this sad and demoral izing time for him. We should make an effort to be welcoming toward her."

Zelda tsked. "Sam's children sure don't like her. Did you see the faces they were making?"

"That doesn't mean anything. They would resent anyone who moved into Sam's life in place of their mother. You can't go by that," I said.

"Very well," said Oma. "The nicer we are to this Carole woman, the more we will learn about her. We will draw our own conclusions. Now I must find my Sam! I see him so seldom."

"Oma, why don't you take the next few days off? I can handle the inn."

Oma looked at me in surprise.

"Yes!" said Zelda. "What do they call that? A staycation? You never take any time off. Holly is here and I would be delighted to help her. You don't want any gifts. This will be a present from Holly and me." She held her palm out to me and I high-fived her.

"You girls!" Oma consulted her calendar. "It is not possible. At four o'clock I have a bride coming with her parents to see the inn."

Zelda tsked at her. "Did you or did you not bring Holly on board so she could do some of these things?"

Oma gazed at me. "Surely you have plans."

"Yes. I have a bride and her parents coming at four."

Oma smiled. "Then I will do exactly as you two suggest. I can spend time with my Sam and I can snoop on this Carole."

Zelda mock-coughed. "You mean entertain her."

"It is my poor English. Always I am making silly mistakes." Oma winked at us.

I opened the door and found Dad there, ready to knock. "I hope I'm not interrupting anything."

"Not a thing." I motioned to Zelda and the two of us scurried past Dad.

I whispered to Zelda, "Are there any other surprises in store for Oma? Like a visit from Aunt Margaret?"

"Sadly, no."

"Okay, I'm going to block rooms for Aunt Margaret and Josh, just in case."

With those rooms blocked, we only had one vacancy. So far, it didn't appear that we had any troublemakers staying with us. I hoped it would stay that way for Dad's visit.

Zelda nudged me with her elbow.

I looked up from the computer as my mom walked through the automatic glass doors.

"Good morning," she trilled. "I was picking up the gift I planned to give Oma and was told she doesn't want any presents! That can't be true."

I sucked in a big breath of air. Should I warn her that Dad was in Oma's office? Or that he was in Wagtail? "I'm sorry, Mom. I hope you can return it. Oma says the pleasure of our company is all she wants. Nothing else."

"Holly, I know you better than that. I'm sure you got her something."

"Honest, Mom. I haven't!"

"She tells us every day," said Zelda. "Sometimes twice!"

"You two are up to something." Mom eyed us. "What's going on?"

At that exact moment, the door to the office opened and Dad stepped out into the registration lobby.

Four

❧ ❧ ❧ ❧

A long painful moment of silence passed as my mother and father stared at each other in shock. It had been close to twenty years since they had been in the same state, much less in the same room.

I sucked in a deep breath and held it.

"Sam?"

"Nell?"

That was followed by an awkward hug.

"How silly of me. I should have realized you would be here for Oma's birthday," said Mom.

"Did you come all the way from California?" asked Dad.

Mom glanced at me. "Didn't Holly tell you? My parents and I moved back here."

Dad frowned at her. "Just . . . the three of you?"

"We found the perfect house. You'll have to stop by while you're here. I know they'd love to see you. How long are you staying?"

"We'll be here through next week. The kids will be on spring break, and I want to spend some time with Oma."

"Why don't you drop by my house for hors d'oeuvres before dinner on Saturday? Holly and Zelda can show you where it is."

"Nell, you don't have to go to any trouble on my account."

"Nonsense! Let's see, dinner is at six, so how about four o'clock? Just some light nibblies. I'll make the deviled eggs you like so much."

"You remember that?"

Mom laughed. A solid, comfortable laugh. "How could I forget? I'll see you then." She waved at us, knocked on Oma's open door, and disappeared inside.

I could hear her asking if Oma really didn't want gifts

Dad shot me a look and I would have sworn he heaved a sigh of relief. He gazed upward at the stairs and a moment later, Carole made her appearance.

She had changed into tight jeans that were torn at the knees. One sleeve of her top hung down so that it exposed her shoulder She held up her phone and snapped a selfie as she walked down the stairs.

"See you later," said Dad, heading toward the sliding doors.

Carole hurried toward him awkwardly in high heels. "Honey! Wait up."

They almost made it out the door before Mom saw them. Almost.

The glass doors closed behind them and Carole slung her arm around Dad as they walked away.

Mom stopped in front of the registration desk. "I have seen photographs of Sam's wife and children. None of them look like that."

"He and his wife have separated. We didn't know. Her

name is Carole. Carole Hobson. He didn't bring her with him. She showed up to surprise him."

"That's . . . I was going to say that's a shame, but it's just odd," said Mom.

"You didn't tell me that you were getting a divorce until you showed up here," I pointed out.

"No. I didn't. But I'm still not seeing anyone. Isn't she closer to your age?"

"I wouldn't worry about it, Nell," said Zelda, "she's probably just a rebound date."

With an innocent expression, Mom quickly said, "Worry? Oh, sweetheart, you have it all wrong. He can do whatever he wants. He hasn't been my husband for a very long time."

But she looked back at the glass doors again. They were long gone from view. "I guess I have some food shopping to do. Zelda, I hope you'll come, too."

"I wouldn't miss it, Nell."

Oma, Lucy, and Mike left shortly after Mom did, and my day was consumed by ordinary inn business. First, I booked a solo fishing expedition for Frank Burton and let him know his boat would be delivered to the inn dock at seven in the evening. It was modern and much snazzier than our little boat.

When Zelda took a break, two men who looked remarkably alike arrived in the lobby with backpacks.

"Welcome to the Sugar Maple Inn," I said.

"Um, we don't have reservations. Do you have a room available with two beds?" The one who asked was slightly taller than the other one, about six feet, I thought. Both had short curly brown hair that verged on red. Their noses were identical, but their eyes differed.

"You're in luck! Name, please?"

They looked at each other.

The taller one said, "P. Mellor."

When I asked for an address, P seemed hesitant. He gave me an address in Vermont.

"How long would you like to stay?"

Again, they exchanged a look before P said, "Maybe three nights? Could be less, I'm not sure."

"Could just be tonight," said the other one.

I smiled at them. "You are free to check out at any time, Mr.—Mellor? Are you brothers? You look alike."

The shorter one said, "Yes. I'm Ted and he's Paul."

I didn't miss the fact that Paul gave his brother a swift kick.

"We're glad to have you staying with us. May I have your credit card, please?"

"I'm paying with cash. Is that okay?"

"Certainly." It was highly unusual, though. Almost no one paid in cash anymore. Had they robbed a bank? Paul handed me enough cash to pay for three nights.

"Um, one thing," said Paul. "Is it possible to put a block on our names? We're trying to avoid phone calls."

"You can disconnect the phone in your room. That way you wouldn't hear it ring."

"The point," said Paul, nervously picking at a seam on his backpack, "is we don't want people to know that we're here."

"Right. We need to get away," explained Ted. "We need a break. No girlfriends!"

"No Mom," grumbled Paul. "If they know we're here, they'll keep bothering us." Paul shot me a very forced and uncertain grin. "Could you ask the inn operator not to confirm that we're here?"

"Thanks for thinking that we're big enough to have a full-time inn operator. I can certainly inform the staff."

The relief on their faces was remarkable. They thanked me profusely and seemed much more comfortable. "Do you need assistance with your luggage?"

"No. All we have is what you see." Paul hoisted his backpack.

"All right, then; follow me." I led them to the elevator and tried to make casual conversation. "Have you been hiking?"

After a pause, Ted said, "Yes! How did you know?"

"We get a lot of people who are backpacking on the mountain. Wagtail is a nice place to take a break." But I didn't believe them. Backpackers often had some beard growth, and these two looked clean shaven.

The elevator door opened, and I led them to their room. I gave them the rundown on meals. "I'm Holly. Please call me if you need anything."

I walked away from their room feeling a little bit uneasy. They seemed nice enough, but they were clearly trying to hide from someone. Paul had sounded a little grumpy about "Mom," so maybe it was all quite innocent.

Back at the registration desk, I posted a note not to confirm the registration of Paul or Ted Mellor if anyone called looking for them.

Zelda returned from lunch, and I took a few minutes to grab a berry smoothie.

At exactly four o'clock, the bride, her parents, and their two basset hounds arrived for a tour of the inn. Trixie and Gingersnap accompanied us as I showed them indoor and outdoor locations for the service and the meal. When we were finally back in the office, Zelda delivered a small tray of appetizers, another loaded with pastries for them to nosh on while they perused photographs of other weddings at the inn, and a selection of cookies for their dogs.

Tent or no tent? Would we provide the cake? Sit down dinner or buffet? It seemed like each question prompted more options that had to be explained.

Most of all, they wanted to include the basset hounds in the ceremony and celebration. The dogs were very well behaved even when they romped with Trixie and Ginger-snap in the empty lobby.

On their way out the door, I overheard the mom say, "The Sugar Maple Inn just moved to the number one position as far as I'm concerned. There wasn't a single place our dogs couldn't go with us."

That evening, I kept an eye out for Aunt Margaret, but she didn't show up.

I woke the next morning much as I had the day before—staring into Radar's eyes. I sat up in bed. "What are you doing here again?"

He flapped his tail against the down comforter.

Twinkletoes stretched and yawned as if it were perfectly normal that Radar would be on our bed. Trixie seemed a little jealous, though. She pushed her nose under my arm in an effort to get closer.

I hugged her to me. "Feel like another ride in the boat?"

She wagged her tail.

Returning Radar was now a bit of a problem. If I followed my normal routine, showered, and went downstairs for breakfast, Oma would see him again and I would have to lie to her and claim he wasn't Josh's dog. A white lie, of course, but she would be suspicious, and I really hated to spoil Josh's surprise.

But maybe if I crept out of the inn now? Oma was usually an early bird, but I bet she had been up late with Dad last night.

I dressed in jeans and a white top, grabbed an olive utility jacket, and pulled it on as we rushed out the door.

The inn was still quiet, except for the soft whir of the elevator, which meant it had come all the way up to the third floor, where there were no guest rooms. Someone probably pushed the wrong button. The heady smell of coffee

brewing reminded me that I had intended to bring Josh
and Dana some supplies if they didn't come to the inn. I
paused at the second-floor storeroom for blankets. Scents
of cinnamon and baking bread wafted up the stairs.

I glanced at the open dining area to the right side of the
stairs as I sneaked down them. One of our guests, Judy
Davis, sat at a table with a basket of breakfast breads and
a mug of coffee in front of her. Petite with a penchant for
turquoise and pink, she had arrived without her husband
but had brought along her two cats, Sassy and Patience.
Sassy, a long-haired mostly black cat with white slippers
and whiskers, had the same sort of confidence as Twinkletoes. Her glowing golden eyes didn't miss a thing. Judy
kept them on leashes, which was probably a good idea since
they were relatively new to Wagtail. Patience, a tabby with
a white bib and green eyes, seemed to be a calmer snuggle
bunny. They noticed me right away and watched me.

Holmes was building a vacation home for Judy and her
husband. They were so excited about it that Judy had become a regular guest at the inn. She made frequent trips
to Wagtail to check on the progress and select various
items for their home. This was her first visit with her cats.
She was staying in the cat wing, where each room featured a screened porch with a tree for cats to climb.

Brendan drank coffee at another table. He had made
friends with Patience and petted her like someone who
had cats.

I dashed into the kitchen for some breakfast breads to
take with me. Hoping to avoid Oma, I hurried through the
corridor to the reception lobby, out the door, and down to
the dock, with Twinkletoes and the dogs running ahead of
me. I wondered how they knew where I planned to go.
The dogs paused to do their business while I collected the
life jackets.

As I put one on Radar, I asked, "How do you cross the lake? You're not wet."

With all four of us safely suited up, we puttered across the lake again. A few fishing boats were out in the morning mist, but the world was peacefully quiet, save for our motor.

When we reached the other side and the motor was off, it was blissfully tranquil, as though humans didn't exist. Birds chirped and flew back and forth over our heads. Ducks and Canada geese swam around placidly, dunking their heads under water from time to time.

I docked the boat, tossed our life vests inside, and grabbed the blankets and breads I had brought.

Once again, Radar led the way to the tent. The remains of a campfire smoldered. The fire hadn't been out long, given the scent of smoke in the air.

"Josh?" I didn't want to barge in on them. The tent was zipped up. It was early and they might still be sleeping.

"Josh? Dana!" I called a little louder. I gazed at Radar. Why wasn't he barking at the tent to see them?

Ugh. What if they weren't there? Maybe they'd rented a room after all. Well, I certainly wasn't going to leave sweet Radar behind all by himself!

Trixie seemed more interested in the tent than Radar, which I thought odd. Even Twinkletoes sniffed the side of the tent.

And then Trixie howled. A mournful howl. Long and melancholy.

I thought my heart skipped a beat. Trixie was good at communicating by barking and I had heard that particular howl before.

Someone was dead.

Five

❀ ❀ ❀ ❀

"Josh!" I screamed. "No!" I unzipped the mesh door in haste and peered inside. "Josh?"

Only one sleeping bag lay in the tent, bulked up by the person inside it. One? That wasn't good. Had Josh left Dana behind, or had she taken off and abandoned him?

I tried one last time, very loud, "Josh!"

I dropped the blankets on the ground, hunched over, crept inside, and kneeled next to him. I pushed the mummy-style sleeping bag gently. "Joshie?"

Something brushed my ankle and I screamed again. But it was just Twinkletoes, who had crept past me toward the head of the sleeping bag.

Edging sideways, I followed her, afraid of what I would find.

The sleeping bag was zipped up as far as it would go. A hood covered the hair. Only two open, unmoving eyes were visible.

Trixie howled again, which didn't help my nerves one bit. I zipped the sleeping bag open just a few inches and bent back the material far enough to uncover the person's face.

It wasn't Josh.

The man who stared back at me was Frank Burton, who had wanted to go night fishing. He looked to be in his thirties, with a scraggly beard and premature hair loss. I reached out to touch his neck and find a pulse, but I didn't have to. His skin was cold. Even the sleeping bag couldn't keep him warm anymore.

"C'mon, Trixie." I backed out of the tent. I stood by the glowing embers of the fire and tried using my phone, but I couldn't get a signal.

Where were Josh and Dana? I considered yelling for them, but as I gazed around at the evergreens behind the tent, the site suddenly felt very lonely and isolated. I called the dogs and Twinkletoes and made a mad dash to the boat as fast as I could go. Glad to be out of the woods and on the more openly visible shoreline, I tried my phone again. But even by the water I couldn't get a signal.

I suited up the dogs and looked around for Twinkletoes. She had jumped into another small skiff that was docked. "C'mon, Twinkletoes," I called.

She ignored me.

I walked over to the boat. She was pawing at something. I tried picking her up, but she fought me and went right back to work. There couldn't be a mouse in the little boat, could there? The sun reflected on something thin. I reached in and was able to wiggle it out. When I held it up, I realized that it was an earring. A thin gold shepherd's hook held a mother-of-pearl circle and below it, another piece of mother-of-pearl in the shape of a teardrop. I was no expert on jewelry, but it was finely crafted, not a cheap piece.

I peered closer and saw the 18K stamp on it, designating it as gold. Someone would be very upset about losing that earring. I pocketed it and picked up Twinkletoes.

"Thank you very much. You have a good eye for jewelry." I buckled her life vest and placed her into the correct boat. We puttered back to the inn.

While I removed their life vests, a strange feeling came over me. Like someone might be watching. I looked around. Twinkletoes scampered up the hill. Radar and Trixie joyfully rolled on their backs in the grass.

My gaze drifted up to the inn, where the sun reflected on something in a window. It was brief. So brief that I wondered if I had imagined it. But then I realized that someone was watching from the floor-to-ceiling windows in the Dogwood Room; I couldn't make out who it was.

Officer Dave Quinlan often ate breakfast at the inn free of charge. In her position as mayor, Oma liked to keep up with local news and hear what had transpired in town while we slept. She also claimed that a police presence at the inn deterred criminals.

I always smiled when she said that because Wagtail didn't have a lot of criminal types lurking about. And those who were inclined to snatch a purse, or the like, probably weren't the sort of people who would check into the inn. But I never pointed that out to Oma because I liked Dave and was more than happy to have him stop by for breakfast. With any luck, he was at the inn now.

I hurried up the hill to the registration lobby, which felt like a safe haven in spite of the figure in the window. After all, I often gazed out of my windows. Who wouldn't want to look at beautiful Dogwood Lake?

People were up and about, and the sounds of voices and clinking silverware in the dining area were reassuring as we passed through the main lobby.

Oma sat at a table with Officer Dave. Gingersnap lounged

at her feet. I made a beeline for Dave. Just the man I needed to speak to.

Dave had actually attained the rank of sergeant, but out of long habit, everyone fondly addressed him as Officer Dave. He was actually part of the Snowball Mountain police force but was assigned to Wagtail and lived there as well. He had three officers under him now but still used the inn's office when he needed to interrogate someone.

"Holly!" said Oma. "You are pale. Are you sick? And why is that dog back?"

I looked at their breakfast plates. Dave had a few bites left.

I sat down in an empty chair and spoke in a soft voice so guests wouldn't overhear. "The dog that resembles Josh's dog came back to the inn last night, so I took the boat across the lake to return him this morning. There's a tent, a simple A-frame style, where—" I paused. Josh. It was Josh's tent. At least I thought it was. I skipped that part. "A campfire was smoldering. And there's a dead man in the tent."

That got Dave's attention. "Who is it?"

"Frank Burton. He was a guest of the inn." I knew what would happen next, and I really wanted some breakfast. You'd think finding a corpse would have eliminated my appetite, but I guessed the fresh air had left me hungry. I nabbed a breakfast roll and shared it with the dogs. Twinkletoes patted my hand with her paw. It was her way of saying "Me, too!" For a cat, she was surprisingly fond of bread.

Shelley brought me a mug of steaming tea.

"Thank you, Shelley! I needed this!"

Shelley started to rattle off the day's specials. I interrupted her. "I don't think I'll have time to eat, but maybe you could bring Twinkletoes some turkey and whatever you have ready for the dogs?"

"What's going on?" she whispered.

"Someone died," I whispered back.

"Who?"

"A guest, but it wasn't here."

She shot me an appalled look, nodded, and hurried to the kitchen.

"Where exactly did you see this person?" asked Dave.

We excused ourselves and walked out onto the terrace. I pointed across the lake. "See that little pier jutting out? That's the tent. Right there on the opposite shore. Radar and Trixie went straight to it both times."

"Both times? You were there before?"

"I went yesterday morning to take Radar back."

"Why was this man camping if he was a guest of the inn?"

"I don't know. I didn't see him there the previous day." I took a deep breath and ratted on my cousin. "I couldn't say this in front of Oma. Josh is here for her birthday. He was camping in that tent, but he didn't want Oma to know. He wants to surprise her. He's with a woman named Dana." I explained the entire Josh story sequentially.

Dave stared across the lake quietly for what felt like a long time.

I didn't know what *he* was thinking, but I knew what worried me. Someone had killed Frank and left him in Josh and Dana's tent. The most logical conclusion was that *they* had murdered him and taken off. There had to be another explanation. There just had to be!

We returned to the table inside. Officer Dave thanked Oma for breakfast and walked away. I could see him raise his phone to his ear.

"What a terrible thing. Could you tell how he died?" asked Oma.

I shook my head. "I didn't unzip the sleeping bag all the way."

"Did you see blood?"

I had to think about that. "Actually, I didn't. That's odd, isn't it?"

"Maybe he wasn't murdered. Maybe he died of natural causes," said Oma.

Shelley arrived with breakfast for Twinkletoes and the dogs. Trixie danced around on her hind legs in excitement.

Shelley set a plate in front of me filled with pancakes. Cooked apples slid off them.

I stared at it. I had just seen a dead person. I was pretty sure I shouldn't be hungry, but I was, and I knew from experience that the next part would take hours. I tried not to eat as fast as the dogs were consuming their breakfasts.

By the time Dave returned, I had made more than a dent in the pancakes.

"I've called for backup and an ambulance from Snowball. I'll go get the police boat and meet you at the dock."

"Okay. Fifteen minutes?" I asked.

"Sounds about right."

When he left, Oma asked softly, "Does this involve Joshua?"

How to answer that? The unexpected death of a man we didn't really know had changed everything. After all, he was in Josh's tent. At least I thought it was the same tent. Maybe it was a different tent that looked like Josh's! Those green tents all looked alike. "I hope not, Oma. He desperately wanted to surprise you."

A faint smile crossed her lips. "That sounds like our Joshie. Is he in trouble?"

"Oma, I should have known you would figure it out. I'm sorry I didn't tell you, but I wanted to help him surprise you. I have to be honest. He could be in trouble. I think the dead man was inside *their tent*. Maybe they went to get help. Or maybe they spent the night somewhere in Wagtail and Frank used their tent?"

"You say 'they.' Was Margaret with him?"

"I haven't seen or heard from Aunt Margaret. Josh was with a woman named Dana."

Oma nodded. "Margaret always disliked camping. It's surprising that Josh is so fond of it." She rose from her seat. "You will keep me informed. Yes?"

I'd already gone and spoiled the surprise of Josh being in Wagtail. There was no point in hiding anything now. "Of course."

When I finished breakfast, I took a few minutes to dash upstairs and brush my teeth. Then the dogs, Twinkletoes, and I hurried down to the dock. Dave was already there, waiting for us.

He helped me with the life jackets for Twinkletoes and the dogs. In minutes, we were puttering across the lake, with Dave following us in the police boat.

The dogs and Twinkletoes were getting used to these little trips. They leaped from the boat onto the pier and pranced around, eager for us to take off their gear.

Radar could hardly wait. The second his life jacket was off, he shot toward the tent, with Officer Dave on his heels.

The campsite was exactly as I had left it. I'd forgotten the blankets and breakfast breads in my haste to notify Dave. I waited outside the tent when he crept inside. I could hear him taking photographs.

"Just like you described," he said when he returned. "Right down to the smoldering embers."

Trixie pawed at something near the fire.

"Trixie. Stop that! You'll burn your paws."

She paid no attention to me.

Dave squatted to inspect what was left of the fire more closely. He used a stick to dig out the thing Trixie had been pawing. He slipped on gloves to pick it up and examine it.

"What did you say this guy's name was?

"Frank Burton."

"Look at this."

I squatted next to him. Trixie had found a scrap of paper that had been mostly burned. But someone had written on it the letter *P*.

"The question is, did someone toss it in the fire, or did it fall there accidentally?"

"Josh? His last name is Paxton." I didn't know Dana's last name. Some people went by their middle names. She could be Patricia Dana for all I knew.

Dave stood up and slid the scrap of paper into an evidence bag. "We'll learn more from the autopsy, but I'd wager that man has been in the tent for hours. Are you certain this is the same place you saw Josh?"

I stood and looked around. "The general location is correct. I can't swear it's the same place. And that's a pretty generic tent. But I'd say the odds are low that Josh and Dana packed theirs up and Frank Burton happened to come along to the same place with the same sort of tent."

Where was the cairn I had seen? I walked over to the spot where the little cairn would have been. And there, on the ground, lay the milky-white quartz pyramid that had topped the pile. "This is the right place, Dave. Someone knocked over the cairn that was here."

"Indicating a possible struggle," he murmured.

"Dave?" called someone from deeper in the woods.

"Over here!" he shouted.

Radar and Trixie barked as twigs snapped underfoot and voices came closer. In seconds, members of the rescue squad appeared along with additional police officers.

"Maybe I should get out of the way," I said.

Dave nodded. "I know where I can find you."

I called Twinkletoes and the dogs and started rounding up the life vests when I heard Dave call me.

"Holly! Do you know where Josh is?"

I could make some guesses. But I didn't know. It worried me. Were they on the run now? "Nope. I honestly don't know."

I hoped that maybe Frank Burton had died of natural causes as Oma suggested. Maybe he was a friend of Josh's. Maybe they'd agreed to leave him the tent for some reason. Maybe they thought he was sleeping when they left. I could think of half a dozen scenarios in which Josh would not have been responsible for Frank's death.

We went through the ritual of suiting up and getting into the boat. We were halfway across the lake when I realized that there should have been another boat—the one Frank had taken out. I cut the engine. We floated with the gentle current while I gazed around for any sign of a boat that might have drifted away. It could be out of sight by now.

I sagged at my next thought. Or Josh and Dana might have taken it to get away.

Six

❖ ❖ ❖ ❖

Back at the inn, Oma had a lot of questions, but I didn't have answers for any of them.

"I have informed the housekeeper not to go into Mr. Burton's room," said Oma. "Dave will want to examine it."

"Good idea."

"I'm taking Sam and the children on a hike. Cook prepared a lunch for us. Will you be all right here?"

Perfect! I wouldn't have to monitor Oma and keep her out of the kitchen. "Of course. Enjoy your hike. Um, is Carole going?"

Oma flapped her hand. "Oh, the Carole! Yes. I forgot about her."

I didn't suppress my smile. Poor Carole. Oma didn't bother to hide her feelings. I had dated a guy named Ben, whom Oma insisted on calling "the Ben." I had explained to her that she was being rude, but she dismissed me, claiming it was her poor English, when she actually spoke English very well. Now Carole was the object of derision.

I was about to remind her that she had decided to be nice to Carole. But I let it go. It was her day and I knew Oma would never actually be rude to Carole.

When Oma had left the registration lobby, Zelda manned the check-in desk and I settled in the office to phone the marina and speak to the person who had arranged Frank Burton's fishing foray. I wasn't quite sure how to ask him about the boat without alarming him. "Thanks for setting up the fishing evening."

"No problem. Do you know what time he'll be back? I have people who'd like to take out the boat. I thought he would have returned by now."

He'd answered my question without my having to ask it. Someone must have untied the boat and let it drift away or have taken it. The most likely suspect being Josh. Could it look any worse for him?

"That's why I'm calling. This morning, Frank was found dead across the lake. There's no sign of the boat. I was hoping he might have returned it."

"Did you say 'dead'? Did he drown?"

I hadn't thought of that as a possibility. Highly unlikely unless someone dragged him out of the lake and put him in the sleeping bag. Besides, he hadn't been wet that I'd noticed. "I don't think they know yet. I'm so sorry about the boat. I'll put out an alert for it. Could you describe it for me?" I promised to let him know if I heard from anyone.

I hung up and placed a post on the online Wagtail community board.

Missing Boat

Please be on the lookout for a blue fiberglass bass boat. It could be docked somewhere or drifting. Contact Holly at the Sugar Maple Inn with any information.

As I hit send, Holmes Richardson raced into the office. He was tall with sandy hair, and the mere sight of him brightened my day. Most importantly, I loved his wonderful sense of humor and easygoing personality. An architect, Holmes had studied and worked in Chicago for years before returning to Wagtail for good. He renovated and built homes now.

"Is it true?" he asked breathlessly. "Is Josh here?"

I was a little relieved. At least Josh and Dana hadn't fled to Holmes for refuge.

Radar loped to Holmes as if he knew him. Trixie, who was used to getting attention from Holmes, yipped and stood on her hind legs until he picked her up.

I'd had a crush on Holmes when we were kids and worked together at the inn every summer. He, Josh, and I had been fast friends. And now that Holmes and I were living in Wagtail, much to the delight of our grandmothers, we were officially an item.

"I'm afraid the answer to that is a firm *maybe*. I saw him yesterday with a woman named Dana. Does that ring any bells for you?"

"No. But it's not like we've kept in touch. You saw him? In town? I can't believe you didn't call me!"

"The circumstances were a little odd." I told him everything that had happened, from waking up with Radar to the boat that had gone missing.

Holmes rubbed his forehead and ran a hand through his hair. "Whoa. Well, we know Josh wouldn't kill anyone." His eyes met mine. "No. No way. That's not possible."

"I want to agree with you, but the facts don't look good for him. And I don't like the way he's treating Radar. Josh left without him! That's not like Josh."

"Maybe it's like Dana." Holmes eyed Radar. "But you're absolutely right. He can't have gone far. Not without his dog. I'd bet anything Josh is around here somewhere."

"I've been trying to figure this out. Where would they have gone? They turned down my offer for them to stay here. We still have a room set aside for them."

"They could be anywhere. Josh knows Wagtail. There are a lot of places where a person might hide out."

"Like where?"

"Deeper in the woods. Or in an unoccupied cabin somewhere on the mountain."

"I'm inclined to think they're in a house or some kind of structure. But why wouldn't they come here? I understood that he wanted to surprise Oma, but now I wonder if that was the real reason they didn't stay here."

"Maybe they were hiding from Frank Burton."

"Okay. Let's assume that was the case. If it was self-defense, then why did they leave? Why didn't Josh report the death to someone?"

Holmes scowled at me.

"They must have taken the boat," I said.

"Why do you think that?"

"Frank had the key. And now the boat is missing."

Holmes scoffed. "There are at least a hundred guys in Wagtail who could start a boat motor without the key."

"That's a scary thought."

"They're not in the habit of stealing boats. But it comes in handy when the keys are accidentally dropped in the water."

"Let's say Josh *borrowed* the boat. Where would he go?" I asked.

"He knows the inn the best, so it wouldn't surprise me a bit if he turned up here. There are some good camping sites along the lake, too."

"They left their tent behind."

"It wouldn't be the first time Josh slept under the stars. But I see what you mean. It seems to get more and more desperate, doesn't it?"

"Unless Frank had a sleeping bag with him, they're down a sleeping bag, too."

I brought up Frank's information on the computer. "Excluding the possibility that Frank was some kind of sick guy who liked to prey on campers, Josh or Dana must have known him. Here we go. He's from New York City." I Googled his name with New York City. "There are a lot of them!" I tried again with his street address. But this time, there was no match.

I rose from the desk and the two of us walked into the registration lobby. "Zelda, did Frank Burton say anything of interest when he checked in? Like why he was here or what he did for a living?" Some people were very chatty and told us all sorts of details about their lives. Others didn't say much at all.

"Mmm, yes. He said he travels sometimes for work but doesn't usually get to stay in a nice place like this."

That wasn't much help.

The glass door slid open and a man in his thirties walked in with an arrangement of long-stemmed pink roses, pink stargazer lilies, giant daisies, and purple gladiolas.

Zelda said, "Hi," in a come-hither voice.

He was cute in a nerdy sort of way, with warm brown eyes and a tanned complexion. His jet-black hair stood up in a trendy cut. He wore rectangular glasses, the kind that didn't have frames. He smiled at her, which made his cheeks puff up like a chipmunk.

He set the arrangement on the check-in counter. "For your Oma."

"I thought Oma didn't want gifts," said Holmes.

"She doesn't. But who would turn this away? They're gorgeous!" I handed the delivery man a tip.

Zelda leaned over the registration desk. "You must be new to Wagtail." She stretched out her hand and cooed, "I'm Zelda."

"Nate." He shook her hand and lingered for a moment. Holmes nudged me.

"Um, Zelda, would this be a good time to take your break?"

She flashed me a pleased grin. "Absolutely. I thought I'd get a latte at Café Chat. Can I bring you anything?"

She didn't wait for a response and was out the door in a flash with Nate.

"Zelda's great. I don't know why she isn't going out with anyone," said Holmes.

I peered at the card on the flowers, but it was in an envelope. "Wonder who they're from."

"Does Oma have a beau I don't know about?" asked Holmes.

"Not that I'm aware of. She likes the owner of The Blue Boar, but I think they're just friends."

"Someone thinks very highly of her," said Holmes.

"Could they be from Josh?"

"Anything is possible, but they're not his style. He would have sent a live plant. But speaking of Josh, I'm going to check around town with some of our friends to see if he has been in touch with any of them."

Brendan Hayward ambled into the lobby. "Excuse me, I was wondering if you have toothbrushes for sale? I could swear I packed mine, but I can't find it anywhere."

I bent over and plucked a cellophane-wrapped toothbrush out of a box and handed it to him. "On the house."

"Brendan?" asked Holmes.

They faced each other.

"Holmes! I never expected to see you here. I thought you were in Chicago."

"I was, but I came back to Wagtail. What are you doing here?"

"My folks are thinking of moving from Snowball to Wagtail, so I thought I'd check it out. Mom says it has changed a lot since we were kids." He glanced at his watch. "I've got to run. I'm meeting Mom for lunch. Good seeing you, Holmes." Brendan jogged up the stairs.

"I played basketball with him when we were in high school."

I lowered my voice. "Wonder why he isn't staying with his parents."

Holmes whispered, "I'm not surprised. I don't think I'd stay with them either if I had a dad like his. He used to come to games and yell at Brendan. You know the kind, putting his kid down all the time. Expecting more of him. Pushing him to play better, harder. I haven't seen his mom in a long time, but as I recall, she was very nice. Anyway, I have to go, too. I'll see you tonight for the big bash at The Blue Boar."

"You're coming to my mom's for hors d'oeuvres, right?"

"Absolutely." Holmes leaned across the desk for a sweet kiss just as Judy Davis walked into the registration lobby with her two cats.

"Aha!" She smiled at us. "I had no idea that you two were a couple."

I could feel a blush rising on my face. "How can I help you, Judy?"

"Is it true that one of the guests was murdered?"

News got around Wagtail fast! Of course, this was a suspicious death, which would make it travel even faster than normal. "That's partly true. One of our guests died. But not here at the inn," I hastened to add. "He was found across the lake. And we don't know the cause of death yet."

She gave me a dubious look. "Should I be concerned? Maybe the cats and I should go home."

Holmes shook his head. "I'm not worried. It's not as though there's someone running around Wagtail attacking people. You're fine here."

Judy relaxed.

"We take the safety of our guests very seriously. I would let you know if I thought you were in danger," I added.

"Did you have any luck picking out light fixtures?" asked Holmes.

As they walked out the sliding glass doors together, I could hear Judy saying, "Yes, just what I had in mind. Holmes, I wanted to ask you if you could build a cat porch like the ones here at the inn. The cats are enjoying it so much."

The doors closed behind them.

A couple of hours later, Oma, Dad, and crew returned to the inn. Naturally, the first thing they saw was the incredible Park Avenue–worthy flower arrangement.

Oma's cheeks flushed pink when I said the flowers were for her. "But I have told everyone 'No gifts.'"

I eyed Dad, but he shook his head in denial. "Oma, you must have forgotten someone."

They clustered around as Oma removed the card from its little envelope. Her smile faded, but the pink in her face deepened quickly.

"Who are they from?" asked Dad.

"You are right, Sam. I forgot someone." Oma spoke briskly, signaling that was all she planned to say. "We will meet back here at ten minutes to four. Yes? That way Holly and I can show you the way to Nell's house."

With that, Oma walked up the stairs to her apartment while we gaped in silence.

When she closed the door to her apartment, Dad asked, "Who are the flowers from?"

I shrugged. "I don't know. That was weird."

"You didn't peek?" asked Carole.

"Carole! No, I did *not* peek."

"Someone certainly likes her." Dad grinned and winked. "We'll get it out of her."

He wrapped his arms around the shoulders of his children, Lucy and Mike. "All right, kids. Don't forget that Oma is German. No being late. She watches the time like a hawk."

"Like that's something new?" asked Mike.

Lucy laughed. "She's just like you, Dad."

As they moseyed upstairs, Casey, our night manager, showed up to take care of the inn while Oma and I celebrated her birthday next door.

The dogs and Twinkletoes followed me up to my apartment. I put the kettle on for a mug of tea and while I waited for it to boil, I went out on the terrace and looked across the lake through my binoculars. A team of police officers searched along the shoreline and a police boat patrolled near the shore. Why would they be doing that? What were they looking for?

Did they believe Frank had been murdered along the lake shore and dragged up to the campsite? That would make sense. They must be looking for clues, like signs of a struggle. Or maybe they were looking for Josh and Dana's footprints. They could have cast the boat out into the water to mislead the police and buy time.

I looked down at Radar, who played happily with Trixie. What was going on with Josh? I didn't mind having Radar around. In fact, I was enjoying his company. But why would Josh abandon Radar?

The shrill shriek of the teakettle interrupted my thoughts. I called the dogs inside and made myself a mug of bracing tea. After a shower, I swept my hair up to be a little dressier for the occasion and stepped into a strapless periwinkle cocktail dress. All I needed were pretty sandals and pearl drop earrings. Which reminded me of the earring Twinkletoes had found in the other skiff. I located it in the pocket of my jacket and placed it on my dresser.

I fastened a pearl collar on Twinkletoes. Trixie seemed eager to wear her collar of little red and pink satin roses, and I found a red bow tie that was perfect for Radar.

The three of them bounded down the stairs ahead of me, undoubtedly knowing from their special attire that we were off to a party.

When I walked into the reception lobby, I could hear Casey saying, "I'm sorry, sir. Oh! Could you hold just a moment, please?"

He punched the hold button on the phone. "Some guy is asking for a Josh Paxton. There's a room blocked for him, but there's no reservation."

"Josh is my cousin. I thought he might show up for Oma's birthday." I held my hand out for the phone and Casey released the hold button.

"Hello, this is Holly Miller. How can I help you?"

A man said, "I'd like to speak with Josh Paxton." His voice had a lilt. Southern, I thought.

I wasn't sure what to say to him. *The police are chasing Josh right now, would you like to leave a message?* Or, *he's not here and he's not likely to show up now that the cops want to talk to him?* What I wanted to say was *How do you know Josh?* But that would be wrong. I responded as I would for any guest.

"Mr. Paxton is not available at the moment. May I take a message for him?"

"Yeah. Tell him the mission is complete and Roo is ready to go when he is."

That was not what I had expected. I didn't know what the man would say, but not that! Mission? I wrote it down and read it back to him. "Anything else, Mr. Roo?"

The man on the phone laughed. "I'm not Roo! Don't worry, he's expecting my call. He'll know who I am. Thanks, y'all have a good day."

Seven

❧ ❧ ❧ ❧ ❧

The unknown caller disconnected on his end and the phone buzzed in my ear.

I stared at the phone in my hand. That was curious. Why hadn't he called Josh's cell phone? It also suggested that Josh had intended to stay at the inn. Or did he simply plan to pick up messages here? Something strange was going on with him.

Casey, who'd been looking over my shoulder and listening in, asked, "Is your cousin a spy or something?"

"No," I said without conviction. "At least not that I know of. He's a pilot. He has spent a lot of time traveling abroad. The last I heard he was running an animal rescue."

I marked the room account with a message notification and tucked the message into the mailbox associated with the room we were holding for him.

"Call me if he arrives, please."

Casey nudged me as Carole and Dad walked into the

lobby. Carole wore a skintight dress that was missing the better part of the middle section and was covered with gold sequins. It wasn't exactly Wagtail style. They *were* from Florida, I reasoned, where people liked to show off their tans and physiques. And where it was a whole lot warmer than Wagtail at this time of year.

Oma, who was rarely flustered, stopped cold when she saw Carole. All she said was, "Can you walk a few blocks in those high heels, Carole, or should we take a golf cart?"

"Oh, honey," said Carole, "aren't you sweet to worry about me. Trust me, I could climb Mount Kilimanjaro in these babies."

The babies in question were undeniably gorgeous, but I knew I couldn't walk in those five-inch heels, not even to cross the lobby.

When Lucy and Mike joined us, we strolled the few blocks to my mom's house, with Trixie, Gingersnap, Twinkletoes, and Radar in the lead. Oma caught up to me and took my arm, letting Dad, Carole, and his children walk ahead. I worried that she didn't feel well or wasn't up to the short walk.

"I have a favor to ask of you," said Oma in a soft voice that the others probably didn't hear.

"Sure, Oma. Anything for you."

"The flowers that arrived were from a secret admirer."

I gasped and grinned. "Ooh, Oma!"

"I am not as amused by this as you are. It feels like someone is stalking me."

"I doubt that. He was probably just too shy to say his name."

"You can find out who this person is. Yes?"

Poor Oma. I was certain that the flowers were simply a lovely gift. What a shame that they were causing her distress. "I can't make promises, but the florist might tell me."

"Yes. Please check into this for me."

"Don't give it another thought. I'll talk to the florist on Monday."

"Thank you, liebling."

We caught up to Dad and his crew. The minute Mom opened the door, Twinkletoes and the dogs scampered into her house as though they lived there. I could hear my other grandparents making a fuss over them. Only Radar took his time, stopping to sniff the premises before entering.

Mom looked terrific. In fact, maybe a little too good. Were those false eyelashes on her fluttering eyes? I tried to hide my grin. There was no question in my mind that she wanted to be beautiful, especially since Dad was accompanied by someone so much younger than the two of them. After all, Mom and Dad had been through a lot together before they went their separate ways.

Happily, my grandparents were surprisingly hospitable to Dad and Carole.

Mom's sister, my cranky Aunt Birdie, fluttered toward me. She was a pain in the neck most of the time, but she had an eye for fashion. She wore a wild cat print dress with a black sequin belt that would have been too flashy for me. But she carried it off with aplomb. It looked very dramatic with the white Cruella de Vil streak in her dark hair. "Is that your father's second wife? She's not old enough to have almost-grown children."

I whispered, "His wife left him. We're not quite sure about the situation between Dad and Carole. She surprised Dad by coming."

"Mmm. I suppose that explains the questionable dress. On the bright side, her tacky dress makes yours look almost acceptable." She frowned at my shoes. "I should take you shoe shopping. Those look like what I wear to do the gardening. Liesel is having a bad influence on you with her old-fashioned ideas about clothes."

Aunt Birdie and Oma tolerated each other, but Birdie was aggravated that I was close to Oma and worked at the inn with her. Even though Birdie rarely had a good thing to say about anyone, I had glimpsed a kinder, softer side and knew there was a heart in her somewhere.

"Is it true that Margaret's son killed a man?" she asked.

Ouch! "We don't know who killed him. Or the cause of death."

A sly smile crossed her lips. "How very diplomatic of you. He always was a wild child. I can't say I'm surprised that he turned out this way given the philistine proclivities of his maternal grandfather. Those genes had to land somewhere, and you certainly didn't get them."

I had never known Oma's husband but had heard rumors that he acquired the inn by winning it in a poker game. I wished I had a cleverly wicked response about her father, but I dearly loved Birdie's father and would never say anything ill-spirited about him.

Luckily, Lucy sidled up to me and tugged me to my siblings. All I could do as I turned away was say, "Let's not go there today, Aunt Birdie."

My mother's children and my dad's children were introducing themselves to one another when one of them asked how they were related.

"Through our dad," explained Lucy.

"That can't be," said Mom's son, Oliver. "I don't think we've ever met him before."

"You share the same half sister," I explained.

They looked at me with confused expressions. My mom and dad tried to explain at the same time. They only managed to confuse everyone more as their words tumbled out simultaneously.

I seized a moment of stunned silence to say, "I'm a half sister to all of you." I pointed at Mike and Lucy. "We have the same dad." Then I pointed at Oliver and Belle. "We have the same mom."

"You're like a bridge between us," said Belle.

That prompted Lucy to declare, "We're Holly-sibs!"

It was a strange situation. They really weren't related at all. Yet somehow, the odd nature of their connection fueled a friendship. They were all about the same age, I reasoned. They probably had a lot in common.

When Dad and Carole went on a tour of the house with my grandfather and the Holly-sibs, I headed for the kitchen. "What can I do to help?" I asked Mom.

She gave me a hug, then handed me a tray. "Make sure your dad gets some of these deviled eggs. They're his favorite."

"Are you wearing fake eyelashes?" I whispered.

"Is it that obvious?"

"Not really. Just to people who see you every day, I guess."

"I debated about them for a long time." Mom removed a tray from the oven. "I hate it when people overdo makeup and end up looking like they stepped off a stage. Is it true that Oma is already calling Sam's friend 'the Carole'?"

"Do you think Oma does that on purpose or that she just can't help herself?"

Mom laughed. "She probably called me 'the Nell' at one time!"

Oma had just walked in and overheard. "I have never called you 'the Nell.' Not even when you and Sam divorced. You have always been my sweet Nell."

Mom handed Bellinis to Oma and me. "Here's to you, Oma. Happy birthday! This girl couldn't have asked for a better or kinder mother-in-law."

We sipped our deliciously peachy drinks. The three of us stood in front of a floor-to-ceiling window that overlooked the garden. Azaleas and rhododendrons bloomed in profusion.

"Nell," said Oma, "if I lived in this house, I believe I would make excuses to bake just so I could be in the kitchen overlooking the beautiful garden."

"I love this view. We're still settling in, but it feels great to be back in Wagtail."

Someone in another room called, "Oma! Oma, where are you?"

Oma hustled toward the doorway with me behind her. But Mom tapped my shoulder and crooked her finger at me.

"Has anyone heard from Margaret?"

I shook my head. "Not a peep."

Mom frowned at me. "I can't believe she would miss her mother's birthday. She was excited about coming."

"You were in touch with her?" I asked.

"Sure. Why not? You say that like it's odd."

"You divorced her brother. I didn't know you had kept in touch."

Mom smiled. "We were friends, honey. I suppose you were too young to remember. She adored you when you were a baby."

I barely remembered Aunt Margaret. I knew she was a child psychologist who lived in Boston. And I thought her husband had died rather young. There were loads of pictures of my dad and his sister in Oma's apartment. Dad had told me once that Margaret was an ace student and valedictorian of her class in high school. He'd warned me never to go to a casino with her because Margaret could count cards and always won at blackjack, which had gotten them banned from two casinos when they were in college.

I joined the others in the living room, where I found Carole flirting with Holmes.

"You're so handsome," she gushed. "If I had known that Virginia mountain men were so good-looking, I would have come to Wagtail years ago."

Oh, barf!

She reached out and toyed with his sleeve. "Are you a lumberjack?"

I nearly spewed my Bellini.

Holmes finally noticed me. I just grinned at him and lifted my glass in a teasing toast.

"I'm an architect and a contractor. It was very nice meeting you, Carole. Excuse me but I see my girlfriend."

He headed toward me, his eyes wide with discomfort. "Who is that woman?" he whispered after kissing me with a little more passion than he usually did in front of people.

"Dad's new girlfriend."

"Where is your dad?"

I looked around. "I don't know. Maybe he's in the back with Gramps."

"Probably hiding from her," Holmes muttered. "Any news on Josh yet?"

"Nothing from Josh or his mom."

We mingled amiably. Before long it was time to go to The Blue Boar. Holmes and I hung back to help Mom wrap up leftovers and stash them while the others got a head start.

"What does your father see in that woman?" Mom stacked containers and slid them into the fridge.

"Ask Holmes," I suggested.

"Very funny." Holmes handed me a baking sheet to dry. "I bet she was a rebound date, Nell. Sam probably went out with her once and now he can't get rid of her."

"Holmes knows just how clingy she can be," I teased.

Holmes blushed. "She was a little bit forward for a woman who was supposed to be here with someone else."

"Sam is still smarting from the divorce," said Mom. "I

can relate to that. If I had been more clever, I'd have wrangled a date of my own for this weekend."

"Mom, you'll have more fun than he will," I assured her.

The three of us, the dogs, and Twinkletoes walked over to The Blue Boar, which was packed with patrons.

The owner, Thomas, which Oma pronounced *Toe-moss*, spotted us when we entered. "This way, please."

Classical music played softly in the background. Giant chandeliers sparkled overhead. One long wall of floor-to-ceiling windows overlooked the lake and the mountains. Now that it was evening, the distant mountains couldn't be seen, but lights on a few boats and houses shone in the night and charming lanterns glowed outside the restaurant.

Thomas led us to a long table. In a low voice, he said, "Liesel will be very angry with me. You must help me, please."

"What did you do?" I asked.

"I know she only wanted family and close friends, but people started reserving their own tables and before I knew it, the entire restaurant was booked by people who wanted to share her birthday celebration."

"I guess we should have booked the whole restaurant." I looked for Oma. She was in her element greeting friends. "She looks happy. I think she'll forgive you."

"You promise to help me?"

"I promise that I will defend you."

At that moment, Aunt Margaret walked in. I could hardly believe how much she resembled Oma. Even though I didn't remember her, I would have known her anywhere. They had the same alert eyes and pert nose. Oma hugged her like she might never let go. Tears streamed down her face. I couldn't hear what they were saying, but it didn't matter. They had clearly missed each other.

I pulled out my phone and snapped photos of them

and various guests. Oma would enjoy reliving the night later on.

Officer Dave approached Holmes and me. "Is there assigned seating?"

It looked to me as though Oma would sit in the middle of the long table, with Dad on one side of her and Aunt Margaret on the other. "Sit next to me. Oma loves you like you're one of her grandchildren."

We were taking our seats when Radar yelped and ran toward a couple entering the room.

Officer Dave leaned over and whispered, "Is that Josh?"

Sure enough, Josh was introducing his girlfriend to Oma and his mom. He had trimmed his beard very short and had gotten a haircut. He looked much more like the old Josh I knew and loved. Just a little older.

Dana had made an equally remarkable transformation. The messy bun had been replaced by a sleek crossed bun. She wore a sleeveless dress in white with a cutout midriff. The tie-up boots had been replaced by high-heeled white patent leather sandals with ankle straps. Quite a difference from the person I had met across the lake. They had obviously gone shopping.

There was one big truth about living in a small town. We knew too much about one another. For instance, I had seen that white dress at a local clothing store and knew that it carried a hefty price tag. Bigger than hefty, actually. Zelda and I had wondered who would buy it, since showing the midriff wasn't popular in Wagtail. Granted, there were plenty of wealthy residents in Wagtail, but the dress wouldn't appeal to or fit everyone with that fleshy display of the abdomen. It wasn't any of my business, but it did mean that either Josh or Dana had a good amount of money. I didn't imagine that flying an animal rescue plane paid particularly well. Maybe I had been wrong about that.

Or maybe Dana had a lot more money than her mini-skirt, large man's shirt, and boots suggested the first time I met her.

Aunt Margaret and Oma doted on Josh. His presence had brought them more joy than any gift ever could. I was grateful that he showed up.

A chill ran through me. Surely Dave wouldn't ruin Oma's birthday celebration. "Are you going to arrest him?" I hadn't paid attention to Dave's attire and glanced at him to see what he was wearing. I was relieved to see he had dressed in a nice suit instead of his uniform. Josh probably wouldn't realize that Dave was a cop.

He took a deep breath and whispered, "I didn't want to have to tell you this tonight. Dr. Engelknecht is sending Frank to the medical examiner in Roanoke, but on a cursory examination, it appears Frank was strangled. I'm going to take Josh and Dana in for questioning but not until they leave this room. I have officers standing by outside, ready to detain them."

"Thanks for not spoiling Oma's birthday."

Josh and Dana took seats on the other side of the long table, across from his mom, Margaret. Radar had clearly missed him and leaned against Josh's legs.

A procession of servers arrived dressed in black trousers and vests over white shirts. They set a plate before each of us with two crostini on it, one with prosciutto and the other with smoked salmon. I tried not to gobble them, but they were delicious. Twinkletoes and the dogs were served small biscuits, which they snarfed too fast for me to identify.

Creamy shrimp soup arrived next with a small shrimp dish for Twinkletoes and a serving of what appeared to be cod with a shrimp on top for Trixie.

I hated that Josh had wound up in this situation. All I

could do was hope he had some kind of good explanation. "You expected him to come," I muttered to Dave.

Dave nodded. "Of course. Supposedly this party is why he's in Wagtail, right?"

I tried to put it out of my mind. The detainment of Josh would happen soon enough and there wasn't a thing I could do about it. At this point, I had to hope that he hadn't murdered Frank. Hopefully, Josh didn't even know him. Though I had to wonder how he had come to be in Josh's tent if that were the case. There had to be some logical explanation.

Just as I lifted a soup spoon to my mouth, I heard Oma say softly, "Not the Ben!"

Eight

❀ ❀ ❀ ❀

I nearly spilled my soup. Surely I hadn't heard correctly. But when I looked up, my former boyfriend, Ben Hathaway, was entering the room. Emphasis on *former*. The man who had proposed marriage to me through a text. A pity proposal at that. I hadn't heard from him in a long time and assumed he had found someone else and moved on. I certainly had.

But there he was in a distinguished suit and horn-rimmed glasses, wishing Oma a happy birthday and apologizing for arriving so late.

In a loud voice, my father said, "There's my future son-in-law! Glad you could make it!"

Holmes looked at me with raised eyebrows. "Is there something I should know?"

I flashed him a confused look. "No! I have no idea what he's doing here or why my dad would say that." To be honest, I didn't think Holmes was one bit threatened by Ben. The three of us had worked together to solve a few murders in the past. Ben's expertise as a lawyer had come in handy more than once. Still, I wasn't pleased about his sudden appearance.

One of the servers brought him a chair and quickly set a place for him. Ben kissed me on the cheek and was more warmly welcomed by Holmes than by me. And now I had the dubious pleasure of being seated across the table from Holmes and beside Ben. It was a nightmare! What was he doing here? I was afraid to ask.

Trying to choose my words carefully so I wouldn't sound quite as annoyed as I felt, I said, "How nice of you to join us."

"I wouldn't have missed it."

"How did you know about Oma's birthday?" asked Holmes.

"Liesel has used our law firm for several matters. Her birthday popped up on our tickler system. I thought someone should come to wish her well."

Finally, Oma's favorite dish, and quite possibly mine, too, arrived. For a short time Duck Confit with Cherry Sauce absorbed my attention. I forgot all about the Ben, the Carole, and Josh. Trixie and Twinkletoes also dined on duck, but without the cherries. A dollop of mashed potatoes and red Swiss chard had been added to Trixie's bowl. I thought I saw a few peas in Twinkletoes's dish.

Oma was in her element seated between her son and daughter. I wasn't at all sure how it happened, but my mom sat beside my dad. Carole was across from Dad and not looking at all happy about it. I wondered how many other undercurrents of dissatisfaction that I didn't even know about were in progress around the room.

When the dinner dishes had been cleared and champagne was being poured, a few people began to chant "Speech!"

Oma smiled and waved her hand. "No speeches and no

toasts. Just the company of my family and dear friends is all I wish for this evening. I love you all!"

Black Forest cherry cake was served, with its luscious layers of moist chocolate cake separated by heavenly cream and cherries.

My dad, who had a beautiful voice, started us all singing "Happy Birthday."

Oma's slice carried a single candle. She closed her eyes to make a wish, then blew it out.

As the servers came around to pour coffee and tea, I began to tense up. It wouldn't be long now.

Most of all, I wanted to be sure Oma and Margaret weren't with Josh when the police nabbed him. I figured the easiest way to achieve that was to make sure Oma and Margaret left the room first.

I kicked Holmes gently and said, "Excuse me, please." I discreetly motioned to him to follow me.

Unfortunately, Ben watched closely, as if he suspected something was up.

I ducked into the hallway where the restrooms were.

Holmes grinned. "Are we making a mad dash away from Ben?"

Ben peered around the corner.

"I wish. C'mon, Ben. You might as well hear this. There are cops outside waiting to take Josh and Dana in for questioning. I don't want Oma and Margaret to see that. I think the easiest thing would be to stall Josh and Dana. Holmes, you haven't had a chance to talk with Josh yet, so maybe you could amble over with a bottle of champagne and keep them busy while Oma and Margaret leave."

"What's going on?" asked Ben.

I summarized the situation very quickly for him.

He took off his glasses and massaged the ridge of his nose. "Never a dull moment in Wagtail. I'll do what I can to help."

"Thanks, Ben." Holmes slapped him on the shoulder. "Good to see you here again."

Holmes's warm outgoing nature was one of the things that I loved about him. He was the embodiment of a guy who had never met a stranger. I was a little more reserved and admired his ability to befriend everyone. Even my former boyfriend.

I was pleased when Holmes wrapped his arm around me as we returned to our seats. Maybe he hoped to send Ben a little sign after all! Or maybe he was just being Holmes.

When the festivities broke up, Dave was the first one out the door. Holmes immediately headed for his old friend Josh. But my plan to make sure Oma and Aunt Margaret would not see Josh being detained was sliding out of control. I hadn't counted on all the people who were stopping Oma to say hello and give her their good wishes on her birthday. Not to mention the people who recognized Margaret and clambered for her attention because they hadn't seen her in a decade.

I picked up Twinkletoes and Trixie so they wouldn't be underfoot as people milled around.

Dave walked over to me. "Did you make some kind of arrangement for them to get away?" He rarely spoke in such a gruff tone.

"No. I just didn't want them detained in front of Oma and Margaret. That would spoil their memories of this day and it would be horrible for them."

"Then where are Josh and Dana?" he asked.

I looked for Holmes but didn't see him. "Oh! I guess they're outside now."

Margaret and Oma were strolling through the doorway, followed by a lot of people. The room was clearing fast.

"Holly Miller, I will arrest *you* if you assisted them in some way."

I rolled my eyes.

"She said she didn't." I turned to find Ben behind me.

Holmes walked toward us. "Whew! I didn't think I'd ever coax them outside."

Officer Dave scowled, and I realized that he was wearing an earpiece. "Where did you leave them, Holmes?"

"At the front entrance." A flush of red rose up his neck. "I didn't want them to think I was walking them into a trap."

"Looks like they might have suspected it," said Dave. "They're gone."

"What?" I lowered Trixie and Twinkletoes to the floor. "How is that possible?"

Radar loped back into the room, his nose to the carpet.

"No, no, no," said Holmes. "That can't be. I was with them. They have to be out there. Your people must have missed them."

"Doggone it! They probably doubled back to mix with the crowd." Officer Dave spoke into a handset as he ran from the room.

"Unless they're still in the building," I said.

Holmes, Ben, and I rushed for the door.

When we were in the empty hallway, Ben said, "I'll check the men's room."

"I'm not sure you have to," I said in a whisper, pointing at Radar, who was sniffing the floor and appeared to be following a scent.

Trixie ran toward her friend and lowered her nose to the floor to find out what smelled so interesting.

Radar trotted forward with his nose down.

Trixie and Twinkletoes followed him. Holmes, Ben, and I were right behind them.

Radar came to an abrupt stop at a glass door that led to the balcony. He reared up on his hind legs and placed his front paws on the door.

Ben, Holmes, and I crowded together behind him to look out.

Holmes shoved the door open and all of us rushed onto the balcony that overlooked the lake. Thanks to moonlight and a couple of spotlights on the side of the building, we could make out Josh and Dana staggering to their feet below.

"Josh!" I called, trying to keep my voice low. "What are you doing?"

Holmes was a little louder. "Have you lost your mind? You could have broken your neck jumping off this balcony."

"Shh." Josh gave Dana a hand getting up. "We're okay."

Dana didn't look okay to me. She limped when she took a few steps. "Josh, why are you running? It only makes you look guilty."

"Guilty? We haven't done anything."

"Then why are you jumping off balconies?" asked Holmes.

"I need to protect Dana. Listen, I could use your help instead of your criticism."

"What do you need?" asked Holmes.

"Cover. Whistle if you see anyone following us, will you?"

Ben spoke softly. "Don't do it. If they're guilty, you could be aiding and abetting."

"We can't do that, Josh," said Holmes. "I don't understand. If you didn't murder that guy—"

"Murder? Who's dead?" Josh gazed up at us with a bewildered look on his face.

"Frank Burton," said Holmes.

Josh held up his palms and shook his head as if he knew nothing about it. Then he ducked under Dana's arm to help her walk and they disappeared into the trees, Dana still limping.

"If I were a cop, I'd say they were acting guilty," said Ben.

"But you heard Josh," I protested. "He looked genuinely surprised that Frank Burton is dead. I don't think they killed him."

"Then why are they on the run, or the limp as the case may be?" asked Ben in a snide tone.

My eyes met Holmes's. Neither of us had an explanation.

A long moment of silence passed before Ben said, "I understand that he's your cousin and a friend. But his behavior makes no sense. Why did they come here tonight if they were afraid of getting caught? And why run from the police if they didn't kill anyone?"

"Maybe Josh got into a fight with him and thought Frank was alive when they ran from their tent," said Holmes.

"Unlikely," I said sadly. "Frank was strangled."

"Okay, that's a problem," said Holmes. "But someone else could have come along and strangled him after they left."

"You won't know unless they go in for questioning," said Ben.

"I wonder where they're going." We stepped inside. "The weather is nice during the day, but it's still cold at night."

"They must be staying someplace," said Holmes. "They were well-dressed and groomed. They didn't look as though they'd been roughing it."

"Who was Josh's best friend in Wagtail?" asked Ben.

"Me." Holmes ran a hand through his hair. "Why would that matter?"

"If I were on the run, I would go to my best friend. At least for the night. The cops would know how to locate my parents or family members, but they might not know who my friends were."

Ben had a point.

"That's probably what most people would do." I gave Holmes a questioning look.

"They didn't come to me last night. That's for sure." Holmes thought for a moment. "Josh doesn't know where I live. He would think—"

"Would think what?" I asked.

"Would he go to the house I lived in as a kid?" Holmes raised his eyebrows hopefully.

"Your parents' house?" asked Ben.

"They don't live there anymore. They sold it and moved. They're still in Wagtail, but Josh wouldn't know any of that."

"Then let's go," said Ben. "How well do you know the people who bought the house?"

"I've met them a few times. They're nice people." Holmes gazed at me. "What do you think, Holly?"

I had a different idea. "I wonder if Radar would track them."

Ben, who had little understanding of animals, snorted. "Right. Like he'd be able to do that. He came back in here. What does that tell you?"

I shook my head in disbelief. "That he returned with them when they doubled back but they closed the door so he couldn't jump off the balcony."

"Ahh. Then he's much smarter than I thought," Ben said sarcastically.

Holmes gave Ben an odd look. "Holly's right. But I see flashlights down there right now. We don't want to lead the cops to them. We'll go home, change clothes, and meet back here in an hour."

Nine

❦ ❦ ❦ ❦

"In the dark of night?" Ben scoffed. "No, thanks."

"I'll meet you back here, Holmes." I called Trixie, Twin-kletoes, and Radar and headed for the door.

I could hear Ben asking Holmes, "You're not serious? They're adults. It's not like they're lost. They're hiding from the cops on purpose. Why would you want to find them?"

Holmes caught up to me. "Don't you have any close friends, Ben? People you'd do anything for?"

"Uh, sure. But not crawling through the woods at night."

We had reached the front door. I saw Officer Dave and recognized some police milling about. "Shh. Talk about what a great meal we had."

"I don't think it could be beat." Holmes slid his hand into mine and locked our fingers. "That cake was the best ever."

"Thomas is talented." I squeezed Holmes's hand. "And everything was so beautifully plated."

Out of the corner of my eye, I noted Officer Dave eyeing us. "Good night, Dave!"

"Good night," he called back.

But I knew he had his eyes on us. If anyone had a clue about Josh's whereabouts, it would be Holmes and me.

Holmes left on a golf cart to go home and change out of his suit. Ben and I continued walking toward the inn.

"It was nice of you to come." I said it more to make conversation than anything else.

"I've missed you, Holly."

Gack. That was the last thing I wanted to hear. "Are you kidding? There's so much to do in Washington."

"Yeah. It's not the same without a friend to talk with. Look what happened tonight! I've only been here a few hours. I've already been to a fantastic dinner, participated in hunting fugitives, and been part of the discussion about them. Nothing like that ever happens to me at home. Okay, sometimes I go to a nice dinner, but none of the other stuff."

"That's not exactly the norm around here, Ben." We walked up the stairs to the main entrance of the inn.

"That's not how it looks to me. There's always something going on. And the townspeople are so nice. Holly, I'm tired of being alone on holidays."

We were in the lobby. I didn't know of a nice way to ask where he was staying. He had walked back to the inn with me, which led me to believe he intended to stay with us. I stopped at the bottom of the grand staircase and cheerily asked, "Where are you staying?"

"With you." He said it without a second of hesitation. "When I called to book a room, Zelda said you were full up. Casey said to take my bag up to your apartment."

No. Just no! "If Josh and Dana don't come back to the inn tonight, you can stay in the room I set aside for them."

Ben's grin melted away. "Oh. Okay."

He walked up the stairs with me. Trixie, Twinkletoes, and Radar waited for us at the top, outside my door.

I unlocked it and sure enough, Ben's bags were waiting just inside. "Help yourself to whatever is in the kitchen. I'm going to change."

Trixie, Radar, and Twinkletoes followed me to my bedroom. Trixie and Twinkletoes sat side by side, gazing at me with worried expressions. Could they know that Ben had encouraged me to give them up years ago?

I bent to tickle them under their chins. "It's okay. I'm not going anywhere, and neither are you." I whispered, "He'll probably be gone by tomorrow afternoon."

Ben, who had never lived with an animal of any kind, would have made fun of me for talking to them. But I knew they understood certain words. Probably many more than I realized.

They seemed to relax a little, although when Ben shouted to me, "I didn't bring any boots," Twinkletoes turned her head in his direction and hissed.

I had to stifle my laugh. Ben had once tried to attract cats by rubbing his clothes with catnip. It had worked, but apparently, Twinkletoes remembered him for who he really was, the man who wanted me to ditch her.

I replaced their festive collars with their regular ones, along with their GPS collars in case one of them took off and got lost. In addition, I fastened a light on Radar's collar so we could see him more easily in the dark.

I changed into a black turtleneck and soft black jogger pants. Alas, I didn't have running shoes in black, but there was nothing I could do about that now. I grabbed a black jacket in case it was getting colder and opened the door to find Ben in jeans and a black turtleneck.

"Ready?" he asked.

"I thought you weren't coming."

He shrugged. "You two bozos need me. How else will you stay out of trouble?"

"Okay. Let's go."

We walked downstairs and could hear Oma, Margaret, and Dad having a great time in the Dogwood Room. Part of me longed to join them, but Josh's welfare was at stake.

Saturday nights in Wagtail were usually busy and that night was no exception. People crowded into restaurants and bars and walked along the sidewalks, gazing into brightly lit shop windows.

The Blue Boar was close to the inn, so we didn't have far to go. The trickiest part was slipping around the outside of the building without attracting attention.

Ben hunched over like a guilty thief.

"Stand up straight and look like you know what you're doing," I whispered.

"But I feel so sneaky."

"We're not doing anything wrong."

"We're trespassing!"

"Thomas is a family friend. He wouldn't mind if we crossed his property to get to the woods."

Ben grumbled incoherently.

We waited at the edge of the woods. I held Radar so he wouldn't get a head start and lose us. Holmes arrived shortly after we did.

I set Radar on the ground, as close as possible to the spot where we had last seen Josh and Dana, and switched on the light attached to his collar. He sniffed the ground, his tail wagging. He concentrated on a small area and for a couple of minutes, I thought he might not follow their tracks, but then, without lifting his nose, he entered the woods.

Holmes and I high-fived and silently followed him.

Ben was right behind us. "How did he do that? What

if he's following someone else? He doesn't know where he's going. We're crazy for following an animal with a brain the size of a nut."

"Shh!" I hissed.

"Oh, right. Like it might distract him?"

I wondered if Ben would ever stop talking when we heard a branch snap.

Holmes stopped and whispered, "Was that one of you?"

"It sounded farther back," I whispered.

"Wasn't me." Ben grabbed the back of my jacket like a child would grab hold of his mom.

We stood motionless, craning to hear any other sounds. Radar's light was getting farther away.

"We're going to lose Radar," I said softly.

Holmes nodded, and we began our little trek again.

The lights of Tequila Mockingbird, a local bar and restaurant, shone through the trees as we came closer.

The light on Radar disappeared under the outdoor dining deck. I caught a glimpse of the white fur on Trixie and Twinkletoes just before they, too, disappeared into the darkness under the deck.

We hurried to catch up to them. Radar kept going until he broke into a cleared lot where a house was under construction. The roof and walls were already in place.

"I don't believe this," whispered Holmes. "This is the house I'm building for the Davises."

The structure loomed before us, gray in the darkness of night.

"That's a big deck," I whispered.

"Half of it will be a screened porch," hissed Holmes. "It runs the length of the house."

"It's beautiful." Even though it wasn't finished yet, it exuded country cottage charm. "Does it have running water and electricity?"

Holmes grunted. "It's all wired, but there are no lights

or sinks or showers yet. Drywall is scheduled to start on Monday. Ben, you stay out here in case they try to escape through the back."

"Me? All alone? Why do I have to do that?"

"It's not like you have to tackle them," said Holmes. "We don't have time to bicker. Radar and Trixie must have found a way inside. I don't see them anywhere."

In the woods behind us, someone grunted. Twigs snapped, followed by a loud groan.

Holmes turned his flashlight in the direction of the groan and cautiously walked toward it. I was right behind him.

"You two are nuts," Ben huffed. "I'm calling Officer Dave."

Another moan came from the woods and a phone began to ring somewhere.

Heavy footsteps pounded away from us.

Holmes shouted, "Hey! Hey, stop!"

I aimed my flashlight at a dark mound on the ground.

Ten

❀ ❀ ❀ ❀

The glow of my flashlight illuminated a man lying on his belly. I kneeled next to him. "Are you okay?"

His phone was ringing. I leaned forward for a better look at his face. Dave! "Dave, are you conscious?"

He opened an eye. "Holly," he groaned. "Was that Josh?"

"Josh?" That possibility hadn't even occurred to me. I expected Josh to be in the house that was under construction. "I don't know who hit you. We didn't get a good look. We heard someone running away."

"I didn't get a look at him. Where'd he hit you?" asked Holmes.

"Back of my head. He must have used a bat or something hard." With my help, Dave turned and howled in pain. He eased himself into a sitting position. The pain must have eased because he loosened the grip he had on my arm and felt the back of his head.

I could hear Holmes on the phone mobilizing his rescue friends and Dr. Engelknecht.

Dave tried to stand up.

"No you don't," I said. "Wait for the rescue crew. Dr. Engelknecht will want a CAT scan of your noggin."

Trixie and Twinkletoes bounded toward us and immediately demanded attention from Dave.

"I'm sorry," I said. "Let me take them away from you."

"It's okay," Dave muttered.

Twinkletoes curled up in his lap and purred.

Radar's absence was highly suspicious and led me to think that he had found Josh and Dana in the house.

"Where were you going?" he asked.

I might as well be honest about that. "We hoped Radar might follow Josh and Dana's trail."

"I guessed that was the case. I thought you'd never get back."

"You were waiting for us?"

He nodded. "Ouch! Ugh."

"Try to keep still."

He closed his eyes and slowly stroked Twinkletoes. "I guess you didn't find them."

"No." It wasn't a lie. I didn't know if they were in Judy Davis's house or not. "Is someone after you?"

"Lots of people. But I'd bet on Josh and his girlfriend."

"That doesn't make any sense. Why would Josh hit you over the head if he was tailing *you*?"

"That's not the right question. Why would Josh tail me is a better one. You must have been heading toward something he didn't want me to find."

At that moment, a collection of flashlights danced in the night like crazed oversize fireflies. Voices called out, "Holmes? Dave? Where are you?"

Trixie yelped and ran toward the lights, barking.

They descended on Dave, which Twinkletoes found annoyingly rude. She fled his lap and watched from a distance.

Dr. Engelknecht checked Dave out. "I suspect a broken fibula and you probably have a concussion, too."

"Fibula? Where's that?" asked Dave.

"It's the smaller bone in your calf. Won't know for sure until we get an X-ray. I'm sending you over to the hospital in Snowball."

"Can't you just do it here in Wagtail? I've got a murder investigation in progress."

"Sorry, Dave. I'm not taking chances with the blow you received to the head. You need a CAT scan. Chances are good that they'll release you by morning."

In a matter of minutes poor Dave lay on a stretcher that was carried out to the road on the other side of the house. The golf cart that had been modified as a little ambulance took off to transfer Dave to a real ambulance at the edge of town. Holmes, Trixie, Twinkletoes, and I were left in a dark and silent backyard.

Only then did I remember Ben. I turned in a slow circle, aiming my flashlight around the backyard. "Where did Ben go?"

Holmes pointed at the house. We walked around to a side door.

Josh opened it as if he was waiting for us. "Welcome! Is that guy okay?"

"No. He's not." I couldn't keep the anger out of my tone.

Josh led us to Ben and Dana, who sat on the floor in what I guessed to be a great room. Ben's flashlight sat on its end, offering the only light in the room. The dim glow reminded me of slumber parties and ghost stories on Halloween.

Easygoing Holmes's first words were, "You do realize that this is private property?"

Josh appeared surprised.

I was, too, but when I thought about it, I realized that as the contractor, Holmes was probably responsible to the owner, not to mention concerned about liability if the house was damaged or someone was injured on the property.

"When did you become such a beast?" asked Josh. "The two of you used to be fun."

"Since we became responsible adults," Holmes grumbled. "Did you kill Frank?"

"Ben has been telling us about him. I can't believe that you think we murdered him." Josh sounded incredulous. "We didn't even know him, much less that he was dead."

"My husband is after me," said Dana in a tiny voice.

Josh looked at her. "You don't have to explain, Dana."

"I want to. They don't understand. Josh has been trying to protect me. If he finds me . . ."

My eyes met Holmes's. If they didn't know Frank, why did he go to their campsite? I wasn't buying it. Could he have been her husband? "Frank is dead. You no longer have anything to fear."

"Frank wasn't her husband." Josh reached for Dana's hand and squeezed it. "Now do you understand?"

Holmes's voice softened. "You think Dana's husband killed Frank?"

Josh nodded. "It could have been us he murdered. We're lucky we got out of there when we did."

I wanted to be sympathetic. But why did they run from the police?

"Look, I'm sorry, but you can't stay here. It's not an option. The house and land do not belong to me. Not to mention that it's under construction. Do you know how many dangerous pitfalls there are in here? It's a work in progress," said Holmes. "Holly has been holding a room for you at the inn. You'll be safer there anyway."

Ben nodded. "In the morning, I'll go to the police with you."

I was willing to bet that they wouldn't be at the inn in the morning. But there wasn't anything I could do about that, unless . . . "I think you should go to the cops now. They don't take an injury to one of their own lightly. The more you cooperate with them on finding the person who attacked Dave, the better. Because, come daylight, they'll be fanning out in Wagtail, on the hunt."

My phone vibrated. I had a text from Dave.

Need your help. Am in Snowball ER.

When I looked up from my phone, Josh was making a fuss about going to the police and Holmes was telling him to quit griping and get his stuff together.

Although the hospital wasn't far from the Snowball police station, there would be four people in the car, and I had to assume the complaints would continue. Not that the bellyaching would stop me from catching a ride with them, but it might be easier to drive myself and not have to wait for them.

"Dave just texted me from the hospital. He needs help. Maybe it would be best if Ben and Holmes drove you to the police station." I waved at them and said I would see them later. I called Radar, who seemed reluctant to go with me but finally joined his pals Trixie and Twinkletoes for the walk back to the inn.

I strode out to the street and took a minute to figure out exactly where I was. Trixie and Twinkletoes knew. They dashed along the street to a house that looked very familiar as I approached it. My mom's house.

A Sugar Maple Inn golf cart was parked in the driveway. Maybe Aunt Margaret had gone over to Mom's for a visit.

In any event, we weren't far from home. We walked past stores and restaurants and in a matter of minutes, the Sugar Maple Inn loomed ahead of us, inviting lights glowing from the windows.

Trixie, Twinkletoes, and Radar waited for me at the front porch. I always felt big and bumbling when they raced ahead, graceful and swift.

I opened the door and immediately heard a chorus of voices calling our names from the Dogwood Room.

Oma, Aunt Margaret, Dad's kids, and the Carole waved to me.

Uh-oh. This was bound to be uncomfortable. Unless Josh was staying in touch with his mom, which I seriously doubted, I was the one who would be the bearer of bad news.

"Hi!" I said as I walked over to the open area we called the Dogwood Room. It overlooked the lake and featured a gorgeous stone fireplace. "It looks like you're having fun."

"Where have you been?" asked Oma.

"Is your dad with you?" asked Carole.

"Have you seen Josh? We lost him after dinner," said Aunt Margaret.

I tried to choose my words carefully. "I have not seen Dad, but I was with Josh and Dana. Officer Dave was in an accident and taken to the emergency room, so I'm going to bring these three rascals up to my apartment and then head over to Snowball to check on Dave."

"Dave?" Oma cried. "Our Dave? What happened?"

"Yes, our Officer Dave. Dr. Engelknecht thinks he broke a bone in his leg."

"But this is terrible. Should I go with you?" asked Oma.

"I don't know how long I'll be there. They might even let me bring him home. It's probably best if you stay here and entertain everyone. After all, they came to see *you*."

"Ach, yes. Of course."

"Where is Josh?" Aunt Margaret sounded miffed.

Oma spoke softly. "I have told Margaret about the man in their tent."

That was helpful. "Holmes and Ben are taking Josh and

Dana to talk with the police. I believe they plan to come to the inn when they're done."

"Well, I assumed that. Where else would they go?" Aunt Margaret's fingers were tightly coiled into a fist.

Aha. She didn't know the entire story. I nodded. "Come on, you three."

"Holly," said Oma. "Bring Dave back here. He doesn't have anyone at home to help him."

Once again, I nodded. We were filling up fast. Dave and Ben might have to share my guest room.

I ran up the stairs as fast as I could. In my apartment, I closed the dog door so they would stay put during my absence. I brought each of them a snack. While they ate, I said, "Stay in here. No running out, okay? I'll be back in a couple of hours."

I grabbed my purse, closed the door behind me, and locked it. I paused briefly but didn't hear any whining. They were probably worn out. It had been a busy day.

Hoping to avoid Aunt Margaret and questions about Josh, I walked down the grand staircase to the second floor, then turned and strode along the hallway to the back stairs that led to the registration lobby. I picked up keys to a golf cart and let myself out the sliding glass doors. The cool crisp night air woke me up and gave me a second wind. I left the golf cart at the parking lot on the edge of town and drove my car down the mountain and over to Snowball.

The emergency room was surprisingly quiet. I stopped at the nursing station. "I'm looking for Dave Quinlan, please."

The nurse didn't move her head. Only her eyes looked up in my direction. "Are you family?"

Oh no! Had I come all the way to Snowball for naught? The HIPAA laws made everything so complicated. "No. He asked me to come."

"Name?"

"Holly Miller."

Now her head moved. She jumped up from her seat. "We've been waiting for you."

"For me?"

The nurse opened a door and announced, "She's here!" She turned to me on her way out. "I'll bring the discharge papers and instructions."

"Hi!" I edged around the bed in the tiny room. "How are you feeling?"

"Relieved that you're here. Thanks for coming, Holly. I can't wait to get out of this place."

"Is everything all right? Your text said—"

"I'll tell you about it on the way home."

"Okay. Where am I taking you? Oma thinks you should come to the inn, but I have to warn you that you won't have a private room. You'll be staying in my spare room with Ben."

"I'm sorry to be such a pill. But that works for me, if you don't mind."

"No problem, although I suspect your mother won't be happy about it."

"Mom doesn't know yet. I don't want her to worry, or worse, to come to my house and watch me sleep."

The doctor burst into the room. "You must be Holly." He handed me a sheaf of papers. "Call Dr. Engelknecht immediately if he experiences any pain in his head, even a headache. He'll need to see an orthopedist on Monday or Tuesday. For now, he needs to keep weight off his leg, but he should be up and moving around."

Half an hour later, the discharge papers had been signed and a lovely man helped Dave into the passenger seat of my car.

We had just left the parking lot when Dave asked, "Has anyone come to the inn to check for evidence in Frank's room?"

"Not that I'm aware of."

"Good. They gave me meds, so I might drift off. I want to be clear on this. I need you to help me go into the room and take photographs. Wear gloves so you won't leave your fingerprints. I'm not asking you to touch any of his possessions. But I need thorough photos of what is in the room."

"Should I open drawers and closets?"

"Yes."

"What if I find a briefcase?"

"I'll be there with you. I can open briefcases and wallets and take pictures. Don't touch or rearrange anything."

"What are we looking for?"

He didn't answer. I looked over at him. He had nodded off.

Eleven

❁ ❁ ❁ ❁ ❁

I was driving up Wagtail Mountain when Dave snorted and woke with a start. He massaged his face with his hands. "Did you ever find Josh?"

"Yes. Ben and Holmes took Josh and Dana to the Snowball police." I could feel Dave watching me in the dark. "They're there now."

"Where were they?"

"In a house Holmes is building."

"With Holmes's knowledge and consent?"

"Without. In fact, he was very firm with them. They cannot stay there."

"Could Josh be the one who attacked me from behind?"

"I seriously doubt it. Ben entered the house and found them while we were with you."

He looked out the window. "Good to know."

"What's going on, Dave?"

His head leaned back, and I could hear exhaustion in his voice when he muttered, "I don't know. I honestly don't know."

I let him doze the rest of the way home.

"We're almost there, Dave." I tapped his arm lightly.

He woke and the guys at the Wagtail parking lot helped Dave from my car to the golf cart.

"Has Holmes come back yet?" I asked them.

"Not yet."

I thanked them and drove to Dave's house. Holding out my hand for the key, I said, "I'll get Duchess. Is there anything else you need for the night?"

He rattled off a short list, mostly shaving items and a change of clothes. Duchess was whining when I opened the door. "Go on, sweetie. He's right outside. You're coming with us."

Duchess, a long-haired white dog worthy of her regal name, bolted for the golf cart. I went inside, found a duffle bag, and tossed in everything I thought he might want. We could return during the day for the rest.

Careful to lock up, I tossed the bag into the golf cart and handed him the key.

It was late when I pulled into the inn's portico. "Stay here. I'll be right back with a wheelchair."

"I don't need a wheelchair." Dave stuck his good leg out at me and tried to stand.

It was cruel of me not to help, but he was so tired and doped up that I didn't think he could do it. Better that he realized it while he could fall back on the seat than when we were in the elevator.

"Gaah!" Dave moaned and stopped moving. "Okay, go get it."

I unlocked the sliding doors and fetched a wheelchair that we kept on hand for emergencies like this one. With a lot of moaning and grumbling, Dave was finally in the seat, and I was able to roll him into the inn.

When I opened the door to my apartment, Trixie, Twinkletoes, and Radar greeted us with enthusiasm. Trixie and Radar sniffed Duchess and circled one another. Twinkletoes had the audacity to jump on Dave's lap.

He looked completely worn out.

"Should I help you change into pajamas?"

He shook his head. "I don't want to be a burden."

I figured he would need help, but it was a good sign that he wanted to do things on his own.

I took Trixie and Radar downstairs with me and parked the golf cart where it belonged while the two of them roamed.

I checked my phone but didn't have any messages from Holmes, Ben, or Josh. I hoped that wasn't a bad sign.

Back in my apartment, Dave napped in the wheelchair. I served dinner to Duchess and a snack to everyone else so they wouldn't try to eat the food in her bowl. Twinkletoes jumped up on her favorite chair and carefully washed her face. The dogs settled on the sofa. They were pooped.

I, on the other hand, was wide awake and very surprised when Dave woke and wheeled himself to the door. "Any chance you could help me with Frank's room before my meds wear off?"

It was as good a time as any. Maybe doing it now while most people were asleep or heading for bed was a good choice. "I'll get the keys and come back for you."

I tiptoed downstairs to retrieve the house keys. For the safety of guests, we left sufficient lighting on through the night. The last thing we needed was someone tripping in the dark. The only entrance or exit was the main door to the inn, so we dimmed the lights a bit in the registration lobby. It was quiet there. No one was up and about, at least

not in that part of the building. I let myself into the inn
office, nabbed a key to Frank's room, then returned to
collect Dave.

He waited by the door, amazingly alert and eager. His
phone lay on his lap along with two pairs of gloves. "I found
the gloves under the kitchen sink. Hope that's okay."

"It's fine."

The dogs and Twinkletoes had settled in and were
snoozing when we left. Keys tightly in hand, I rolled Dave
to the elevator, which we took to the second floor of the
main building. We passed the rooms where Carole and my
half siblings slept. In accordance with the dog and cat theme
of Wagtail, Oma had named the guest rooms for animal
activities. Fetch, where Frank had stayed, was near the
grand staircase.

I pulled gloves over my hands. Dave did the same. Then
I slid the key into the lock and turned it. A flick of the light
switch at the door illuminated the room. After a quick check
of the bathroom and closet to be sure no one lurked inside, I was satisfied that we were alone and rolled Dave
inside, closed the door, and locked it.

Curtains in a soft slightly heathered blue buffalo check
framed the window that faced Wagtail. A matching blue
comforter lay on the bed. In fact, the pillows had been
plumped up properly, too. That made sense because Frank
had never come back last night.

Dave handed me his phone. I snapped a photo of the
bed from several sides.

A duffle bag lay on the luggage rack, neatly zipped
closed. I took pictures as I walked through the room so I
would catch it exactly as it looked when we entered, before we handled anything.

A black toiletry bag lay next to the sink in the bathroom. It was also neatly zipped closed. Towels had been

used, or unfolded at least. Two hung in an orderly fashion on the towel rack. A stack of folded towels was piled neatly on the vanity. I was beginning to think Frank was a very fastidious person.

Dave unzipped the bag and spread the sides apart. "Photograph the contents, please."

I didn't see anything of particular interest. Mostly shaving items.

Dave rolled into the bedroom and opened the drawer of the bedside table. Frank had left absolutely nothing in it.

He hadn't hung anything in the closet. There were no extra shoes, coats, or bags.

The dresser drawers were similarly empty.

"He didn't intend to stay very long," murmured Dave.

"Maybe he planned to depart when he returned from his boating trip. The room has a packed-and-ready-to-check-out look about it."

That left the duffle bag. It was a medium size, in dark green waxed canvas, with leather straps. I photographed the outside. Good quality but neither extravagant nor eye-catching. Zippered pockets run around the outside. Very practical for flight tickets and the like that needed to be within easy reach. I unzipped each of them and photographed the contents. Five pairs of socks, a map of Wagtail, sunscreen, mosquito repellent, a paperback of John Grisham's *The Judge's List*, a stash of peanut butter cups, and a couple of charging cables. Nothing that the average visitor wouldn't have in their luggage. Dave removed everything from the interior of the bag, but there wasn't much. A couple of flannel shirts and two T-shirts. A pair of jeans. Some underwear. And a laptop.

We left the bag exactly the way we found it, with everything zipped up. I turned to take one last look around the room. It really was unremarkable. Frank Burton liked peanut butter and thrillers. He was neat and tidy. I was sorry this nice man had been killed.

On our way out, I glanced in the bathroom where something caught my eye. It gleamed in the pile of towels on the vanity. I looked at it more closely and a chill ran through me.

Twelve

I stared right into a camera lens. I scuttled past it in a hurry.

"Did you see that?" I whispered to Dave.

"See what?"

"A camera."

"What?"

I backed up his wheelchair. "Between the towels," I whispered, which I immediately realized was silly because the camera had already caught us. It probably even picked up audio sounds.

Had Frank set it up so he would know if anyone had entered the room? Or had someone else set it up so they would know if Frank had returned?

I shuddered at the thought that we had probably been videoed. I skirted around Dave's wheelchair and entered the bathroom. Moving the towels cautiously, I peeled them back for a better look. It was a white box, about three inches square and one inch thick. It had a camera and a light, which I presumed was motion activated. It was aimed directly at the doorway to the bathroom, which anyone entering the room would pass. Anyone going in or out would be caught by the camera.

But who had the app? Who was the person with access to the videos? Had Frank set this up himself or was someone spying on him?

My heart pounded. Frank Burton wasn't the nice average guy I had thought. Either he was afraid of someone and needed to know if anyone had entered the room while he was out, or someone didn't believe he was dead and was waiting for Frank to return and collect his belongings.

I knew one thing for sure. We had to get out of there, pronto! I snapped a couple of photos and returned the towels to their previous position as fast as I could.

When I stepped out of the bathroom, I pushed the wheelchair away, then hid behind the wall and stretched my arm out to hold my phone where I thought it would catch a photo of the mostly hidden camera. I quickly took a picture. Anyone watching would know who I was. It was too late for that. But it was all I could think of to do. Even if we took the camera with us, the person who set it up would still have access to the video.

I forced myself to slow down so I wouldn't be noisy and wake guests. As calmly as I could, I opened the door and pushed the wheelchair out into the hallway. When I heard the soft sound of footsteps, it took all my willpower not to gasp. I held my breath as I saw a man pass by the end of the hallway. I didn't think he had seen us. Leaving Dave in the hallway, I scurried toward the man as fast as I could. He disappeared into Oma's apartment, but not before I could identify him. It was my dad.

That settled my nerves. I was quietly locking the door

to Fetch when Dave tugged at my shirt and placed a finger over his mouth.

We listened in silence.

I heard Ben greeting Casey downstairs on the main floor.

I pushed the wheelchair inside the elevator.

Dave reached over and selected the main floor. "I want to hear what happened."

He rolled himself out of the elevator and toward Ben in the lobby. "You're back."

Ben rubbed his eyes. "I'm beat. Holly, I'm afraid your cousin Josh is in a mountain of trouble."

I looked around the lobby. "Where is he?"

"Locked up in Snowball. I did my best, but this is a murder charge. They might be released tomorrow but only on a hefty secured bond."

"Oma and Aunt Margaret will flip out."

"Well gosh, Holly. Maybe Josh and Dana shouldn't have murdered Frank Burton."

I bristled at Ben's sarcasm. "Some lawyer you are."

"I wouldn't be quite so snotty about it if I were you. As far as I can tell, you're the main witness."

"But I didn't see them murder him."

"Maybe not. But you're going to end up testifying. It may be circumstantial evidence, but you can testify about the tent, the location, the fact that Frank went out on a boat, and that you discovered him in Josh and Dana's tent."

Ben had sucked the air right out of me.

Casey adjusted his wire-rimmed glasses. "Maybe we need to find the real killer, then."

"Not tonight," muttered Ben. "I'm beat. Let's head up to your apartment."

There was one very small benefit to Josh and Dana's incarceration. We now had their reserved room available for Ben. "Come on. I'll check you in and give you your key."

Ben's expression changed. "I'm not staying with you?"

Dave raised his hand. "I am."

Dave rolled the wheelchair down the hallway to the elevator. Ben and I followed along.

"It's better this way," I said. "You won't have to bunk with Dave in my guest room."

Dave rolled into the elevator to go to my apartment.

I headed to the office to replace the key to Fetch and grab a key for Ben. He came upstairs with me to collect his luggage.

As soon as he stepped into my apartment, Twinkletoes hissed at him. Trixie raced around my ankles, glad that I was back. Radar looked disappointed. Maybe he was hoping Josh would reappear.

I peeked into the guest room. Dave already lay on his back in the bed in a deep slumber. Duchess sneaked in, jumped on the bed as if she were light as a feather, then curled up at the foot of Dave's bed. I pulled a blanket over him, turned off the lights, and coaxed Twinkletoes, Trixie, and Radar out of the room.

I closed the door so none of the other dogs would join Duchess.

"How's Dave?" asked Ben.

"Fast asleep. See you at breakfast," I said, closing the door behind him.

I was exhausted, but I set my alarm to go off in three hours so I could check on Dave. When I lay in bed, with Twinkletoes curled up near my head and Trixie and Radar snoozing beside me, I stared at the ceiling wide awake. Casey had been right. We were going to have to find the real killer.

In a very small way, we had started that by trying to learn more about Frank. His room hadn't revealed much information about him. He was orderly and traveled light.

The hidden camera I found concerned me, though. I hoped it was connected to the laptop in his duffle bag. Otherwise, someone might come looking for me!

I worried about that for a while before I finally drifted off.

I woke with a start when the alarm went off. The sky had turned a dark blue and the sun was beginning to inch up in the sky. I hurried to the guest room and looked in on Dave. I didn't know whether I should wake him or not. But if I didn't, how would I know if he was all right?

"Dave," I said softly. "Dave?" I gave his shoulder a little push.

"Mmm." His eyes opened. "Holly. What is it?"

"What's your name?"

His eyes opened wide. "Did you hit your head or something?"

"No. You did."

"Oh, that. Dave Quinlan."

"Okay. Go back to sleep." Before I closed the door, I looked back at him and thought he had already drifted off again.

I returned to my own bed and fell into a deep sleep.

Mr. Huckle was off on Sunday, so there was no tea or coffee waiting for me. I had become completely spoiled. I peeked in on Dave again. Duchess raised her head briefly to watch me. I could hear the shower running. I knocked on the door. "Do you need help?"

"Nope. I'm fine. Thanks for asking. I found a trash bag and plastic wrap in your kitchen. Hope it's okay that I used them."

"Absolutely!"

After showering and dressing, I found Dave in my living room surrounded by the dogs and Twinkletoes. I offered to push his wheelchair, but he declined and rolled himself toward the elevator. Duchess went with him.

Trixie had an aversion to the elevator, which I suspected came from being locked up in a small space before she adopted me. So the rest of us took the stairs down to the lobby.

Duchess caught up to us and I hustled all the dogs out the door to the doggy bathroom. Twinkletoes remained inside and headed to the dining area.

We soon returned and found Dave drinking coffee at a table with my dad, Aunt Margaret, and Oma.

"Good morning!" I said cheerfully.

Aunt Margaret scowled at me. "Excuse me? My little boy spent the night in a cold barren cell."

"I'm sorry about that, Aunt Margaret."

"Margaret," said Oma. "Joshua is a strong and resilient young man. He will weather this and may be home today in time for dinner."

"I hope you're right. Where is your boyfriend, Holly?" Margaret gazed at me. "He got Josh into this mess. The least he can do is tell me how to bail him out."

"No problem, Margaret," said Dad. "Ben is great. I love that we're going to have a lawyer in the family."

Oma rolled her eyes.

"You have it all wrong," I protested. "I haven't seen Ben in years."

"This is true," said Oma. "The Ben has not come to see Holly in a very long time."

I was about to explain that Holmes was my boyfriend when Dad said, "Now, Mom, don't start in on that young man. I like him. Ben is a solid, dependable fellow and I hope they'll be tying the knot. Soon."

Whoa. How did this happen? I was about to correct my dad when Shelley arrived with Dave's breakfast.

She placed it in front of him. "Brie-stuffed French toast

with raspberries and maple syrup." She filled up his coffee cup and smiled at him. "Holly, can I bring you the same?"

I had suspected for a while that something was brewing between Shelley and Dave. "I think I'll stick to two eggs sunny side up and fresh fruit. Three orders of eggs and turkey for the dogs, and how about some tuna for Twinkletoes?"

Shelley nodded and left for the kitchen.

"All right. Let's get this straight," I said. Unfortunately, that appeared to be a cue for everyone to start talking. Dad insisted on praising Ben, and Margaret loudly blamed Ben for her son's situation.

Oma spoke sharply. "I will not have this from my family. If you intend to argue, then kindly leave the dining area immediately and do your bickering elsewhere. Outside the hearing of our guests. Is that understood?"

The arguing ceased immediately.

Ben ambled in and pulled up a chair. "Good morning, everyone."

He looked as tired as I felt.

Margaret glared at him.

"You must be Holly's aunt Margaret," he said. "We spoke last night about a bond for Josh."

"What are you doing having breakfast? There's no time to waste. I need to get Josh out of there." Aunt Margaret spoke harshly.

If Ben was miffed, he didn't show it.

Shelley arrived with our breakfasts and a cup of coffee for Ben. "Thanks, Shelley," he said politely. "I'll have the same as Dave." When she left, he turned to Aunt Margaret. "There's not much more I can do for you at this point. You need to phone the number I gave you. He'll meet you at the jail. Once you sign the surety bond, Josh will be released."

"Ben is very competent." Dad winked at me.

I was going to have to have a talk with him and straighten him out on the Ben situation.

"At this point it's a matter of payment," said Ben.

"Then what? Isn't it your job to get him off the hook?" asked Aunt Margaret.

"I believe that's my territory," said Dave. "It's not up to me to prove his innocence, but it is my job to find out exactly what happened."

"You? Won't they send a replacement cop for you?"

"Let me worry about that."

"That's another thing," said Ben. "Josh has got to talk with me. I need to know his version of what happened."

"Nothing happened! My Josh is a good man." Margaret's face was flushing red.

The Josh I had known was kind and gentle, so I tended to agree with Aunt Margaret. He had enjoyed playing jokes on people, but they were always funny and never malicious.

Ben remained calm. "Then why was a dead man in his sleeping bag?"

As I gazed around the table, it became apparent that I wasn't the only one who was slightly aghast.

Aunt Margaret held her head high, stood up, and gracefully walked away.

I shot Ben an angry look. How could he say something like that to Josh's mother and grandmother? Granted, he had a point, but he had no business phrasing it so brutally to Josh's family. I had never spent much time with Aunt Margaret, except perhaps as my mother suggested when I was too young to remember. I wasn't sure how she handled crises.

One by one, people excused themselves from the table until only Dave, Ben, and I were left. I savored my tea and selected a chocolate croissant from the bread basket on the table. "How are you feeling, Dave?"

"Fine. A little annoyed that I'll have to baby my leg.

Especially with a murder to investigate. And I'll have to call my mom shortly."

"Holly and I can be your legs. What do you need?" asked Ben.

"Not if you're representing Josh or Dana," said Dave.

Ben smiled. "I see what you mean. It's a conflict-of-interest problem. Well, let me know if there's anything I can do. Gosh, look at the time. I'd better hurry."

"Are you going to see Josh?" I asked.

"Not unless your Aunt Margaret wants me to. She's the one who needs to go ante up money for Josh's bond. Your dad wants to go across the lake to see Josh's campsite."

"And you're going with him?" I nearly choked on my tea.

"Yeah. Thought we'd have a look around. Get the lay of the land."

My first instinct was horror. Dad spending time with Ben couldn't be a good thing. But as I thought about it, I changed my mind. Maybe it *would* be a good thing. Dad grew up here. He knew the lake and the woods. Ben was a city slicker through and through. I was willing to bet the short boat trip would be a disaster.

"Have fun!" I said cheerily as he left.

"What is with your dad and Ben?" asked Dave.

"I have no idea. But I'm hoping their little outdoor adventure will put an end to Dad's high praise of Ben. Have you gone through the pictures of Frank's room we took last night?"

He pulled out his phone, flicked through the images, and stopped dead on a picture of the camera in the bathroom.

Thirteen

. ❀ . ❀ . ❀ .

Dave cocked his head. Without saying a word, he scanned the diners.

We were doing a fairly brisk business at Sunday brunch. Judy Davis ate with Jenny Franklin, a local woman who owned Purrfectly Meowvelous. Beyond them was a family with four rambunctious children. An elderly man sat alone, savoring his coffee while reading a newspaper. I recognized the owner of Tall Tails, the bookstore, and his companion. The tables were full, but no one looked nefarious or out of place. "Who are you looking for?"

"Someone has us on video."

"I'm hoping it was Frank who set up the camera."

Dave flipped back through the other photos, examining each quietly. "Looks like this was the only camera in the room. I don't see one anywhere else. Dana denies knowing him."

"Do you believe her? I know young women often marry

older men, but Dana and Frank don't seem like a match."
I smiled at Shelley as she refilled my tea. "Thanks!"

"The presence of the camera changes everything. It
certainly suggests that he was on the lookout for someone
who was after him. Unfortunately, I think that someone
found him." Dave sipped his coffee. "I'd like to see what's
on his laptop. I'll have to get someone on it."

Just then, Oma returned. "I am glad to find you still
here. Dave, perhaps you can help us post bond for Josh
and his friend. I don't know where to start and Margaret
is so upset that she cannot think straight."

"I would be happy to help you, Liesel. Ben's bail bondsman is expecting to hear from her, so it should be fairly
easy."

"Holly, would you mind watching the inn?" asked Oma.
"Margaret is in no condition to drive. We'll be going to
Snowball as soon as we can pick them up."

"No problem." And then I remembered the tea for Oma's
birthday. She had to be back by two in the afternoon. Yikes!
I needed to think of an excuse to get her back here by
then. "Um, I do have plans at two o'clock. I hope you can
spring Josh by then?"

"Plans?" she asked.

Rats, I hoped she wouldn't ask me any questions. Eye
doctor? Dentist? Neither of them were open on Sunday. "I
promised Aunt Birdie that I would help her with her website." It was a lie, but just a little white lie so that Oma
would be surprised. Besides, Oma and Aunt Birdie weren't
close, so it was highly unlikely that the truth would be
discovered before this afternoon at two anyway. I smiled
at Oma.

"I see. I will do my best."

Oh no. "Maybe I could cancel with Birdie so I could
take Aunt Margaret?"

"I think I will drive her this time. I would enjoy some time alone with my daughter. I see her so rarely. But thank you for offering, Holly."

Oma offered to push Dave's wheelchair, but he insisted on wheeling himself.

I went up to my apartment to brush my teeth and then headed for the office. Zelda had the day off. Mom had volunteered to cover for us during the tea, which I thought very generous of her.

Unexpectedly, two police officers arrived to search Frank's room officially. I texted Dave, then showed them the way and unlocked the door for them. Snowball wasn't large enough to have a big forensics crew, so they had to do it themselves. Dave rolled into the room and watched what they were doing.

"Did you get the bond straightened out?" I asked.

"Sure. No big deal. They just need to drive over to Snowball to make the payment."

When I returned to the office, I found Zelda with Nate, the fellow who had delivered flowers for Oma.

"Hi, Holly! You remember Nate."

"I do. You delivered the beautiful bouquet."

"I'm giving him a tour of the inn."

"It's a very special place," said Nate. "I love the old stonework."

They entered the little gift shop, where Nate promptly bought a Sugar Maple Inn T-shirt and a raspberry-filled Lindt chocolate bar. When he paid, I couldn't help noticing the Breitling watch he wore. They weren't exactly in the price range of the average flower delivery person. Of course, he could have inherited it or received it as a gift.

Nate grinned at me, and those adorable chipmunk cheeks plumped up. "Zelda says you're having a tea party this afternoon. Maybe I could give you a hand arranging tables and chairs?"

I looked at Zelda. She was beaming.

"That's really nice of you, but—"

Behind him Zelda was nodding vigorously. I continued anyway. "—it's just for employees. I hate to have you do the work and then not be invited."

"That's okay. I'm not sure a ladies' tea is up my alley. Maybe Zelda could sneak a few leftovers for me. I'm new to Wagtail and I don't have any other plans today, so I would be happy to help."

"All right." I could hear voices behind me. The two cops had finished with Frank's room.

I turned my attention to them.

"Here's the key. Thank you for giving us access to the room."

"Did you find anything of interest?"

The cop didn't even pause. "Nope."

I knew they had to have found the camera. I guessed they weren't supposed to reveal anything. And they must have taken possession of the duffle bag. One of them carried a good-size sack.

One of the cops suddenly said, "Brendan? Is that you?"

Brendan Hayward was passing by. He stopped and clapped a hand on the cop's shoulder. "Bobby Simmons! Dad mentioned that you joined the police force. You look great, man!"

"What are you doing here?"

"My folks are selling the house in Snowball and Mom insisted I come get what I want. She threatened to throw out my baseball card collection!" He laughed. "And she's pushing Dad to move to Wagtail, so I'm scoping out houses with her."

"We have to get together for a drink while you're here. Hair of the Dog today around five?"

"That would be great! See you then."

My gaze fell on Nate, who listened attentively.

When Brendan and the cops left, Nate said, "Zelda tells me one of your guests was murdered. Is that why the cops were here?"

I tried to make light of it, as much as I could anyway. "I'm afraid someone was murdered. But not here in the inn."

"I'm so sorry. That must be awful for all of you. Did you know him well?"

"No. We barely knew him at all."

"I'm sure it's still a shock." He turned to Zelda. "Let's go move some chairs."

I returned to the office, where Dave had collapsed in a comfy chair, his leg elevated on a footstool. Twinkletoes had curled up on his lap. I left him to keep an eye on things and told him to text me if anyone needed help.

I found our housekeeper and let her know Frank's room was ready to be cleaned for Josh and Dana. Relieved to have a room for them, I put together a wine and cheese basket and carried it up to their room. Trixie, Radar, and Duchess tailed my every step.

Then I headed to the private kitchen and looked in the magic refrigerator for lunch. When Holmes, Josh, and I were kids, we had named the fridge. A lot of the inn's leftovers were delivered to needy families, but some of the leftovers went into the refrigerator for our consumption. It seemed like it was never empty, hence the name *magic*.

It didn't disappoint. Cold fried chicken, potato salad, and guacamole sounded just about perfect for lunch. There were also chicken dinners for the dogs and Twinkletoes. Tortilla chips and chocolate chip cookies were on the counter. I grabbed some sodas, loaded a tray, and rolled a small feast down to the office.

Dave had nodded off. He jerked awake when I arrived. "Food. Looks good."

I fed the dogs and Twinkletoes, then settled on the sofa

for lunch. "The police wouldn't tell me if they found anything of interest."

Dave shook his head. "Only the camera. They were pretty excited about it. Now to get into that laptop. Sometimes I wish I were a computer genius so I could do it myself. There's a guy at the police station in Snowball who knows all that stuff. But it takes a while. Now we sit and wait."

"Aside from the possibility that that's where the photos went, what are you hoping to find?"

"Who he is. Why he was here. Hey, did you have anyone check out the day he died?"

"I see what you're getting at. Someone could have killed him and then beat a hasty exit out of Wagtail before anyone was the wiser. Nope. No one has checked out in days."

"So the killer could still be here at the inn. Calmly watching as we try to figure out what happened."

I shuddered at the thought.

I heard the sliding glass doors open and rose to see who was coming in.

Oma, Mom, Margaret, Josh, and Dana entered.

"Congratulations on being sprung!" I said with a grin.

Dana shot me a look that let me know she did not find that amusing. "I would like my room key. I need to wash off the stench of prison."

She approached the registration desk. I nabbed the key and walked around to the stairs. Normally I would have asked about luggage that I could carry, but Josh held two rolling suitcases, one larger than the other. He could pull them easily. "This way, please."

Dana frowned at me. "I can find it myself. This isn't the MGM Grand, you know."

Oma raised her eyebrows and Margaret's eyes widened.

"Fine." I handed her the key and returned to the desk.

She clearly had no idea where to go and wandered into the hallway toward the main lobby.

"That was awfully rude," said Margaret. "Am I wrong to think that someone whose bond I just paid might be a little more polite to us? And I believe you're putting her up gratis. Far more comfortably than a tent in the woods."

"Mom, she spent the night in jail. It's not surprising that she's a little grouchy." Josh turned tired eyes at us.

"You spent the night in the slammer, too, but you're not being rude to Holly," said Margaret.

"I should help Dana," said Josh.

I didn't think he knew where their room was, either. He hadn't been to Wagtail in a long time.

"Just a minute, please," said his mother. "Now that your girlfriend is gone, I'd like to have a word with you." Margaret crooked her finger and he followed her into the office.

Dave must have been listening because he quickly rolled the wheelchair out of the office. Twinkletoes jumped off his lap and onto the registration desk.

Josh closed the door behind him.

"My mom is on her way to take me to get crutches in Snowball," said Dave. "I'm meeting her at the parking lot. I hope I'll be back tonight, but I'm not sure. Do you mind if Duchess stays with you?"

"She's always welcome."

A Wagtail taxi pulled up outside. They were golf carts that served the same purpose as taxis.

"That would be my chariot. Thanks for all your help!" Dave rolled toward the sliding doors and they opened automatically.

I checked the time. One forty-five. I needed to keep Oma busy for fifteen minutes.

She tiptoed to the office door and leaned her ear against it. Mom and I followed suit.

Margaret's voice came through loud and clear. "Joshua, you know that I have tried to stay out of your adult life, even when I thought your choices might not be the wisest. But this goes beyond the pale."

"I didn't murder anyone, Mom."

"I know that. I mean Dana. You're having an affair with a married woman." Aunt Margaret's voice grew shrill.

"I'm protecting her."

"In my day they called it something else."

"Mom, you don't understand. Her husband is a horrible man. She grew up with a drunk and abusive father. She lived in terror because she never knew what might trigger his ire. He battered her mom until she couldn't take it anymore. But when she fled, she left Dana behind to take his abuse. She never heard from her mother again."

"That's very sad. I'm sorry she had a tragic childhood, but that does not excuse your inappropriate behavior with a woman who is married to someone else."

"She married a man who was just like her father."

Margaret's voice was softer when she asked, "Where did you meet Dana?"

"I was at Orly Airport in Paris, having breakfast before a flight to Istanbul to pick up some golden retrievers. Dana came up to me and asked if I would mind if she shared my table. When she heard that I was flying to Turkey, she asked if she could go with me. I thought it would be nice to have company along for the trip, and everything developed from there."

"So that was when she told you about her cruel husband?"

"Yeah."

"Josh, honey, she's not a puppy that you can rescue and rehome."

"Mom . . ."

"Oh, honey," said Margaret. "You have always been

such a kind person. Even as a child you wanted to rescue everything, even the spiders I desperately wanted to smash. But Dana isn't a kitten or a lost dog. This time you can't whisk her away to safety. You can't rescue her from herself."

"I realize that, Mom. But she needs help. It would be nice if you could help me instead of making Dana out to be a wild woman."

"Just how long have the two of you been together?"

"About three months."

"And you're supporting this woman?"

"Mom, I'd like to marry her."

Fourteen

* * * * *

A long silence followed. "Has she filed for divorce?" asked Margaret.

"Yes. She submitted the paperwork to get things started."

"Well, that's *some* comfort. I'm going to be honest with you, Josh. She could be the most wonderful woman in the world, but something doesn't smell right."

"Aww, Mom. You're overprotective. I know you'll come to love Dana like I do."

"I think I'll like her better when she's single again. You really shouldn't be involved with a married woman. Especially one who has a violent husband!"

"She needs me. No one else ever stood by her, helped her."

"Josh, sweetheart, your kind nature is one of your best features. But don't let it get you in trouble. If her husband is looking for her, what do you think is going to happen when he finds her? You're putting yourself in a terrible situation."

"You worry too much."

"Honey, someone has been murdered. Look how much trouble you're in now!"

"That's not Dana's fault."

"Of course it is. If you didn't know Dana, her crazy husband wouldn't be pursuing you."

"Mom, anyone could have killed him. His death probably doesn't have anything to do with Dana."

"And yet you were arrested. Joshua, you're all I have left. Nothing in this entire world is more important to me than you. Can you imagine what your father would say about this?"

"Mom! Don't start that."

"You know what he would say."

"What Dad would say is irrelevant. I love her, Mom. That's all that matters."

There was a pause, and Oma gestured for us to move away from the door. I hurried behind the desk, Mom stood across from me, and Oma straightened brochures about local attractions.

As I understood it, Margaret had taken her husband's death quite hard. I could understand how she felt about Josh and why she was overly protective of him.

The office door opened. Josh sidled up to the registration desk. "So where is our room?"

I was so tempted to tell him we weren't the MGM Grand and he should find it himself, but I wasn't that small. Plus, his girlfriend had said it, not Josh. But I had to wonder how he could be so blasé about everything that had happened. If someone had been murdered in my sleeping bag, I would be freaking out!

I took another key, in case she was still wandering or had run off somewhere. "Follow me."

I led him up the stairs and then along the corridor. The dogs trotted along behind us. We neared the grand staircase. I knocked on the door first. No one answered. I unlocked it and led Josh inside. "Breakfast and lunch are served downstairs, but not dinner. The magic refrigerator is still in the private kitchen, so I'm sure you can find something there if you're hungry and you don't want to go out." I bent to kiss Radar on his nose. "I'll miss you!"

Josh peered in the bathroom. "Dana isn't here."

I held up my palms and shrugged. "Maybe she wandered down to the cat wing."

"There's a cat wing?"

"There is. And a very cozy little library as well."

He still held the room key in his hand. "I guess I'd better go find her. She has a tendency to break into tears when she's frustrated."

I tried not to show my surprise. She was a grown woman, not a child. Besides, I had offered to show her to the room, and she snapped at me. I simply said, "Let me know if you need extra pillows or anything."

He followed me out of the room and locked the door. "Which way is the cat wing?"

"First and second floors that way." I pointed past the grand staircase.

Josh grinned at me. "It's hard to believe that I used to know every nook and cranny in this place. Everything has changed."

I nodded. "The inn and Wagtail are very different than they were when we were kids." I turned to walk away.

"Hey, Holly!"

I turned to look back at him. Josh strode toward me and embraced me in a big bear hug. "It's good to see you again."

I watched him hurry away in search of Dana. In the greater scheme of things, that hug wasn't important, but it meant the world to me. It took me back in time and assured me that the old fun and sweet Josh hadn't really changed.

I glanced at my watch. Two o'clock! I hurried down the grand staircase and texted Oma.

Could you please come to the dining area?

She replied.

On my way.

I waved as Casey, the night clerk, and a couple of servers hurried toward the terrace.

Oma walked briskly through the hallway toward me, Gingersnap by her side. "Is there a problem?"

"It's out on the terrace."

I opened the door for her. As she and Gingersnap stepped outside, our employees struck up a chorus of "Happy Birthday."

Oma looked around, genuinely surprised. "You did this for me? It's beautiful!"

It was. A brightly colored umbrella shaded each of the round tables from the sun. They were formally set for afternoon tea, with double-tiered tea cake servers laden with petit fours, miniature éclairs, cream puffs, scones, dainty triangular sandwiches, tiny lemon tarts, and an assortment of cookies, including dog and cat cookies meant for Gingersnap and her friends like Elvis, Trixie, and Twinkletoes.

The tea was set up on a long table, self-serve, so no one would have to work. On the same table stood a Dobos torte, with a classic glistening caramelized sugar top. The caramel had been cut into triangular wedges that stood on their sides, leaning slightly like a fan. Another Dobos torte had already been sliced and laid on plates so everyone could help themselves.

They had hired a string quartet that played softly in the

background. There wasn't one bit of wind off the lake and the sun shone strong, high in the sky.

Oma was whisked away and embraced by employees. I guessed from her surprise and the chatter that not a single word about the tea had leaked to her. I watched my Oma for a moment, admiring her. She truly was loved by the people who worked at the inn.

Shelley came up to me. "We're at the same table. We drew numbers from a bowl to choose who would get to sit at Oma's table."

I couldn't believe how much trouble they had gone to, and how kind they were to come up with such an equitable plan. "Great!"

"I'll bring you some tea."

"You will not. You go sit down and I'll bring you tea for a change."

She stared at me and tried to hide a smile. "Okay."

I fetched the tea and brought an additional pot to the table. I walked around the table, pouring tea, then decided to pour for everyone before I sat down to enjoy the goodies.

Shelley whispered to me, "I have a date tonight!"

Dave had asked her out in spite of his broken leg? "With Dave?"

She shook her head and sipped tea. "Only in my dreams. I like Dave a lot, but he never asks me out. I only see him here when I'm working or if I happen to run into him in town. We wouldn't have to do anything fancy. I'd be thrilled with a picnic or a walk in the woods with Duchess. But the only time I really see him is when he comes here for breakfast. Maybe I'm just misinterpreting his interest."

"I don't think so. That's odd. He never struck me as the shy type. Maybe he's one of those guys who is afraid of being turned down?"

"I know! A shy cop? They're not afraid of anything! I don't know what to think about Dave."

"So who are you going out with?"

"Brendan."

"I was there when he checked in. He's very handsome!"

"I'm excited about a real date. It feels like forever since I was on one. I'm as giddy as a schoolgirl. We're going out to dinner." Shelley selected a miniature éclair. "He's tall and strong with that gorgeous hair. And he's so sweet! He's been getting up early for breakfast every morning, just so he can see me before the day gets hectic."

"Wow. He must be very attracted to you."

"I hope so!"

Marina, the most reliable member of our cleaning crew, leaned toward us. "Is it true that nice Mr. Burton was murdered?"

"You talked with him?" I asked.

"Yes, he was very nice to me. And he kept his room so neat."

"Did he say what he was doing in Wagtail?"

"Not really. He said it must be nice to live in Wagtail, with the lake and the woods and wildlife. So I asked where he was from and he said New York. I told him I thought they had lakes and trees in New York, too. He told me it's very nice upstate but he usually works in the city."

Cook said, "Rumor has it that your cousin murdered him."

What could I say? "I seriously doubt it. Josh is a very kindhearted person. He rescues animals."

"You want to hear something gross?" asked Marina, the housekeeper. "Josh and his girlfriend are staying in the dead man's room. Where I am from, we would be afraid his ghost would find us and torture us for killing him."

Eww. Well, now that she put it that way, I could see why that might not have been the best room choice for them. But I could hardly ask someone else to swap rooms. *I'm sorry to inconvenience you, but would you mind changing rooms? You see, my cousin and his girlfriend would be uncomfortable sleeping in the room previously occupied by the man they murdered, so I'd like to move you in there.* Definitely not Hotel Management 101.

As they spoke, I realized just how much the Sugar Maple Inn and its reputation could suffer. Not only was the murdered man a guest of the inn, but his alleged murderer was a member of the Miller family! I had been so worried about Josh that it hadn't occurred to me just how bad this would look for the inn.

Right then and there, I knew it was up to me to find the killer. That was our only chance. I had to believe that it wasn't Josh. There must be someone else who had been across the lake that night.

Two people knew more about what had happened. The key was to separate them. Dana seemed to have some magical power over Josh. I wondered if her neediness appealed to him, as Aunt Margaret had implied. I had to get each of them alone.

I excused myself and made a second round with the teapots. Then I loaded a rolling serving cart with tea, cups, plates, napkins, and a three-tier server filled with goodies. I rolled it down to Mom and Aunt Margaret in the registration lobby.

They were laughing about something so hard that tears ran down their cheeks. "You two are having a good time!"

"It's been too long." Aunt Margaret wiped tears from her face.

"I brought you some treats from the tea so you wouldn't miss out. Thanks for watching the inn."

"I feel a little guilty," said Mom. "It's been wonderful to catch up with Margaret. And not much has happened here."

"All the better. Enjoy!"

On my way back to the tea, I heard someone call my name.

Carole hurried toward me. "Have you seen your dad?"

"The last I heard he was going across the lake. But that was hours ago. He should be back by now."

She huffed and her shoulders sagged. "I thought this trip would be an opportunity for us to get closer, but I've hardly seen him."

"I'm sorry, Carole. He hasn't been here in a very long time. I think he wanted to spend time with his mom. Add in his children and sister, and he's just been really busy."

"I thought he would include me, not ignore me."

I felt sorry for her. Dad wasn't interested in her. His children and his mother didn't like her, and here she was, all alone in a town where she didn't know anyone. "I'm sorry it turned out this way for you. You must have friends and family who dote on their pets. Maybe you could do some early holiday shopping?"

"I guess so."

For a fleeting moment, I thought about hooking her up with Ben. The Carole and the Ben. A perfect match! But I had bigger problems on my hands at the moment, so I cheerily said, "Have fun!" and hurried back to the tea.

When I returned, candles had been lit on the Dobos torte, they were singing "Happy Birthday" again, and then Oma made a wish and blew out the candles.

I helped Mr. Huckle pass out slices of Dobos torte before returning to my seat with my own slice of the seven-layer wonder with chocolate hazelnut buttercream. Chatter around the table came to a halt as everyone ate the torte. Yum! What a treat. No wonder it was Oma's favorite.

Aunt Margaret hurried in, her face flushed. "There's someone here to see you."

I ate the one last bite that remained on my plate, sipped

my tea, and excused myself again. When we were out of earshot, I asked, "What's wrong?"

"It's a cop." Her eyes were wide and she looked scared.

"A cop? Did he ask for Josh or Dana?"

"He says he's replacing Dave!"

Shelley's teacup dropped from her hand and broke as it crashed on the table and flipped her plate over. "Oh, I'm so sorry! What a mess."

Twinkletoes peered over the top of the table, dismayed by the racket.

I left everyone else to deal with the mess. Margaret and I hustled to the reception lobby. Sure enough, a uniformed cop waited there. In his fifties, I guessed, mostly because he'd lost a good bit of his hair. The graying remainder had been cut short. His glasses were tinted, and he wore a hefty mustache that was still mostly brown with some silver creeping in.

I smiled at him. "Hi. I'm Holly Miller. How can I help you?"

"Sergeant Hayward." He didn't bother to show me any identification. "I need to see Frank Burton's room, but this lady won't let me in." He gestured toward Mom.

"I'm sorry, but it was cleaned and other guests are staying there now."

His beefy face turned red. "You contaminated the crime scene?"

"We did *not*. Two policemen came to examine the room and when they left, they turned it over to me and told me it could be rented again."

"What cops? Did they show you any identification?"

"No. But you haven't, either. I believe Sergeant Quinlan knew them."

"Oh. Officer Dave." He sneered when he said it.

I couldn't help wondering if he was jealous.

"Figures. Well, your darling Officer Dave isn't in charge

of this matter. I am. He's done with this cushy job. I have seniority and I'm ready to take over this podunk town and relax."

Trixie, who stood next to me, growled softly.

I stared at the grumpy man. Was Dave's job really in jeopardy? Anyone could break a leg. It made sense to replace Dave while he was on the mend, but not permanently! "I am happy to help you however I can. But Mr. Burton's belongings were removed from his room and taken away. I would imagine they are in your evidence room now."

"What a little smarty pants you are. Did you pick that up on TV? Like watching crime dramas, do you? Well, let me tell you that real life isn't anything like TV. This case is going to be handled by the book. I hear there are some complications because one of your relatives is a suspect, but you better be straight up with me. Your Officer Dave is history. I'm in charge now and I will not tolerate any sass. Am I clear?"

Trixie growled again.

Hayward? Was this the harsh father of Brendan? Why was he so angry with Dave? And why was he lecturing me? I hadn't done anything wrong. Not that he knew about, anyway. But suddenly, I was very glad that Dave had skirted the rules by asking me to help him take photographs of the room. I didn't quite trust this guy.

"What can I do for you?" I asked sweetly.

"Where is Joshua Paxton?"

Aunt Margaret gasped, which didn't help the situation one bit.

Fifteen

❖ ✿ ❖ ✿ ❖

Josh had undoubtedly been questioned while he was in police custody and he had been legitimately released. I stuck to the simplest version of the truth. "I don't know."

"I called his room, but no one answers," said Mom.

"Then I guess he's out somewhere." I shrugged.

Sergeant Hayward eyed Aunt Margaret. "Do you have knowledge of his whereabouts?"

Aunt Margaret froze.

I wrapped an arm around her waist. "He's her son."

"Is he now? Was he a problem child? Did he bully other kids?"

"He did not. And he hasn't killed anyone, either."

I could feel her body tensing and feared what she might

say, so I hurried to get rid of this cop. "When he returns, we'll let him know that you'd like to speak with him." I released Aunt Margaret and walked toward the sliding doors, as though I was escorting him out of the inn. At least I hoped he would instinctively realize that and leave.

If he noticed at all, he had other ideas. "That won't be necessary. I'll be right here." He sat down on a love seat and made himself comfortable.

If he thought one of us would notify Josh or give away his current location, he was dead wrong.

I relieved Mom, who made a big deal of collecting the teacups and putting them back on the tray.

"I told Cook to leave everything. I'll wash up later. He put so much effort into the celebration that I thought cleanup duty was the least I could do."

"Honey, we can do that!" Mom surreptitiously motioned to Margaret to follow her. The two of them disappeared down the hallway with the serving cart.

Because no one would be checking in, I had planned to lock the office and the doors. But now I was stuck with Sergeant Grouchy, who looked like he was dozing.

For an hour, I took care of paperwork, moving from the office to the registration desk and back again.

Guests came and went, glancing at the uniformed man snoring loudly on the love seat.

Brothers Paul and Ted returned. Paul approached the desk. He spoke so softly that I had to lean forward to hear him. "Has anyone asked for us yet?"

"Not that I'm aware of."

He smiled. "That's great! Thank you!"

Ted nudged him and pointed toward Sergeant Hayward. The smile quickly disappeared from Paul's face and the two of them hurried up the stairs. I didn't know what to make of those two.

When Ben and my dad returned, I laid a finger over my mouth so they wouldn't wake him. I wrote on a scrap of paper **He's waiting for Josh!** and held it up for them to read.

Dad's eyes widened. He and Ben tiptoed through to the hallway.

Just before six, I looked up from my work to see Josh and Dana outside heading for the sliding doors. I waved my hands at them and hurried to lock the doors. I pointed for them to go around to the main lobby. They looked confused. I didn't think they could see Sergeant Hayward from where they stood.

I posted a sign informing guests that the registration entrance was closed and, like Dad, tiptoed out of there.

I arrived at the main lobby just in time to see Mom and Aunt Margaret shuttling Josh and Dana into the private family kitchen.

"Hurry!" Aunt Margaret pleaded.

Great. Now we were harboring them. They weren't fugitives, I reasoned. Still, Sergeant Hayward would never believe that we hadn't hidden them. And he would be right.

I held the door open long enough for Trixie, Radar, and Duchess to zoom through. Twinkletoes was already in the kitchen, lounging in a comfy armchair.

When Dad and Aunt Margaret were children, Oma worried that they needed private family time, away from the guests. She set up the family kitchen like a cozy country kitchen, with a cooktop and oven, a fireplace, and a huge farmhouse table big enough for homework and dining.

"Now," said Mom, "tell us what's going on."

"No, no, no!" Aunt Margaret whispered. "He'll hear us in here."

"He who?" Dana's forehead crinkled with worry.

Aunt Margaret told them about Sergeant Hayward.

"He won't hear us," said Josh. "Holmes and I used to try to listen to Holly and Oma when they were in here."

I smiled at the memories. "We always knew you were out there, so we whispered."

"No. We're not taking chances. This guy is unreasonable. I'm afraid he's trying to make a name for himself or something," said Aunt Margaret. "Maybe we should talk in Oma's apartment."

Mom gazed briefly in the direction of the hidden staircase that led to my place. "How about Holly's apartment?"

I nodded. "Fine with me."

"No cops!" Dana protested.

"Dave left this morning to pick up crutches in Snowball."

Dana gave me a look like she was going to cry. Really? A grown woman using tears to get her way?

Josh tilted his head at me.

"All right. Fine! I'll run upstairs to see if he's there." I opened the door to the hidden stairs. All the dogs followed me.

The door at the top, two flights up, swung open into my dining room. It was quiet in my apartment. I peeked in the guest bedroom on the chance that Dave had had enough of his mother and had retreated to the inn. But he wasn't there.

With three dogs behind me, I hurried back down to the kitchen. "All clear."

"Wonderful. I was just making cocktails." Mom handed me a tray of delicious-looking snacks she must have found in the magic refrigerator. "Just a nibble before dinner."

I carried it upstairs and everyone followed me, drinks in hand.

Aunt Margaret immediately toured my apartment. "I might have stayed in Wagtail if I could have had a pad like this!"

Mom chuckled. "No, you wouldn't have. You desperately wanted to leave Wagtail."

"That's true. It's so different now. When I was growing up, I was convinced there was a big world out there beyond Wagtail Mountain that I had to see."

I gave each dog and Twinkletoes a snack, and we settled down. It didn't take long for Aunt Margaret to ask, "Dana, what brings you to Wagtail?"

Josh said, "Mom—"

She cut him off with a look. "Dana?"

"Well, um, my husband is looking for me. Josh told me he was coming here for his grandmother's birthday, and it sounded like a great place to go."

"Honey, why are you hiding from your husband?" asked Mom.

"He is not a kind man. I . . . I married him when I was very young and didn't understand the sort of man that he was. At the time, I was eager to get away from my father and his strict rules. He had an archaic view of women. We were supposed to wear skirts to our ankles and long sleeves at all times. We weren't allowed to wear any colors except black and subtle hues of dark blue. We couldn't cut our hair, and no makeup was permitted. We weren't allowed to work outside the home. Women were only good for bearing children, cleaning, and cooking. I'm afraid I rebelled. They say you marry a man like your father, and I guess I did, except with beatings thrown in."

We sat in silent horror for a moment.

"I'm so sorry," said Mom. "Should we assume, then, that your husband killed Frank Burton? Perhaps he mistook him for Josh?"

Aunt Margaret gasped at the implication. "You mean he intends to murder Josh? That's why you're hiding?"

Dana nodded vigorously. "He must realize by now that Josh is helping me escape his cruelty. He's a terribly jealous man. Josh has been so good to me. I didn't think I could ever trust a man again, but Josh has been wonderful." She flashed a smile at him.

I wanted to get to facts. "Then Frank Burton was not your husband?"

"No."

Dana sure knew how to clam up. "Did you know Frank Burton?"

Dana and Josh shook their heads.

"What did he say to you?" I asked.

"We never even saw him," said Josh.

"How can that be?" Mom sounded dubious.

"We left to go to Wagtail. He must have arrived after we were gone." Josh ate a cracker topped with cheese as if he wasn't one bit concerned.

"But you left your tent and a sleeping bag?" I asked doubtfully.

"That was my fault." Dana giggled. "I saw a spider crawl into the sleeping bag, and I wasn't ever going to sleep in it again!"

For a split second, Josh listened to her as though hearing this for the first time. But then he grinned and gazed at her with adoration. I had a bad feeling there wasn't a thing in the world Dana could do or say that he wouldn't find enchanting.

"What about the tent?" My tone was a little harsher than I intended.

Josh's lips pulled tight. "We left in a hurry."

"Why?" asked Aunt Margaret.

"We were afraid her husband had found us."

Why did we have to pull every little detail out of them? "What made you think that?"

Josh flicked a glance at Dana. "Dana thought someone was watching her."

"Did you see someone, Dana?" asked Mom.

"No. You know that creepy feeling. Women can tell these things."

This woman was thinking that Dana wanted to get out of there and made up that story. How many other stories had she invented to get her way? Maybe she was tired of sleeping in a tent. "So you thought it preferable to camp out in a house that is under construction?"

"It wasn't ideal, but no one would have found us there," said Josh, obviously overlooking the fact that we discovered him without much trouble.

"What is your husband's name?" I asked, hoping he wasn't one of the guests at the inn.

"Mack Carrington," said Dana.

"What does he do for a living?"

"He's a computer geek. I don't know exactly. That computer stuff is beyond me. He helps people with programming or something. Um, is there a ladies' room I could use?"

"Of course." I showed Dana to the bathroom attached to my bedroom.

When I returned, Mom asked Josh, "Did she say anything that was true just now?"

Josh picked up another cracker. "Sure. Her husband really is looking for her."

Mom's eyes narrowed. "And how exactly do you know that?"

"Dana feels him," said Josh. "We've had a couple of close encounters. Mom, I want you to know how much I appreciate you putting up money for our bond."

Aunt Margaret gazed at her son with pure adoration. "Sweetheart, I just wish you weren't in this mess. What if her husband wants to murder you?"

Josh nodded. "That's why we've been evading him. I thought for sure that he wouldn't find us here, but obviously he has."

Dana returned from the bathroom and took a seat.

"We should notify the police," said Aunt Margaret.

"No! We have to get out of town!" Dana jumped to her feet. "Right now!"

"Not so fast." Aunt Margaret held out her hand. "You are probably safer here in Wagtail than you would be on the run."

"I can't stay here. You don't understand. He knows where we are. Josh, we have to go." Dana clung to Josh and gazed into his eyes not unlike Trixie when she wanted a cookie.

"Dana!" Mom spoke with authority. "Calm down, dear. Margaret is correct. You are better off here at the inn. We'll all be on the lookout for him. And he won't take a chance hurting you here. There are far too many ears and eyes. You won't have this kind of security anywhere else."

I wasn't quite satisfied with Dana's explanation. "Just a minute. You just said that you didn't see anyone. How do you know your husband is here? Maybe the person you felt watching you was Frank."

Dana's eyes widened. "I can feel his presence."

Baloney! "You flew in on Josh's plane, right?"

Josh nodded.

"So how would your husband track you? How would he know you were with Josh?"

"He has money and connections. He probably hired someone to find me."

"I'm so sorry, dear," said Mom. "Men can be very persistent."

"Dana, could you provide a photograph of your husband, so we'll know who we're looking for?" I asked.

Josh smiled at her gently. "Dana, Aunt Nell is right. You're so used to being on the run that you don't realize this is an opportunity to finally catch him and live normally again."

"Catch him? No! I have to disappear. Go someplace where he'll never find me."

"No," Josh said firmly. "You'll be looking over your shoulder your whole life. Never comfortable, never happy. This comes to an end now. Even if they can't prove he's a murderer, the police can charge him with stalking."

"You have no idea who you're dealing with. He has connections everywhere!" Dana screeched in a tone so high that Duchess howled.

"All the more reason not to run," said Aunt Margaret.

"If he finds me, he'll kill me. And probably Josh, too." Dana clutched Josh's arm so hard that her fingers were turning white.

Aunt Margaret paled at the thought.

"But don't you see?" I asked. "Josh is right. The way to stop this is to locate him. If the police arrest him for Frank's murder, then you're in the clear and you won't have to worry about him anymore. He'll be convicted and you will be free to live your lives. The key is to catch him."

"He'll never be arrested. And if he is, he'll get out. I know him. I've seen how powerful Mack is."

"Holly," said Mom, "would you be a dear and run down to the kitchen for another pitcher of these drinks? I left one in the fridge."

"Of course." The dogs followed me down the stairs again. Even Radar accompanied us.

To my surprise, Oma, Dave, the Ben, and Dad were noshing on leftovers from the magic refrigerator. Duchess made a beeline for Dave, her tail wagging like crazy.

The mood was jolly, and they greeted me with enthusiasm.

"You're back!" I said to Dave.

He reached over and patted crutches. "Mom dropped me off here so I could return the wheelchair. Liesel saw me and offered me some dinner. But I'll be heading home afterward. I'm a little unsteady on the crutches, but I think I can manage. Thanks for letting me stay over with you."

"Where is Josh?" asked Oma.

"Upstairs in my apartment. Mom and Aunt Margaret are getting to know Dana."

"Oh? Has she shared anything interesting?" asked Dave.

"Probably just the same things she told the police. She had a strict father and a husband who beat her. She's terrified of her husband and thinks he's on her trail or that he hired someone to find her."

Dad stopped eating. "That's great for Josh. Clearly, the brutal husband would have been Frank's killer." He looked to Dave for confirmation. "Right?"

"Not necessarily," said Dave. "It depends on whether the husband is actually here, when he arrived, and whether he has an alibi. But he's certainly someone the police would want to talk to."

"Aha. The jealous husband," said Oma. "We need to watch our Joshua. He may be in danger from this man."

"Do you think we can pay some off-duty officers to hang out here until the police find this guy?" I asked Oma.

"Better yet, what about local people?" asked Dave. "I bet Holmes and I could put together a group in no time. What do you know about the husband?"

"Not much. I think she said he was some kind of computer specialist, but she didn't go into detail. In fact, she was sort of sketchy about it."

"Do you have a picture of him?"

"I've asked Dana for one. I'll get it to you—"

At that moment, clattering and loud voices arose. We jumped up and rushed into the lobby, with the dogs leading the way and Dave limping along behind on his crutches.

Dana ran past us. Still on the stairs, Josh called out to her, "Dana! Dana! Wait!"

He flew by us. Radar barked as he ran alongside Josh. Dana flung open the door and fled into the night, followed by Josh and Radar.

Oma, Dad, Dave, Ben, Duchess, Trixie, and I followed them as far as the front porch. We watched helplessly as they disappeared into the dark on the Green, the park in the middle of Wagtail.

Sixteen

❁   ❁   ❁   ❁   ❁

"I guess we're going to have a tough time getting a picture of Dana's husband," said Ben.

"Maybe they will return." Oma tsked. "They have nowhere else to go."

"That didn't stop them before. They preferred to sleep in an unfinished house when they could have come here. I even offered to get them a room somewhere else." I picked up Twinkletoes.

"Josh has the Miller family stubbornness," Dad said.

"So it runs in the family. I thought it was just Holly." Ben grinned at me.

Oma sighed. "There is nothing we can do now. Holly, bring your mother and Margaret down to the kitchen to join us for dinner."

As the others filed into the kitchen, I called Holmes. If Josh caught up with Dana, they might ask around to find out where he lived and head for Holmes's place, which was nicely secluded on the mountain. I explained what happened. "Or they might go back to the house under construction."

"They might, but they're going to have a tough time getting inside. I've been working like crazy. I have more to do, but it's secured pretty well now. They could always break a glass door or a window, but there are no easy ways to enter the house."

Holmes promised to let me know if they showed up.

I trudged up the stairs to my apartment to fetch Mom and Aunt Margaret. When we joined the others in the kitchen, I realized that a seat had been saved for me next to Ben. I took a deep breath. Everyone was already glum and worried about Josh and the irate husband. It probably wasn't the best time to pitch a fuss about seating arrangements.

I located filet mignon for cats in the magic refrigerator, which I dished out for Twinkletoes. Beef stew for dogs sounded appealing. I heated it a little bit for them and placed bowls of it on the floor before selecting my own dinner from items someone had lined up on the island like a buffet.

Aunt Margaret offered me wine, but I declined. I had a bad feeling that things might get worse. After all, what if Dana was correct and the irate husband was here looking for Josh? What if he showed up at the inn? Would we even know? We had no idea what he looked like. Unless he informed us that he was Dana's husband, we would probably be gracious to him.

I took my seat next to Ben, ate my roast beef sandwich, and listened to Aunt Margaret.

"I always hoped Josh would find a nice girl. And I want to keep an open mind about anyone he loves. But Dana seems like trouble. Am I wrong to feel that way?"

Dad shook his head. "I think you are well within your rights to believe that about Dana. Josh has such a kind heart. Always has. But I don't know about this situation. A married woman flying around the world with a single guy? And that little display a few minutes ago doesn't build confidence in her. She's obviously American. Did she tell you where she's from?"

"No. I don't even remember her last name." Aunt Margaret stared at a forkful of macaroni and cheese as if *it* had caused her dismay.

"Carrington," said Dave.

"What else do you know about her?" asked Oma.

Dave cocked his head to the side. "Can't tell you much."

"Well, I intend to find out more. I don't care if that makes me a nosy no-good interfering mom. I'm not letting her ruin Josh's life." Aunt Margaret refilled her wineglass.

Dad watched her with a grin.

"What's so funny?" she asked.

"Oh, Margaret. That young man has you wrapped around his finger. You would do anything for him. Not to mention that you can't stop that kind of love. History is replete with disapproving parents. And those stories rarely turn out well."

Aunt Margaret narrowed her eyes at him. "Maybe you could help me."

Dad burst into laughter.

"You two are teasing," said Oma, "but I must remind you that our Joshua is a murder suspect. It is imperative that we find out if Dana's husband could be the killer."

Aunt Margaret sagged. "You see? Do you see why I don't have good feelings about Dana? Look what she's gotten him into. And now she has run off, heaven knows why. We don't even know where they are."

"She does seem high-strung," I said. "But I would be, too, if I thought my husband was looking for me and might kill me. Did you say anything that caused her to be so upset that she ran out?"

Aunt Margaret looked at Mom. "I don't think so. She was anxious to leave Wagtail to elude her husband. But we don't even know if he's here. She could be imagining that."

Mom nodded. "I don't know why she can't understand that the two of them are safer in Wagtail. Especially if they stay at the inn. They'd be surrounded by people who would help them. You could assist them in avoiding that pesky Sergeant Hayward, too."

"Hayward!" I said. "He's after your job. He's been hanging around the inn."

Dave moaned. "His wife likes Wagtail and has him convinced that this is a cushy job. I'll admit that the crime we have is somewhat different than that in Snowball, but just because this is a smaller resort doesn't mean nothing ever happens here."

Dad smiled at Mom. Frankly, I was surprised by the amicable relationship between my parents. For years I avoided mentioning them to each other and had even worried about having them both attend the same event in the future, like my wedding. Not that one was planned or in the offing yet, but I had worried about it anyway. So it came not only as a surprise but as a huge relief to me that they could be civil to each other. Everyone present was in good cheer, even though we were all concerned about Josh.

After demolishing the remaining pieces of Dobos torte with decaf coffee and tea, no one moved from the table. I collected the dishes and washed them, declining a hand from anyone, especially Ben.

Later on, when Dave left for home and I went up to my apartment, I hit my computer to see if I could find any photos or information on Mack Carrington. Dave would be able to search police files, which I thought would probably be more useful than my general search. Although I found several Mack Carringtons, I was able to eliminate most of them based on their ages. I seriously doubted that men under twenty or over eighty could be her husband.

Dave called to let me know that if Dana's husband had a police record, it didn't pop up anywhere.

I went to bed early and caught up on much-needed sleep.

I opened my eyes in the morning half expecting to see Radar on my bed. But he wasn't there.

The sun shone warm and bright, but Josh's problems weighed heavily on me. I checked my phone for messages immediately, but there was nothing from Holmes about Josh or Dana.

After a shower, I donned a casual yet professional rose-colored dress and hurried downstairs. Oma, Dad, and Margaret ate breakfast with gloomy expressions.

I ushered Trixie outside to do her business, feeling a little odd since only one dog was with me. Duchess had gone home with Dave.

On our return to the dining area, Twinkletoes was already eating. I slid into a chair at Oma's table. "Did Josh come back?"

Aunt Margaret ran an uneasy hand along her neck. "I stayed in their room last night. I thought for sure they would return for their things. You know, try to sneak in during the night and be gone before dawn perhaps. But they never came."

Shelley showed up with a mug of coffee for me. "How did it go last night?" I whispered.

"It was so much fun!" she whispered back.

"What are you two talking about?" asked Oma.

"Girl stuff," Shelley said. "The specials are shrimp and

grits, lemon waffles with blackberry compote, and ricotta pancakes with blueberries."

"I think I'll try the waffles. Is there one for Trixie?"

"Yup. No lemon, of course. It's bits of waffle mixed with chicken liver and sweet potato. Sounds awful, but dogs love it."

"Okay, we'll try that."

Shelley shuttled away.

"Where would they go, Holly?" asked Oma.

"I talked with Holmes. He said the house under construction is now secure, so I guess that's out. Maybe Josh has friends here? He received a strange message. Something about Roo being ready when he was."

"The airport!" Margaret exclaimed. "Roo is the name of his airplane. From 'kangaroo' because he hops around to different places."

Dad shook his head. "Not impossible, but highly unlikely. Unless they rented a car, they would have to hike down the mountain, which is a long trek, and then hitch a ride to the airport. Holly, would the people at the parking lot be able to tell you if they arrived in a car?"

"I'll check with them. They're pretty reasonable about giving me information because I know the mayor."

Oma blushed and flapped her hand. "Nonsense. They are very nice people. But Sam makes a good point. Hiking down the mountain is difficult."

I nodded in agreement. "I don't know much about Dana, but she doesn't strike me as an outdoorsy person."

Shelley arrived with our meals. I was glad to see Trixie dig into hers. She wasn't a picky eater in general but this was new to her.

"People reach deep for courage when they are driven by fear," said Oma.

"They can't keep running." Aunt Margaret picked up a chocolate croissant, tore off a tiny piece, and nibbled on it. "They started in Paris, which makes it all the less likely that her husband has even a clue where they are now. For months they traveled around Europe. How would he know that they flew to the United States?"

"They have to file flight plans," said Dad. "If you knew who to call, I suppose you could get that information."

There was also the issue of the bonds Aunt Margaret had paid, but I thought it better not to mention that she might not get her money back if they had left. They all knew about it anyway. "I guess you have tried to call Josh's cell phone?"

She scowled at me. "Of course I have. Either he's not responding or it needs charging."

My eyes met Oma's. She shook her head as though she didn't understand what Josh was doing. I didn't, either. "Holly, I have plans today. Can you watch the inn as you offered? Also, the Cat Fest begins on Friday, and we need a few things. I have a list in my office. Could you run errands around town when I return?"

"I'd be happy to do that. No problem at all."

Oma smiled at me. "Thank you, Holly."

Margaret sighed. "I wish you had asked Josh to take over the inn. He wouldn't be in this fix now. He never would have met that vixen."

Oma rested her hand over Margaret's. "Joshua has a need to travel and fly. He would never have been happy tied down to the inn."

"And look where it got him," Aunt Margaret grumbled.

"Margaret, you cannot think that way. This did not happen because of his job."

Aunt Margaret turned toward me. "You must have some idea where he could be."

I didn't have a clue. "Me? I called Holmes because I thought Josh might seek shelter at his place. I think we should all keep our eyes open. Especially for Radar."

I excused myself and phoned the parking lot at the out-skirts of Wagtail to ask if they had a record of a car for Josh Miller or Dana Carrington.

"Nope. I was on duty when they arrived. They caught a taxi from the airport and took a Wagtail taxi to the other side of the lake. Leastways that's what I heard Josh say to the driver."

"Can you put up a notice to call me if they show up?"

He chuckled. "You're a step behind Officer Dave. We put up the notice last night. Have you got any pictures of them?"

"I do! I'll text them to you right now." I disconnected the call and found pictures of Dana and Josh at Oma's birthday celebration. I sent them over immediately and returned to the dining table.

"Dave beat us to it. They're already on the lookout for Josh and Dana. They arrived in a taxi from the airport so they don't have a vehicle at their disposal."

After breakfast, I did my morning rounds of the inn to be sure everything was in order. Brendan had placed his suitcase outside his room. The door was open, and I could see him looking around the room.

"Are you checking out?" I asked.

"I'm afraid so. I really enjoyed my stay, but it makes more sense for me to bunk with my parents right now. They're putting their house on the market and there's so much to do. I thought this would be a nice little vacation for me, but after thirty years in the same house, they have accumulated a lot of stuff. It will be easier for my mom if I'm there. Last night she called me five times in one hour!"

"You're a good son to help them. I'm sure they appreciate it."

I continued on my way and ran into Judy Davis in the cat wing. "Good morning!"

"Oh, Holly! I'm so glad to see you." She lowered her voice. "Have they caught the killer yet?"

"Not yet. But they're working on it."

"I heard it was that Mr. Burton who was killed."

It surprised me that she knew his name. "Yes. It was."

"He was a bit cold. I have met such nice people here but some very curious ones as well. Like those brothers, for instance. At least I think they're brothers because they look so much alike. They come down to breakfast early like I do. But they always eat elsewhere. And whenever I see them, they act like they're sneaking around. Do you think they could have killed Mr. Burton?"

To be honest, the thought hadn't even crossed my mind. I thought they were up to something but—murder? "Thank you, Judy. I'll pass that information on to the police."

"I hope you don't mind me telling you these things. I don't like to butt in, but I would feel so much better if the killer was apprehended."

"I can assure you that the police are working on it."

"That's a relief. I'm off to see your Holmes now. I have to make tile selections!"

"That sounds like fun."

"You can't imagine how many decisions one has to make when building a house. But I love it and wouldn't have it any other way." She hurried along the corridor.

I wrapped up my tour of the inn at the library. When I finished, I spied Dave eating breakfast with Ben and stopped by their table. "I see you're making out all right, Dave. How do you feel?"

"Better, thanks. I have an appointment with an ortho-pedist today."

"Good luck! Does Duchess need to go outside?

"Ben took her out," said Dave.

Ben? The man who didn't "do" dogs or cats? "I'll be in the office. Do you need anything?"

Ben waved a croissant at me. "Any news on Josh?"

"No one knows where Josh is. He never came back last night."

I left the two of them eating breakfast, got myself a mug of tea, and hustled down to the office with Trixie and Twinkletoes, wondering why Ben was still in Wagtail. Didn't he have to get back to work?

Zelda had taken extra care with her appearance that day. Her beautiful long blond hair had been curled in the latest fashion and she wore more makeup than usual. "You look lovely."

Her eyes fairly sparkled when she said, "I have a date tonight. He's picking me up here after work."

"And who is this lucky fellow?"

"Nate!"

"The flower delivery guy?"

"Oh, Holly! He's so nice. And very smart. Maybe it's because I'm getting older, but I appreciate a man who's intelligent and interesting. I'm through with men who are self-absorbed and think the world revolves around them."

"Funny how that happens. Our priorities change, I guess."

"Please don't tell me you're reconsidering Ben."

I nearly snorted the tea I had just sipped. "Why would you say that?"

"Your father adores him. I heard him call Ben 'son' this morning! So I thought maybe something was going on between the two of you."

"No. No way. I have got to talk to Dad about this. I keep meaning to, but so much has been going on that I haven't had a minute alone with him."

No sooner had I said that than Oma and Dad appeared.

"Will you be all right running the inn today, Holly?" asked Oma.

"Of course. What are you two up to?"

Dad glanced around the lobby.

Oma laughed at him. "We're sneaking out. Just mother and son today. No grandchildren are invited."

"And not the Carole or Margaret, either," said Dad. "We'd better hurry before one of them catches us and tags along."

They snickered as they hurried to the sliding glass doors.

"That's adorable," said Zelda.

I settled in the office, delighted to see an email from the bride's father telling me they would like to book the inn for their wedding and needed a substantial number of rooms as well.

I spent the next few hours working up a contract and blocking rooms for them. Ben came in looking for Dad.

"He left hours ago."

"Where did he go?"

"I honestly don't know."

"Did anyone hear from Josh?"

At that exact moment, Aunt Margaret arrived and asked the same questions.

"Why don't the two of you take a golf cart and drive around for a couple of hours. Check out places where they might be hiding. Phone the airport to see if Josh's plane is still there."

I could tell my last suggestion terrified Margaret. Someone had to do it. I picked up the phone and called the airport. "Hi! This is Holly Miller from the Sugar Maple Inn in Wagtail. My cousin, Joshua Paxton, flew in on a plane called Roo?"

The man on the other end knew who I was talking about.

"Wonderful! Can you tell me if the plane is still there?"

He confirmed that it was. I thanked him and hung up the phone.

"Well?" asked Aunt Margaret.

"Roo is still at the airport."

Aunt Margaret stared at me.

"What's wrong?" I asked.

"I don't know whether to be relieved or upset."

"Go with relieved. They're still here somewhere."

Zelda leaned in the doorway to the office. "Mr. Zimmerman is on line four."

"I'm sorry. I have to take this call." I clicked on line four. "Hello, Mr. Zimmerman."

Aunt Margaret and Ben wandered out of the office.

Oma and Dad didn't return until late in the afternoon, but I could tell they had enjoyed their special day together. The two of them settled in the office.

Zelda changed into a pretty green dress for her date, and I hurried out with Trixie and Twinkletoes to shop for local items to add to gift baskets for our guests who would come for the Cat Fest.

Trixie had a ball trying out clever new toys in the stores. One man had created trendy cat grass planters that were pretty enough to place on coffee tables. I also bought plush cat kicker toys, salmon treats, mouse-shaped cookies for cats, larger iced mouse-shaped cookies for their people, and T-shirts with cat slogans on them.

On my way back to the inn, I stopped at the florist. The owner greeted us with dog and cat treats when Twinkletoes, Trixie, and I entered the store. I knew the owner fairly well because I bought arrangements from him regularly for the family graves. "I wanted to thank you for the gorgeous arrangement you made for Oma. It was spectacular."

"I thought it came out well."

"Could you tell me who the flowers were from?"

He snickered a little. "Snooping, are you? I'm afraid I can't help you there."

"You must have his name. I'm sure he paid by credit card."

He grinned at me. "I'm afraid not. I recall the transaction well. I don't get paid in cash much anymore and certainly not for a fancy arrangement." That rang a bell with me. The Mellor brothers had paid in cash.

"So the buyer was here? In the store? You saw him or them?"

"I certainly did. But there was only one."

"If he were a local, you would have recognized him. So it must have been someone from out of town."

"I would think so. He didn't tell me. But he knew Oma."

"He said that?"

"He implied it. Asked me if I knew her and what kinds of flowers she likes."

"What did he look like?"

"He was a fairly young fellow. I thought it might have been Josh. He was about the right age."

Josh? But why wouldn't he have signed his name on the card? I opened my phone and located a picture I had taken of Oma and Josh at her birthday dinner. I handed him the phone. "Was it this man? He might have had a beard."

He shook his head and handed my phone back to me. "No, that's not him. He didn't have a beard, either. This fellow was clean shaven. Nice-looking, with glasses."

Ben! I scrolled back a few years to find a photograph of Ben. It was a little dated, but he hadn't changed too much. I handed the phone back. "How about this guy?"

"Nope. Our fellow had on those glasses that don't have frames. You know what I'm talking about? The arms screw right into the glass. I looked at them at my optometrist's store. They're very expensive. Out of my ballpark."

And just like that, I knew who Oma's secret admirer was.

Seventeen

❁ ❁ ❁ ❁

It had to be Nate. The flower delivery guy.

I was thoroughly confused. "That was the man who delivered the flowers. Nate. But he works for you."

"No, he doesn't,"

I thought back. Had I misunderstood? I didn't think so. He must have made that up. "Let me get this straight. He came into your shop, asked what kinds of flowers Oma likes, and then paid you cash for them?"

"Sounds about right. Except I don't think he called her Oma. I believe he asked what kind of flowers Mrs. Miller liked. What with it being her birthday and all, I assumed he meant your Oma. But I inquired to be sure. 'For Oma's birthday?' I asked him. And he said he didn't know it was her birthday, but that was all the better and he was glad I had told him."

I wished I had a photograph of Nate to verify that we were talking about the same man. We had to be. As far as I knew, no one else had sent flowers to Oma. But why not sign the card? Why pretend it was from a mysterious admirer? And why bring flowers to Oma at all? He wasn't an age where he could have been an old beau. And someone who knew her probably wouldn't have asked about Mrs. Miller. There was nothing to do but thank the florist and be on my way.

I strolled home mulling over that information. It didn't have to be Nate. Surely other residents of Wagtail or visitors to town wore rimless glasses. They weren't as uncommon as they used to be. But I was seriously concerned about the man, whoever he was. How did he know Oma? Why bring her flowers? Why lie about working at the florist?

The sun was setting as we walked. Trixie and Twinkletoes raced ahead of me, meeting up with other dogs and cats whom they knew.

I stopped and gazed in the window of the store where Dana had bought her expensive dress. But as I turned to look, out of the corner of my eye I saw someone dart to the side. Pretending to be interested in the store next to it, I angled myself so I could look back. People, dogs, and cats crowded the sidewalk. It could have been anything. Cats were well known to dart suddenly and then scamper away. That was probably what it was.

I walked on, then stopped to look into the show window of Tall Tails, the bookstore. Once again, I felt as though someone had zoomed into hiding.

Two could play that game. I ambled in what I hoped looked like a casual manner. I wanted to pick up Trixie and Twinkletoes so they wouldn't give me away, but my hands were full of shopping bags. I darted into a store and hurried to the show window to see who might pass by. My money was on Josh or Dana. I didn't know why one of them would be following me, but I couldn't imagine who else it could be.

Unfortunately, it was hard to pick out a person. Holmes

walked by. He didn't seem to be looking for anyone. Shortly behind him was Carole, who appeared bored.

I didn't see Josh or Dana. I must be feeling edgier than I thought what with Josh being a murder suspect. It couldn't be Nate because he was with Zelda. I could ask her about Nate tomorrow.

We entered the inn through the main lobby. It was quiet as it usually was at this time of day. We didn't serve dinner, so most of our guests were out and about in town. I deposited the items in our storage and assembly room. It was a fairly good size, with no windows, and shelves on three walls. We stocked extra items there for our little Sugar Maple Inn store. And we placed luggage there for people who needed to check out but weren't leaving Wagtail for a few hours. It was actually a multipurpose room, with long tables in the center for assembling baskets or preparing flower arrangements. One of my tasks this week would be to put together the gift baskets so they would be in guest rooms when people arrived for the Cat Fest.

But for now, I was more concerned about Nate. When I locked the storage room door, Twinkletoes was nowhere to be seen. I unlocked the door again to be sure she wasn't inside. She wasn't.

Trixie pranced in the hallway, anxiously waiting for me. As soon as the lock clanked in place, she took off toward the main lobby. I hurried after her, imagining a crisis. *Please don't do the howl of death!*

She disappeared through the dog door to the private kitchen. I gulped hard, afraid of the worst, and flung open the door. Oma, Mom, Dad, Aunt Margaret, Ben, and Officer Dave were gathered at the kitchen table. Twinkletoes had snuggled in Oma's lap.

I glanced around. Everyone seemed to be in good humor.

"Holly! Have you eaten?" asked Oma. She swiped one hand through the air. "Even if you have, you should join us."

"Wine?" asked Aunt Margaret.

I was still uneasy about Nate and thought I should keep my wits about me. "No, thanks, Aunt Margaret. Any word from Josh?"

"We were just talking about them," said Dad. "Wagtail isn't that big, yet none of us have seen him."

Dave heaved a sigh. "I haven't been able to find a marriage record for Mack and Dana Carrington, either. There are men named Mack Carrington, but I can't find one in the tech industry."

Aunt Margaret went pale. "What are you saying? What does that mean?"

Dave sighed. "It's a big world with a lot of people and I could have missed the records, but I'm beginning to wonder if she's fibbing."

"Didn't she show you identification?" Ben asked.

"She did on Saturday night. She had a passport and a driver's license in the name of Dana Carrington. But she might not be truthful about her husband's real name."

Aunt Margaret's eyes were wide with horror. She held a hand over her mouth.

"What you're saying is that we don't know if anything she told us is true." Mom pulled a covered dish out of the fridge. "But she's scared of someone."

"Maybe she's scared of the police because she murdered Frank." Aunt Margaret's voice had a tremor in it. "And I stupidly paid her bond as a favor to Josh! We have to find them!"

Mom opened the oven and removed heated serving dishes, which she placed on the island so we could help ourselves. I handed out plates and set the table.

"It is concerning that he has not been in contact with any of us," said Oma. "It is going on twenty-four hours now."

As I listened, I couldn't help wondering if Nate was the

person Dana feared. Was he dating Zelda to get inside the inn and nose around to learn if Dana was there? Delivering the flowers would be a clever ruse to visit the inn and maybe catch a glimpse of Josh or Dana. A chill ran down my back. Zelda was a font of information about who was staying at the inn, and she wouldn't have thought twice before telling him about Oma's birthday and all the family members coming to visit, including Josh. I took a deep breath. He hadn't looked like a cruel person, not that a cruel person would look much different from anyone else, yet somehow something didn't add up. "He might be here. In Wagtail."

Aunt Margaret nearly spilled her drink. "How do you know?"

"I'm not sure, but I think I met him. His name is Nate, or at least that's what he said."

Oma gasped. I had everyone's full attention.

"Nate is the one who delivered Oma's flowers. I checked with the florist today. It appears that he paid cash for the flowers and the florist told him it was Oma's birthday. Then he signed the card as Oma's secret admirer. In fact, he was here yesterday, too. Zelda gave him a tour of the inn. He helped arrange the chairs on the terrace for Oma's tea." I nearly choked when I added, "And now, I think Zelda is out on a date with him."

Dad said, "Aww, Hollypop, she'll be fine."

"This is Zelda we're talking about. The one who married an awful man and then spent years trying to get back on her feet financially after he took all her savings."

"I forgot about him," Oma said. "She doesn't have the best taste in men, does she?"

I was worried about Zelda. I had to tell her. I pulled out my phone and texted her, phrasing my words carefully. I needed to know where she was without saying anything that would alarm her. Or something that she might repeat to him that would put him on alert. It was harder than I thought. I kept it very simple.

Are you on your date with Nate?

I watched my phone to see if Zelda would respond. Fortunately, she did. But she had merely left a checkmark on my text. All I knew was that she was with a possible killer.

"So, what do we do now, Dave?" asked Oma.

"We need to locate Zelda," I said.

Before I could say more, Dave held up his hand. "Don't text or call her yet. We don't want her to let anything slip or to make her act anxious or out of the norm. It's probably better if we find her. Given the time, I'd guess they were in a restaurant or a bar. I'll phone Snowball and have them send officers over to look for Zelda and Nate."

Dad shook his head. "They won't know Zelda or Nate, not to mention that between calling them in to work and driving time, it will be an hour or more before they arrive. I think we should look for her."

Dave held up his palms. "No, no, no. If this guy murdered Frank, then he's very dangerous. He should be taken into custody by the police, not by a bunch of untrained and unarmed citizens. He might even be carrying a gun or some other weapon."

I swallowed hard, imagining that poor Zelda was with him.

"Okay," said Dad. "We won't try to detain him. We'll just watch them. That way Zelda will be somewhat safer, and we can follow them if they go somewhere else."

Dave frowned. "I can't stop you from looking for them. For the record, I am against this. Don't try to take him into custody or anything. Your only job is to locate Zelda and tell me where she is. It shouldn't be too difficult. There are only so many places a person would go to dinner on a first date."

"We'll team up," said Dad. "Nell and I can try the place with the funny name."

"Tequila Mockingbird," said Mom.

"Right. And we'll also visit Hair of the Dog on the other side of town. Holly, you take Ben and check the restaurants along the Green, like Hot Hog and The Blue Boar. Margaret, you stay here with Oma and let us know if you hear from Joshua. If he contacts anyone, it will be you."

I didn't like being teamed up with Ben one bit. Even worse, he looked almost giddy about his assignment. I was tempted to suggest that Dad come with me and Ben go with Mom, but the way Mom and Dad were gazing at each other stopped me. They had been spending a lot of time together. And it hadn't slipped my notice that Dad had been coming in late. I supposed I should be happy about this development, but I worried that whatever had driven them apart before would rear its ugly head again.

In any event, it wasn't the time to argue or make a fuss. Finding Zelda was more important than anything else at the moment. We all needed to focus on Zelda.

I dashed upstairs for a light jacket. Twinkletoes followed me. But when she saw Ben waiting at the bottom of the grand staircase, she hissed at him and refused to go a step farther.

Trixie, Ben, and I headed straight to the restaurants and bars along the Green. We had no luck at The Blue Boar, which wasn't surprising since it was the priciest place in town. They weren't at the Italian place or the Greek restaurant, either.

Ben told me all about his adventure across the lake with my dad. Much to my dismay, he hadn't fallen into the water. But he definitely wasn't fond of boats, nor was he interested in fishing. I hoped Dad had picked up on that. "Did you find anything helpful at their campsite?"

"No. The police did a good job of collecting every-thing. The only thing that was left were ashes from the fire. But it wasn't a total loss. Your dad and I have a better understanding of where Josh and Dana were and the basic lay of the land. It's much easier to imagine now." Ben sighed. "But I still don't understand the beauty of sitting still in a boat with a fishing rod. It was cold out in the wind, and as far as I can tell, nothing happens."

"Did you actually try fishing?"

"No. We saw people fishing. I would have been bored in three minutes. Not my sport, for sure."

"And there are the worms." I knew he would hate pick-ing up anything that wriggled.

Ben turned slightly green. "Very funny. Your dad told me a lot of people use other types of bait made of nonlive components."

Maybe the day hadn't been a total loss. I turned my head to hide my smile from him and spotted someone with long blond hair at a table inside Farm & Fork, one of the newer establishments in town. I hadn't eaten there yet, but I had heard about the farm-to-table restaurant. It was supposed to be excellent, and it was right up Zelda's alley.

I nudged Ben. "Think that's her?"

"Could be. Let's go in."

I opened the door and strode inside, stunned by the num-ber of plants. I had never been in a restaurant with so much vegetation inside. Some hung from the ceiling and some acted as separators between tables. I edged past the host-ess while Ben engaged her in a discussion about the restau-rant and what it served.

The greenery happened to be particularly useful for the task at hand. I was able to peek around a huge fern to see the blonde from the front. It was definitely Zelda. I scooted behind other plants and could make out Nate's glasses.

I hurried back to Ben and pretended to be excited about the restaurant. Nodding at him, I exclaimed, "It's so charming! Do you think we could have the table in that corner?" I hoped I hadn't miscalculated how well we could watch them from there.

The hostess, who had been buttered up by Ben, readily agreed. She led us to a table in a cozy nook and handed us menus. We sat side by side on a bench instead of across from each other, which I didn't care for at all, but we had a great view of Zelda between the plants. I could see Nate's back, too.

Trixie jumped up on the bench and wedged between us. I whispered "Thanks" to her and kissed the top of her head.

I pulled out my phone and quickly texted Officer Dave to let him know that we had found Zelda and Nate at Farm & Fork and had her under surveillance.

I looked up and glanced at Zelda through the fern. She was thoroughly engaged with Nate and her meal and didn't appear to have noticed us. Not yet anyway. But Dr. Engelknecht spotted us.

He stopped at our table. "Ben! It's good to see you back in town."

Ben stood and shook his hand. "It's great to be back. I've missed Wagtail."

Dr. Engelknecht raised his eyebrows and glanced at me. "Wagtail has a lot to offer. How's the Frank Burton murder investigation coming, Holly? Is it true that they arrested your cousin?"

Ben started to answer. I gave him a swift kick under the table.

"Dave is still working on the case," I said.

"He's supposed to be resting up." Dr. Engelknecht frowned at me.

"Think of him as the mastermind. Everyone is bringing him information," I explained.

"Okay, then. That's much better. Is he staying with his mom?"

"No. He was at the inn with me, but now that he's on crutches, he's able to get around at home."

Dr. Engelknecht eyed me and tilted his head. "He stayed with you?"

I didn't know what kinds of conclusions he was jumping to, but I had a feeling Holmes would be getting a report about Ben and Dave from him. I smiled sweetly as though that thought had not crossed my mind. "He needed help the first night."

When Dr. Engelknecht returned to his table, Ben said, "I guess we should order dinner. Would you like wine?"

I was irritated that he sounded like we were on a date when we were only here because Zelda could be in danger!

The waitress approached to take our orders.

"What do you think about fettuccine Alfredo with asparagus?" Ben nudged me and whispered, "We have to order something."

He was right, of course. I glanced at the menu. "I'll have the fish baked in parchment with spring veggies, please."

Ben ordered wine, but I stayed with plain iced tea. What was he thinking? We had to be alert!

Actually, Zelda and Nate appeared to be having a really good time. When I saw Nate laughing with Zelda and passing a bite of something to share with her, I found it hard to believe that he'd abused Dana and was an awful man. Of course, his pleasant demeanor toward Zelda didn't mean anything. I suspected that a lot of people had two sides and could probably switch between them in a heartbeat.

Ben raised his wineglass to toast. "Together again after all these years."

Oh dear!

Trixie must have picked up on my dismay because she growled.

I tried hard not to laugh. I clinked my water glass with his wineglass while saying, "Not exactly. We're only here for Zelda."

"Okay, think that way if you like." He took a sip of his wine. "This is pretty good. So how are things with you and Holmes?"

"Great!" I wasn't exaggerating.

"That's not what I heard."

Dad. It had to be Dad. What was his problem with Holmes? "Well, if your source was my dad, then you received unreliable information."

"I don't see an engagement ring."

I immediately crossed my arms, thus burying my bare hands. "I don't have to be engaged to be happy. Holmes and I have a good relationship. Now, would you mind concentrating on Zelda?"

"That's so like you, trying to avoid the subject of our relationship."

"We don't *have* a relationship," I muttered.

"Holmes is a nice guy, but wouldn't you be happier with a real job again back in the city?"

And there it was. The very thing I had turned down years ago. I resented his insinuation that I wasn't happy with my life. Quite the contrary!

Trixie whined as though she understood the implications of what he was suggesting, specifically that she would be left behind.

I stared at him in shock. "No. I love my life here." I turned back toward Zelda, who had picked up her purse.

Nate pushed back his chair and stood up, blocking my

view of Zelda until they passed behind the huge fern on their way out.

"They're leaving!" I said, jumping to my feet.

I seized my purse as Trixie leaped to the floor. She looked up at me as if she was waiting for my next move.

"Our food hasn't arrived," said Ben.

He had to be kidding. A vague thought that Dad and Ben might have arranged this flicked through my mind. It was ridiculous. They couldn't have known that we would have to watch Zelda.

I should have wished him bon appétit, but I blurted, "I'm following them."

I was on my way when I heard him shout, "But our food hasn't come yet!"

Trixie by my side, we hurried out to the street. Luckily, Zelda and Nate were still in sight. They turned right onto one of the trails through the Green.

I dictated a text to Dave.

Zelda and Nate left the restaurant. They've turned east into the Green. I'm tailing them.

Eighteen

❁ ❁ ❁ ❁

Trixie loved the Green. She darted around, sniffing interesting scents of dogs, cats, and her archenemies—squirrels! I could only hope that she wouldn't run ahead to her friend Zelda. But so far, there were too many intriguing smells.

The lampposts in the Green shed enough light to walk safely through the park, but not so much that one could see far ahead. The trees loomed large and dark in the night. Crickets chirped their universal song. It soothed my anxiety, as though everything were right in the world.

Zelda and Nate paused ahead of me under a light. Zelda looked up at Nate, who bent his head to kiss her.

Nooo! I wanted to separate them. To warn Zelda so she wouldn't be disappointed when Nate was arrested or when she learned that he might be married to Dana. But it was probably already too late for that. Zelda would be broken-hearted. And what was a married man doing kissing Zelda anyway? The rat!

I sank into the shadows and waited silently. Dad had been right about the police in Snowball taking too long to get to Wagtail. I had to stick with them.

But my little dodge into a darker nook proved surprising. On the path, the shadowy figure of a man stopped short and gazed around. I scooped up Trixie, slid off my jacket, and covered her white fur with it. Stroking her so she would remain quiet and wouldn't squirm, I watched the other person. I had no reason to imagine that he was following me. But why had he stopped walking? Most people would simply continue on their way.

Unless it was Ben. That was a good bet. He appeared to be taller than Ben, but in the shadows, it was hard to tell.

Zelda and Nate were walking again. But the person in the shadows remained still. My best bet was to catch up to Zelda and Nate.

I darted toward them, stepping on a twig that broke with a snap. In the still of the night, it seemed incredibly loud.

Footsteps sped up behind me.

Clutching Trixie, I ran in the direction of Zelda and Nate. The footsteps pounded behind me now, but I didn't dare stop to see who it was. "Zelda!" I called.

But it was Nate who turned around and gazed at me. I caught up to him, panting. "Where is Zelda? I thought she was with you."

"She got a text from someone about an emergency at the inn."

A quiver ran through me. Chances were good that there wasn't an emergency and they had used that excuse to lure her away from Nate. But why? Were the police here and closing in on him? Did they want him to be alone?

I dared to look behind me. A couple strolled toward us holding hands. Their cocker spaniel ran to me and sniffed Trixie.

There was no sign of the shadow that had been after me. It couldn't have been the couple. I set Trixie on the ground. She and the cocker spaniel were instant friends, politely getting to know each other.

"Oh look!" said the woman. "Honey has a new friend. What's her name?" she asked.

"Trixie."

Nate said, "Excuse me. I need to get going."

Oh swell. Now what? "Of course." I nodded at him, and while the woman fussed over the dogs, I glanced at my cell phone. The only messages were from a very annoyed Ben, who had sent me photos of what he was eating and now wanted to know where I was. If there had been a genuine emergency at the inn, I felt certain someone would have texted or called me.

"Nice meeting you," I said to the cocker spaniel's mom. "I'm sorry, but we're running late. Maybe we'll see you and Honey again."

I hurried off in the direction Nate had gone. Trixie ran alongside me. When I had him in sight, I held up my phone and dictated a message to Dave.

Zelda has gone to the inn. I'm still tailing Nate. Where are the police?

But Nate made an abrupt U-turn and was coming straight toward me! I picked up Trixie again and left the path. Sticks and dried leaves from the previous fall crunched under my shoes. But at that moment, I didn't know what else I could do. I held Trixie tight, hoping she wouldn't whine—or worse, bark! I peered from behind a tree.

Nate strode by purposefully, as if he had a plan. If he had seen or heard me, he gave no indication of it.

As soon as I thought it safe, I crept out to the trail and hurried to catch up to Nate.

Unfortunately, I heard footsteps behind me again. The lights from stores began to show through the trees and I could hear the dull murmur of voices. I breathed easier knowing I would be back on the sidewalk in the safety of crowds in a minute or two.

"Holly, stop!" It was a young voice. A girl's voice.

Breathing heavily, Lucy caught up to me. "Hurry. There's someone following me."

I took her hand and we dashed toward the sidewalk.

Nate had slowed to a stroll on the sidewalk. Lucy and I lingered, catching our breath in front of Purrfectly Meowvelous, a store dedicated to everything a cat could want. I wondered sometimes if they hid catnip around the store because Twinkletoes couldn't resist going inside.

"Are you sure someone was following you?" I kept an eye on the spot where the path we'd been on merged with the sidewalk.

She nodded.

"What are you doing out here by yourself?"

"Belle is out on a date. I felt like a third wheel, you know? I mean, Belle is really nice, but I knew I would be in the way. Oliver and Mike are watching some game at a bar and I left. It was so boring."

I gazed at my sweet half sister. I didn't know her very well. A couple of hurried days at Christmas now and then wasn't enough to build the kind of relationship that most sisters had when they grew up together. But I knew that she missed her mom. If ever there was a time when she needed a sister, it was now.

I would have to be careful and hope that Nate didn't see me. If he did, I would laugh and pretend it was a coincidence.

I gave Lucy a big hug before I looked around for Nate.

If I hadn't been searching for Zelda in restaurants, I might have wondered what Nate was doing. But he acted just as I had, stopping in front of restaurant windows and gazing inside, as if he were looking for someone. I longed to catch up to him and ask him some questions, but I knew I couldn't. He might take off.

Instead, I sat down on a bench with Lucy. Trixie jumped up on her lap.

"Have you eaten dinner?" I asked.

"Not a real dinner. Mike and Oliver are filling up on bar snacks. I like pretzels and nuts okay, but they're not the same as a real dinner."

"Well then, let's go somewhere and grab a bite. I need to send a quick text and then we'll go wherever you like."

Lucy caught up to me. We're going to dinner. Nate is searching restaurants along the Green.

I had just tapped send when Nate turned around and made his way back. I averted my eyes and hoped he didn't think I was watching him.

He walked over to Lucy and me. Oh no! He reached out to pet Trixie, who acted like he was the nicest person she had ever met. So much for a dog's superior instinct about people.

"We meet again."

"Nate—I'm sorry, I don't know your last name."

"Nate is fine. Just Nate."

"Just Nate, this is my sister Lucy."

"It's nice to meet you," she said politely.

"That explains why you look alike."

"Really?" I gazed at Lucy. "Do you think that?"

"No. It's the first time I've heard it."

"I'm sorry Zelda had to break off your date," I said.

He stroked Trixie. "Me too. I hope she can find some time for me tomorrow. She's a really interesting person. I guess you know that she's a pet psychic."

"I do. It's uncanny."

"Does she read for people as well?"

I relaxed a little. The conversation was safe. He had no reason to feel anxious or threatened. "No. Only for animals."

"She was trying to explain how she does it, but I think I'm too stodgy or old-fashioned to comprehend it."

"I can't do it, either. I've tried, but I guess you have to have a knack for it. Trixie likes you. Do you have a dog?"

"Two dogs and a cat. They would love it here!"

"It's too bad that you didn't bring them with you." I stopped speaking abruptly. I'd forgotten that he thought I believed he worked for the florist and lived here.

He didn't respond. I feared I had blown it, but then I realized that *he* was the one who had blown it when he said, *They would love it here*. If he lived in Wagtail, his dogs would be here. And if they were coming, wouldn't he have said, *They will love it here*?

"I won't be here very long." He massaged Trixie's ears.

Aha! I wanted to know more. How to keep him talking? "Oh?" That sounded stupid, but now it was out there. I hastily added, "Are you planning to leave town? Where will you go?"

"Is that your phone buzzing?" he asked.

"Sorry. It's a text." I glanced at the phone. Dave had sent the text.

Where are you?

I wasn't sure how to handle this. Lucy had complicated the situation. I couldn't put her in jeopardy! "We were just going to get a bite. Lucy, do you know where you'd like to eat?"

"Yes! I've been itching to go to Sugar Dog. Can we go there?"

One of the newer restaurants in town, Sugar Dog was more of a café with light meals like soup and sandwiches. It was popular because older dogs who were up for adoption roamed the restaurant. The white fur on faces of older dogs is called *sugar*, hence the name. "That would be fun, but you know Dad isn't going to let you take a dog home. Right?"

Lucy nodded, but she was glum.

"Aw, come on. I'll go with you, if that's okay." Nate smiled at Lucy. "Cheer up. Maybe I'll take a dog home with me."

The situation was growing worse by the moment. I could be the horrible sister who refused to go there, but Nate might want to go with us to another restaurant as well. "Uh, okay. Just let me text this person and then we'll go." I flicked the screen of my phone and wrote:

Lucy is with me. We're going to Sugar Dog for a bite. Nate is coming with us.

"This will be fun." Lucy stood up and waited for me to join the two of them.

Sugar Dog was close by. Nate and Lucy chatted, but I fretted on the way there. This was all wrong. Lucy would fall in love with a dog she couldn't have, and Nate could be a wife beater. Possibly a murderer!

Nate graciously held the door open for us. Six dogs immediately greeted Lucy, their tails wagging as if she was the most wonderful person they had ever met. It occurred to me that the restaurant might be therapeutic for people who felt down or lonely.

I steered her toward a table while Trixie ran around greeting all the dogs.

When Nate pulled his chair back to sit down, he asked, "Who is this?"

He squatted and gently removed a red dachshund who was hiding under our table. He clutched it to him as he sat down. "Who are you?" The dog watched him with worried eyes.

"There's a name on her collar." Lucy held her hand out to the dog to sniff. "Lucy! Just like me! Is that your name, sweetie? It's a sign."

Oh no. It was a bit of a coincidence, I had to admit. "She might be named after Lucille Ball, who was a redhead."

The human Lucy didn't take her hand off the dog, but she looked at me with big green eyes. "It's still a sign." I knew this would happen.

Lucy-the-dog was adorable but very fearful. I could understand that. I was feeling pretty anxious myself, afraid that a battalion of police would raid the place any second in search of Nate. I excused myself and hurried to the ladies' room to phone Dave.

When he answered, I whispered, "This isn't a good time to send cops."

I heard him say, "It's Holly!" He went on, "Don't worry. That's not going to happen. There was some kind of mix-up. Are you all right?"

"Everything is fine. I'll explain later."

We disconnected the call. I washed my hands and looked forward to dinner.

Lucy-the-dog seemed more relaxed when I returned to the table. "I bet she hasn't eaten. She's been too busy being scared."

The server arrived and gasped. "Look at you, Lucy! You made a friend. We were so concerned about her that we almost didn't bring her over here this morning."

"Is she sick?" Lucy stroked the other Lucy's head gently.

"She's afraid of everything. Poor girl. We have no way of knowing what happened to her."

Nate frowned. "Where did she come from?"

"She arrived with a batch of street dogs that were rescued and flown here. She doesn't look a thing like the other dogs. She's not young, but she has had several litters. We're thinking she was used for breeding and then abandoned."

"How awful!" Lucy reached out for her. "May I hold her?"

Nate released Lucy-the-dog into Lucy-the-human's arms.

"How could anyone do that to a sweetie like you?" Lucy-the-dog snuggled into my half sister's arms, but she still had that scared look.

Nate had had dinner earlier with Zelda, so he ordered a fruit tart with a side of doggy ice cream. I went with a spring salad for me and fish stew for Trixie. Lucy ordered a burger.

The server recommended their chicken breast dinner-for-dogs for Lucy. "It comes in small shreds. Offer it to her by hand."

Lucy plopped on the floor and introduced Lucy-the-dog to Trixie. The two girls appeared to like each other if wagging tails were any gauge.

Lucy's burger arrived wrapped in paper so she wouldn't have to continually wash her hands, which I thought brilliant. She and Nate alternated feeding Lucy-the-dog chicken and the doggy ice cream Nate had ordered for her. Much of the fear in her eyes subsided as we talked and ate.

I tried to sound casual. "Where will you go when you leave Wagtail?"

Nate said, "New Jersey."

"Do you have family there?"

"I do."

I wasn't making much progress and for all I knew he was lying. "What do you do in New Jersey?"

His eyes met mine and I realized that I had gone too far. "I, um, I'm a florist."

Aha. Now he remembered the role he was supposed to

be playing. It wasn't easy to make up a fake persona and stick with it. I pretended I hadn't noticed his near slip-up. "That explains the beautiful bouquet."

Nate insisted on paying the check. I reminded myself that I was supposed to think he was a florist or a flower delivery guy and tried to talk him into allowing me to pay. But he was adamant.

I watched carefully as he extracted his wallet and placed bills in the folder that held the check.

He reached for Lucy-the-dog, whose little legs kicked wildly, knocking over a glass of water on him. He took it well and laughed about it, but he excused himself to clean up, leaving his wallet on the table.

I gathered our used paper napkins and scurried around to his side of the table. Mopping up the water with one hand, I flipped his wallet open with the other. And there was exactly what I had hoped for. A driver's license with his picture on it from the state of New Jersey. And the name Nate Carrington.

Nineteen

· *·* *·* *·* *·*

So he probably was Dana's husband! My heart beat like a drum. I had let my guard down and we had had dinner with the man who was chasing Dana! The man who beat her. Had Dana lied about his first name? Or had I misunderstood it? I had relaxed because he seemed okay. I had to protect Lucy. We should be all right as long as we stayed where there were lots of other people. I took deep breaths to calm myself and debated whether I should tell Lucy. I decided against that, I was having trouble acting like nothing was wrong. Lucy would be better off being her usual self.

I was in my seat by the time Nate returned. I felt a very small wave of satisfaction at having obtained his real name, but it was overshadowed by the fact that everything fit into place. He had found the Millers in his search for Dana.

But then my other concern erupted into a tsunami of trouble because Lucy wanted to take Lucy-the-dog with her.

"I can take her to school with me next year."

"Won't you live in a dorm?"

"Yes, but they'll never know. She needs me, Holly!"

I knew this would be a mistake and yet I had gone right along with it.

Lucy-the-dog, who had been close to paralyzed with fright, raised her nose and licked Lucy's chin.

Oh great. "Let's leave Lucy-the-dog here. Tomorrow you can come back with Dad and—"

"No! You know what he'll say, and I'll never see her again."

Why wasn't she out dancing like other people her age?

The server must have overheard our conversation. "We do allow approved people to take dogs home overnight to see if they're a good fit. We know you, Holly. It would be fine if you took Lucy for a trial run. In fact, it might be good for her. She's not doing well in the kennel."

Even better! Now I would be the ogre no matter what happened.

Nate leaned toward Lucy and Lucy-the-dog. "I'll make you a deal, Lucy. If your dad says you can't keep Lucy-the-dog, then I'll take her. I'd like to give this little girl a chance at a better life. What do you say?"

Lucy nodded entirely too eagerly.

I wanted to scream *No! Not the abusive husband!* Everything we knew about Nate indicated that he might be cruel to a dog. He'd been very nice through dinner, and at times I had trouble imagining that he might be a killer or abusive toward Dana. Of course, Lucy-the-dog would be with *us* for the night. Right now it was more important to get the other Lucy safely home. We could deal with Lucy-the-dog tomorrow.

Lucy gazed at me with hope.

"Okay. I can agree to that."

Lucy squealed with glee. Lucy-the-dog was taken aback for a moment, but then she licked Lucy's chin with such happiness that I felt she understood what had just happened.

The server arrived with paperwork, a leash and halter, and a bag full of goodies for dogs as well as advice on helping them settle into a new environment.

We stood up to leave. "Where are you staying?" I asked Nate.

"I have a rental house up on the mountain."

"Thanks for helping me with Lucy." Lucy the half sister gave him a little hug. "I'll take good care of her tonight, I promise!"

"Maybe I should go to the inn with you. Zelda was called to an emergency there. They might need a hand."

My breath caught in my throat. "Oma probably needed her to fill in because I went out. I doubt that it was anything major. They would have called me back to the inn if that were the case."

Nate nodded. "I'd feel better if I went along. Just in case your dad flips out over Lucy-the-dog."

Could he really be concerned about the dog? Or was he making excuses like I was? Or maybe he wanted to see Zelda again!

What could I say? "Okay. That would be nice of you."

"Dad is going to love Lucy. I just know he is!"

Lucy-the-dog walked nicely alongside Trixie on the way back to the inn. I was sure she must be overwhelmed, but I suspected that Trixie's presence and confidence comforted her.

Our arrival at the inn was heralded as if we were conquering warriors. Lucy-the-dog got that frightened look again, but the other Lucy picked her up and introduced her to everyone in the Dogwood Room.

Twinkletoes, who could be picky about whom she liked, sat in judgment, watching the newcomer from a safe seat atop a table.

Lucy-the-dog was receiving so much attention that I didn't think she had noticed Twinkletoes.

Meanwhile, Dave was eyeing Nate. I introduced him to everyone. "Is Zelda still here?"

"Oh, you were her date tonight." Mom patted the sofa next to her. "Come join us."

While everyone was distracted by Lucy-the-dog, I hurried to the inn office and Googled Nate Carrington. His face popped up immediately and the first couple of pages were all links to articles about him. He lived in New Jersey and had started a high-tech game that he sold for millions of dollars. Most of the articles were about his success, but some were about his generous philanthropic donations. I scrolled through photographs until I spotted him with Dana.

"Well, well," I muttered out loud. She was operating under an assumed name. She was actually Phoebe Philips. And as far as I could tell, the two of them were not married. Under a picture of her in a stunning black evening gown, the caption read, *Nate Carrington breaks off his engagement to Phoebe Philips.*

That didn't mean they hadn't reconciled their differences and married afterward.

I was so deep in thought that I shrieked when someone banged on the door.

"It's Dave, Holly. Can you open the door? It's kind of hard with the crutches."

Sheepishly, I opened the door for him, surprised to see Nate with Dave.

"Dave, why don't you sit behind the desk? That way

you'll be more comfortable." I hurried to scroll the screen page back to the photo of Nate so Dave would see it.

Dave kept his composure. I probably should have left, but I was too curious. I sat in a chair near the sofa.

"Nate." Dave looked at him.

"Right. Is this because I may have lied a little? I have a good reason. A few months ago, someone broke into my hotel room and stole things. It's best to keep a low profile."

"What brings you to Wagtail?"

"Vacation."

Dave looked around. "Did you bring a dog or a cat?"

"Is that against the rules? I didn't bring one with me, but if Lucy's dad says she can't keep Lucy-the-dog, I've promised to adopt her."

"Does the name Frank Burton mean anything to you?"

Nate's eyes opened wider, and he sat up straighter. I hoped he wouldn't deny knowing him because it was clear that he did. "Yeah. I've been trying to reach him."

Dave was a professional, so he probably knew much better than I when a person was lying. But I thought Nate was telling the truth.

"Did you plan to meet him here?" asked Dave.

"Kind of. Is he okay? Why are you asking about him?"

"When was the last time you saw him?"

Nate had to think about that. "Um, it's been a long time. I usually do business with him over the phone."

"What kind of business?"

Nate sat back. "Maybe you should tell me what's going on. Is he in trouble?"

"He's dead, Mr. Carrington."

Even I knew the shock on Nate's face was real. He leaned forward, propping his elbows on his knees and wringing his hands. Then he leaned back and ran both hands through his hair. "How? What happened?"

"When did you arrive in town?"

Nate had better be careful. That could easily be checked with the rental office.

"I'm guessing he didn't keel over from natural causes?"

Dave didn't answer.

"You think I killed him? Of course not! He was working for me."

"What exactly was he doing for you?"

Nate closed his eyes and shook his head. When he opened them, he looked in my direction. "I can't believe this is happening. I had nothing to do with his death. You have to believe me. Hey! You could fingerprint me. That will exclude me. Or I'll take a polygraph test."

Dave sat in stoic silence, simply watching him.

"Do I need a lawyer? Maybe I should call my lawyer. Is that okay?" He pulled out his phone.

Dave nodded. "We'll be right outside." He tilted his head at me. I followed him as he hobbled into the empty reception lobby.

"Now that we know Dana was his fiancée, do you think he's stalking her?" I asked in a hushed voice.

"Could be. He came to Wagtail for a reason and it sure wasn't to give Oma flowers."

"Maybe he's still in love with her."

"Or could be that he's fixated on her. Sometimes a person changes their mind and wants to get together again."

"What now?" I asked.

"I'd like to interview him."

"He said he'd drop by the inn tomorrow to check on Lucy-the-dog. See what I mean? Would a killer worry about a dog?"

"One wouldn't think so, but psychology is complicated. Did he ask you questions about Frank Burton?"

I thought back. "Frank's name didn't even come up."

"Curious," said Dave. "Maybe Zelda told him everything he needed to know about Frank."

"I don't think so. That seemed like a genuine reaction when you told him Frank was dead."

Dave picked up the phone. "He could have rented through one of the online apps, but chances are good that he went through a local Realtor." He punched in a number. "Hi, Carter. How are things?"

I couldn't make out the response.

"I'll be okay. It's more of a nuisance than anything else. Listen, do you have a tenant up on the mountain by the name of Nate Carrington? He probably paid cash in advance."

As Dave listened, a smile crossed his face. "Thanks!" He disconnected the call. "Well, he didn't lie about that. I hope his lawyer is encouraging him to be forthcoming, otherwise the interview will be over."

A few minutes later, Nate found us. He held his phone out to Dave. "She'd like to speak with you."

Dave took the call and walked back into the office for privacy.

To his credit, Nate didn't run off. He stayed right there until Dave summoned him.

Nate and I returned and sat down.

"Remember how I said someone broke into my hotel room?" said Nate.

Dave nodded.

"It was my former girlfriend, Phoebe Phillips. They caught her on a hotel camera."

"Where did this happen?" Dave appeared skeptical.

"In Paris." Nate sighed.

But now he had my attention. Wasn't that where Dana and Josh met? It had at least the ring of truth to it.

"Did you report it to the police?" asked Dave.

Nate nodded. "I did. That's how I know about the hotel camera."

"And you followed her here?"

"In a manner of speaking. I had no idea where she was. Paris is a big place and it's easy to travel across Europe. So I called a private detective. He's the one who found her."

"His name?" asked Dave, who was taking notes.

"Frank Burton."

Twenty

❁   ❁   ❁

Dave's pen dropped to the floor.

I hustled to pick it up. His eyes met mine when I handed it to him. Finally, a connection to Frank!

Dave did not look happy. "Surely you can do better than that."

Trixie jumped up to sit beside Nate. He stroked her back as though he was used to dogs. Nate swallowed hard. "What don't you believe? You can contact the commissariat. They can confirm what I've said."

"If Frank was a private investigator, how come that didn't come up when I searched his name?"

Nate nodded. "You won't find him on the web. He keeps a very low profile. The only way to contact him is through someone who has used him before. He has what you might call a high-profile clientele."

"Really. Like who?"

"I don't know the half of them. Rock stars. Fancy lawyers. Models. That's how I found him. I dated a model who was being stalked."

"Phoebe?" I asked.

Nate chuckled. "Definitely not Phoebe. She's pretty, but being a model is hard work. Phoebe would rather take shortcuts."

"What does that mean?" asked Dave.

"She would rather steal from me than have to actually get up out of bed and go to work."

"You think theft is easier?" Dave frowned at him.

"Probably not. I've never done it, so I wouldn't know, but if you do it right and get something valuable enough, you only have to do it once or twice."

"Sounds like you do have experience in that regard."

"Only because I've been on the wrong end of the equation. Phoebe helped herself to plenty when we went out. And that wasn't enough. She had to come back for more."

"Were you ever married to Phoebe?" asked Dave.

"Married?" Nate snorted. "We never married. That was a near miss as far as I'm concerned. Made me shy away from any thoughts of marriage."

"Why is that?"

"She's nuts. Look, I'm a pretty low-key guy. I'll put up with a lot before it grates on me, but Phoebe is out of her mind."

"What exactly did she take from you?" I asked.

"A flash drive."

"Is that like a thumb drive?" I asked.

Nate smiled. "A little better. Here, I have a photo of it." He flicked on his phone and pulled up a photograph to show us. Guessing from the pen next to it, the little white gadget couldn't have been an inch wide, and it was about three inches long. The top of it curved in the shape of a paw and had little pink pads on it.

"That looks like a paw!" I craned my neck to see better.

"Yup! It's a disguise. There's actually a very high-tech secure drive inside, not the generic one that comes in this paw-style flash drive. I thought if it looked like a toy, people would be less inclined to take it. If it were sleek and black with buttons and numbers on it, people would think it might be something important worth locking up."

"Must have been a very valuable flash drive to follow her all the way here." Dave frowned at him.

"It is."

"What's on it?" asked Dave. "Incriminating photographs?"

"The digital wallet to a small fortune in cryptocurrency."

I gasped. "How does that work?"

Nate tilted his head. "If she can figure out my passwords, she can move the money and very likely get away with it."

"You said 'figure out' the passwords?" Dave looked as stunned as I felt.

"Yeah. It's encrypted. I wouldn't just put in passwords. Then anyone who stole it could figure them out and immediately access the money. It's a little bit complicated, but if Phoebe and Josh manage to get into it, then I'll lose all that money. And possibly worse, if they try passwords too many times, it will all vanish. So time is of the essence."

"Why were you traveling with a flash drive that was so valuable?" asked Dave.

"Well, for starters, there's the risk of it being stolen from my home or from a vault. In addition, I was invited to Paris as a speaker at a conference. Tom Guzman was going, too. He's got a small start-up that's heading south fast, but I know how to turn it around. I've offered to buy it from him, but no luck so far. I thought I might need to put down some earnest money or something if we could come to terms. My mistake was forgetting it in my hotel room when I changed clothes for dinner."

"Did Frank know all this?"

"Of course. He had to know what he was up against. Josh and *Dana*—" he accented her name like it was annoying to him "—spent the last three months flying back and forth all over Europe. They typically landed Roo at small airports but never stayed anywhere longer than a night."

"So let me get this straight." Dave looked at his notes. "You were never married to Phoebe, who is using the name Dana."

"Correct."

"Were you physically abusive toward her?"

"Good grief! No! What would make you think that? I grew up as the sole boy in a household with four sisters. I have great respect for women." Nate smiled. "If anything, I was on the receiving end as a kid. Seriously, look at me. I'm a nerd. I like sports okay but never was any good at them. I avoid working out, too. I'm a pretty ordinary guy, and I've never hit a woman in my life."

Either Dana was lying or Nate was. And right now, I was leaning toward believing Nate.

Dave's expression had changed entirely. He sounded much less stern when he said, "I'm sorry to put you through this and I appreciate your candor. I'll be following up, of course."

"So what happened to Frank?"

"He was found in a tent. The medical examiner reports that he died of strangulation." Dave watched Nate's reaction.

"I can't believe this. Why would anyone do that? It had to be connected with another case. He was helping *me*. I wouldn't want him to be dead. Surely you must see that. But I know some of his clients were dealing with people who were a lot more dangerous than Phoebe."

Dave didn't respond, letting him stew and keep talking.

"Do you think he found Dana? I would think he could overpower her."

I agreed with him on that. But my heart sank. Because it was one more thing that pointed toward Josh's guilt.

Dave finally terminated his questioning. "If you think of anything else that could be helpful, please give me a call."

The three of us walked back to the Dogwood Room.

"Are you all right?" I asked Nate.

"I'm a little shaken. I never expected this. I liked Frank. He was a good guy."

"Didn't you wonder why Frank wasn't returning your calls?" asked Dave.

"Sure, I did. But I assumed he was busy. That was when I brought the flowers for your grandmother. I figured Phoebe would be staying here and I knew Frank had booked a room here. It stood to reason that they would hide out at her boyfriend's grandmother's inn. But I never saw either one of them."

"You haven't seen Dana?" asked Dave.

"No. For all I know she's long gone. Unless she's still in Wagtail?"

I probably should have let Dave answer that, but I wasn't getting bad vibes from Nate. "No one knows where they are."

When we reached the Dogwood Room and I saw Lucy-the-dog on my dad's lap, I knew she was a member of the family. She leaned against him and watched everyone else with alert eyes. I gazed at Nate. "I think you're going to have to find another dog."

He smiled. "All that matters is that Lucy-the-dog found a good home. Um, I'm going to take off now. If it's okay, I'd like to text you my number."

"That would be fine." I told him where to send it. I had mixed feelings about that. What if my assessment of Nate was dead wrong?

"If you hear anything from Dana, I'd appreciate knowing where she is. I need to get that flash drive back. And Holly, I apologize for lying to you. I'm sure you understand why. On the chance that Dana and Josh were staying here, I didn't want word getting back to her that I had turned up. She would have left town immediately and I would have been back to square one. You seem like a decent person, and Lucy is really sweet. Lucy-the-dog got very lucky tonight. At least something turned out well."

He said good night to everyone and stroked Lucy-the-dog's head one more time before he left.

Dave sat down and relayed what we had learned about Dana.

"She tricked Josh?" Aunt Margaret's face was turning an ugly shade of red. "I knew she was trouble."

"Why would she pretend to be married?" asked Dad. "That doesn't make any sense."

Lucy looked at him. "It makes perfect sense. She had to concoct a story that would make Josh want to help her. *I stole something very valuable and now they're after me* doesn't exactly inspire a desire to help her."

"She's a thief!" declared Margaret. "A no-good, lower-than-a-worm thief! Dave, can I revoke my bond and get my money back?"

"You can. You have to call the bail bondsman and tell him what you would like to do."

"First thing in the morning!" she declared.

"But Dana will be taken into custody again," Dave pointed out.

Aunt Margaret scowled. "I wonder how Josh will take this news. Will he believe us?"

"I don't know how much money is involved," said Dad, "but you can't be responsible for a liar and a thief. You don't know if she'll turn up for her court date. Look how they're behaving now. I understand why you would pay Josh's bond. He's your son and we do everything we can for our kids. But he was sucked in by a . . . what do they call them—a siren!"

"I pray that she didn't talk him into anything illegal." Aunt Margaret tried to hold back tears.

"You mean like murdering Frank?" asked Ben. "He wouldn't be the first man to spend life in prison for believing a woman's lies."

I shot him a dirty look. Had he no consideration for Margaret's feelings?

I called the dogs and walked outside with them. Even Lucy trotted along with Trixie and Gingersnap. It was a clear night, with loads of stars in the sky. I hoped Josh was okay. I was angry with Dana for sucking Josh in with her tale of woe, which appeared to be nothing but a big fat horrible lie. But someone not too far away under the beautiful starry sky had injured Dave and might just be the same person who killed Frank Burton.

I woke early the next morning, and Trixie and Twinkletoes were not on my bed! I threw on a Sugar Maple Inn robe and dashed into my living room.

Dave sat on my sofa drinking coffee and eating croissants.

Mr. Huckle was in the process of handing dog cookies to Trixie and Duchess. Twinkletoes waited patiently for her cat treat.

"It's nice to have you back, Mr. Huckle."

"I should have been here all along taking care of Officer Dave. Why didn't you phone to tell me there was an emergency?"

"Mr. Huckle, you do so much for us. You deserve time off."

"But it is my pleasure. Dave tells me he spent one night here but is now sleeping at home."

"That's all I can do there," Dave griped. "My mother insists on staying at my house. She hovers over me like a vacuum cleaner, sucking the air out of the room."

Mr. Huckle and I exchanged amused glances. He poured a cup of tea for me and I curled up on the sofa with Twinkletoes.

"Did you see the doctor?" I asked.

"I got lucky with the break. No surgery required. I have to use the crutches, then I'll graduate to a walking boot. I have great news, though. Everything taped on the camera in Frank's room went directly to the laptop in his duffle bag. So he's the one who set it up. He must have suspected or feared that he was being followed."

"That's a relief. At least no one is after us. Did you ever find out what's going on with Sergeant Hayward?" I sipped the warm tea.

"He's trying to horn in while I'm injured."

"Trying?" I asked.

"Technically, I'm on desk duty and they sent Hayward over to fill in for me on the street. I was told on the sly that he thinks he can have my job if he brings in Frank's killer."

"Surely he is mistaken," said Mr. Huckle. "That could not possibly happen. Could it?"

"I'd say it's unlikely but not impossible. There's always some higher-up who wants to shake things up. That would be a nightmare for me."

"But you must have seniority," said Mr. Huckle.

"Not over Hayward. A lot of people don't want the Wagtail beat, but he does. I plan to solve the Burton murder, but I'll need help since I can't get around."

"Count me in! Officer Dave has been bringing me up to date on the dreadful murder of Mr. Burton. Such a shame." Mr. Huckle waved his binoculars. "I stole a peek across the lake. Our friend Radar isn't there this morning."

"Poor Radar. I know he loves Josh, but heaven only knows where they're hiding out."

"Pity that he doesn't have a GPS collar."

I jumped to my feet, alarming Twinkletoes. "But he does! Assuming they didn't take it off him." I kissed Mr. Huckle's cheek. "You're brilliant! I can't believe we didn't think of that." I fetched my phone and used the app to search for Radar's location. "It looks like he's up on the mountain. There's a cabin. Looks like he's in it!"

Dave held his hand out for my phone. "I know that place. It belongs to Jerry Armistead. Go get dressed."

I pulled on jeans and a deep green top with long sleeves that wouldn't make me stand out if I needed to sneak up through trees. I tied my sneakers and grabbed a jacket of a similar hue in case I needed to hide Trixie's white fur again.

When I emerged, Mr. Huckle was gone. I fed Twinkletoes a salmon and chicken combo for breakfast. "I'm sorry, Twinkletoes, but I think you should stay home today. I'm not sure what will happen." As I spoke, I wondered if it would be safe for Trixie. And then I wondered why I was worried about it being safe. For heaven's sake, I was going to find my cousin and his dog. That was all.

"I phoned Jerry while you were changing clothes," said Dave. "The cabin isn't rented out. He'd appreciate it if we checked on it. The key is in a frog."

"A frog?" I laughed. "This I have to see."

Dave took the elevator, but I walked down the stairs with Trixie. I could smell the bacon cooking, and the aroma of coffee wafted through the air. The only early bird was Judy, who sipped from a mug and studied something on her phone.

Trixie and I met up with Dave in the registration lobby. Through the glass doors, I saw someone in a helmet arrive in a four-wheeler.

"That's our ride," said Dave, cocking his head toward the doors.

The driver disembarked and when we stepped outside, he handed us helmets. I peered closer to see who it was.

"Holmes!"

Dave fastened his helmet. "I'm useless with this bum leg. And Holmes's chariot can move a lot faster than a golf cart."

"I didn't know you had this," I said.

"Comes in handy when I'm building or checking out acreage where there's no road."

"I see. So it's not a toy," I teased.

Dave and Holmes snickered.

He put it in gear and I was shocked by how quiet it was.

"Electric," explained Holmes.

It didn't take us long to get to the cabin. I had the GPS app open on my phone and could see the blue dot. When I enlarged the location, the dot appeared inside the cabin.

At Dave's request, Holmes stopped the four-wheeler a short distance from the house.

"Good location for a hideout," I said. "There's no one around here to notice anyone coming or going."

Trixie leaped from the vehicle and raced ahead of us.

It was a beautiful spot. Light green leaves were coming in on tall trees. The woods were tranquil and peaceful. The only sounds came from birds celebrating the arrival of spring. The three of us walked along quietly as though we didn't want to disturb the natural grace of the wild. Even Dave lurched along the dirt driveway without a sound.

But then we heard it. The sound tore at my heart each time. Trixie howled her long mournful song that meant someone was dead.

Twenty-One

❀ ❀ ❀ ❀

Dave stopped. In a whisper, he said, "I'm going to call for backup."

Holmes raised his eyebrows. "Are you sure about that? We don't know what we're dealing with yet. What if Snowball police come out here and it's a dead deer?"

"Trixie has never howled like that unless it was a person," I said in her defense.

"There's always a first time. I'll sneak up there and peek in the windows."

"I can't put you at risk," Dave protested.

But it was too late. Holmes was already jogging toward the house. We watched as he ducked and scurried to a window.

Trixie howled again, giving away our presence to anyone who knew her. But no one opened a door or a window.

Holmes ran back to us. "I don't see anyone in there. Someone could be hiding in a bedroom or a closet, but there's no indication of anyone staying there. No mugs or pizza boxes or anything like that."

"What about Radar?"

"I didn't see him, either."

Dave sighed. "We're too late. Okay, let's go have a look." We approached the house cautiously.

"Anybody see a frog?" Dave gazed around on the ground.

Holmes laughed at him. "Do you have a fear of frogs that I'm not aware of?"

"We're looking for the key. There it is!" A large lantern hung from a hook a few feet away from the door. Inside the lantern were a faux candle, an artificial lily pad, and a fat ceramic frog. I was opening the lantern door when I heard Holmes say, "Uh-oh. It's open."

Holmes and I exchanged a glance.

"Maybe they left in a hurry?" I asked.

"Don't touch anything." Trixie flew by Dave as he entered the house.

I was worried because there was no sign of Radar. I tried to remember if Trixie had ever howled about a deceased dog before. I didn't think so.

The cabin was a cozy little place, with high ceilings and a rustic woodsy décor. A large stone fireplace dominated the main living space. I could imagine a blazing fire with snow falling outside. It looked perfect. I didn't know how it appeared before, but Holmes was right—nothing seemed to be out of place.

I followed Trixie, who was agitated. She ran into the bedroom and howled again. Holmes was right behind me when I stepped into the bedroom. A woman lay on the bed with a comforter drawn up under the chin. Her eyes were wide with horror. A wave of sadness swept over me as I recognized the bleached hair and tanned face. Carole had met a tragic and horrific end.

"Isn't that Carole?" asked Dave.

I nodded. "Did you know her?"

"Not really. She was sweet. Always stopped to ask about my leg when she saw me at the inn."

"Isn't she your dad's girlfriend?" Holmes asked.

"She had a thing for him. But Dad wasn't interested in her. She was bored. Apparently, she thought if she surprised Dad, they would hang out together and get closer. I feel just awful. Why would this have happened to her?"

Dave struggled over to her and gently pulled back the covers. Even I could see the red welts around her neck.

"Looks like another strangulation," said Dave.

"Same MO," said Holmes.

"You watch too much true crime on TV." Dave pulled out his phone and called the police station.

Holmes was right, though. It could have been the same killer. Or it could have been someone who copied the modus operandi of Frank's killer. In any event, it wasn't a coincidence that both of them had been strangled and their bodies had been covered, leaving only their faces exposed.

Trixie stood by my legs. I picked her up. "You were a very good girl. Thank you for telling us we needed to come in here."

Still holding Trixie, I gazed around the room for any indication of a struggle, but everything seemed to be in order. I walked into the bathroom. Towels had been used and left in a pile. A box was in the trash can. I set Trixie down and squatted for a closer look. It was blond hair coloring. Carole had blond hair that I suspected was bleached. But that didn't make any sense. Why would she come to this cabin to color her hair when she could have done that at the inn? Or it could have been Dana who dyed her hair.

I hurried out of the bathroom and took another look at Carole. Her hair was dry, and no dark roots were showing, so it could have been Carole who colored her hair.

Dave turned toward me. "Wait a minute. Where's the GPS tracker that brought us out here?"

Good question. I set Trixie down, turned on the tracker app, and enlarged the image several times. "The app shows it in the cabin. It says, 'You are ten feet from the dog.'"

Holmes snorted. "Trixie is the only dog I see. Are you certain you're not searching for her collar?"

I double-checked to be sure I was looking at the screen for the correct collar. "Nope. I have it right."

Trixie pawed at the back of a sofa repeatedly and finally pulled out the mostly hidden collar. She sat beside it, wagging her tail as though she knew that was the reason we had come.

"Don't touch it!" Dave yelled.

"No problem." Holmes raised his empty hand in the air.

"So Josh and Dana were here," I mused. How could this happen to them again? I groaned, imagining how devastating it would be for Oma and Aunt Margaret. For the first time I wondered if Josh and Dana could be some kind of Bonnie and Clyde, roaming the earth in Josh's plane and leaving devastation behind them. That was absurd, I reasoned. But there was no shaking the truth. Death appeared to follow in their wake.

"The question, I think," said Holmes, "is did someone hide that there intentionally to lure us here? Or was it left behind and forgotten?"

"The presence of the collar doesn't mean they were here," said Dave. "Someone could have found it and brought it here. Or Radar may have been here by himself and someone removed it from his neck."

Holmes patted Dave on the back. "Thanks, Dave. You're a good friend. And you're completely correct. But I think we all know how bad this looks. We can only hope the cops don't find Josh's and Dana's fingerprints in here. If they do . . ."

He looked at me. He didn't need to finish his sentence. We all knew exactly what that would mean. How could they ever overcome something like that at a trial?

"We're back to square one," I said softly. "Where are they?"

The door swung open and Sergeant Hayward strode into the cabin. "Well, well." He gazed straight at me. "You again." His voice was gruff and angry when he saw Dave. "What are you doing here?"

Dave didn't flinch. "We were looking for a dog."

"You can do better than that." He nodded toward Trixie. "That the dog you were looking for?"

I snatched her into my arms.

"You know I'm going to have to report your breaking and entering, right?"

"We entered with the permission of the owner."

I was impressed by Dave's ability to speak in a calm and steady voice.

Hayward's face flushed with anger. "So why'd I get called out here, then?"

"This way." Dave led him to the bedroom.

I could hear Dave's voice murmuring. When they returned, Hayward's face had developed red and white blotches.

"Are you okay?" I asked.

He nodded. "I'd like you to step outside with me. Him first." He pointed at Holmes.

When it was my turn, I handed Trixie to Holmes and followed Hayward outside, where I told him exactly what had happened when we arrived at the house.

"Your fingerprints will tell me if you're lying."

I forced a smile. "I admit to entering the house, but poor Carole was already there."

"You see, what troubles me is that you found the dead

guy a few days ago. Don't you think that's an awfully big coincidence?"

"I wouldn't call it a coincidence. I'd think the two murders were connected in some way."

His face hardened. "I forgot. You're the one who thinks she's a forensics expert."

"I *never* said that."

Several police cars pulled up the driveway. Reinforcements from Snowball, I assumed.

"Listen to me, missy. Your buddy Dave can't protect you anymore. I've got you and your cousin dead to rights on these two murders. I haven't quite figured it all out yet. But I know it's not a coincidence that you turn up when there's a murder."

I was about to explain about Trixie's unique ability to sniff out murder, but he turned and walked toward the people disembarking from cars. I entered the house and retrieved Trixie.

Hayward was so distracted that when Holmes asked if he could leave, Hayward looked at me. "Yeah, you can go. But you might want to get yourself another girlfriend. There's one hour a week visitation where she's going."

Dave said he would catch a ride back with one of the other cops. With the exception of Hayward, they acted friendly toward him. Holmes, Trixie, and I left in the four-wheeler.

"What did Hayward say to you?" I asked.

"Just the regular stuff. Why were we there? When did we get there? Did we see anyone else?" He glanced at me. "He doesn't like you."

"I've noticed that. I'm not *very* worried. I don't see how he can pin anything on me. But I sure would hate it if Dave were reassigned and we were stuck with a grouch like Hayward. Hayward seems to think he has seniority."

Holmes reached over and squeezed my hand. "Dave has got more clout than he admits to."

I certainly hoped so!

When we reached the inn, I asked Holmes to join me for breakfast.

"You bet! I'm starved. And I have to admit it's nice to have a luxurious inn breakfast once in a while. My go-to breakfast is usually oatmeal in the winter and cereal in the summer."

"I bet that's true for most people. I'm terribly spoiled by the breakfasts here. As part owner of the inn, I hereby use my extensive powers to give you an open invitation."

Holmes laughed. "I thank you, kind mistress. Luckily for you, I'm at work very early most days. Especially as we go into the summer months. Have to get work done before it's too hot."

It was a much-needed moment of silliness. But it didn't last long. Trixie leaped from the vehicle, but I lingered for another moment. My voice quivered slightly. "Holmes, do you think Josh killed Frank and Carole?"

Holmes looked straight ahead. "Not the Josh we knew. But this looks bad for him. For Dana, too. Dave is absolutely correct that the GPS collar doesn't mean they were in that cabin. Anyone could have found it and left it there. But I think all three of us know they were there."

He stepped out of the four-wheeler and I followed suit. He reached out to me and hugged me to him. I nestled my head against his chest and he rested his chin on the top of my head. We were devastated and completely broken by the unexpected turn of events.

"Hey! You two are too old to smooch out here."

It was my mom, teasing us.

Holmes kept one arm on my shoulders and placed his other arm on Mom's shoulders. "We have bad news."

"Remember Carole?" I asked.

"The Carole?" asked Mom.

"She was murdered. We found her in a cabin this morning. And there's reason to think that Josh and Dana had been there."

Mom gasped. "That can't be. Carole? You mean the woman who surprised Sam here?"

I nodded.

"That poor child! She was about your age. What happened?"

We filled Mom in on what little we knew.

Mom gripped her forehead. "I think I had better be the one to tell Margaret. She's already beside herself. I don't know if she can take this news."

"You realize that Dad will probably be a suspect, too."

Mom's eyes widened. "This is a nightmare. Well, whether Josh and Dana are innocent or not, if they hadn't already left Wagtail, I suppose they're gone now."

She was right about that. Josh was probably growing that beard again to disguise his face. "They haven't come back for their things, have they?"

Mom shrugged. "What are you getting at?"

"If they're on the run, won't they want their sleeping bag and whatever else they had with them?"

"You can buy a sleeping bag anywhere," said Holmes.

"Right after breakfast, I'm going to change the lock on their door. If they want their things, they'll have to come find me or Oma. No sneaking back into the inn in the middle of the night."

"But honey," said Mom, "that could be dangerous."

"Do you really think Josh would harm me?"

Mom's mouth tightened in an unhappy line. "To tell you the truth, I don't know what to think anymore. In my wildest dreams I never imagined Josh in this situation."

I called Trixie and we entered the inn through the registration lobby.

"Remember," whispered Mom, "don't say anything about this until I have a chance to break it to Margaret."

We assured her we wouldn't say a word. We found Twinkletoes happily finishing a bowl of food.

She meowed at me and rubbed against my ankles. I picked her up. "I thought you were eating breakfast when I left. Did you tell Shelley that you hadn't eaten?"

Twinkletoes purred contentedly and gently placed one paw on the side of my face.

It was already midmorning. Most of the diners had cleared out. Holmes, Mom, and I settled at a table.

Shelley arrived immediately with tea and coffee. "Rumor has it that there was some kind of police commotion up the mountain this morning. Would that have anything to do with your tardy appearance for breakfast?"

Rumor sure got around fast in Wagtail. We didn't say a word.

"I see," she said. "The specials this morning are praline French toast and poached eggs Florentine."

"Is there a doggy version of the poached eggs?" I asked.

"Sure is. A little bit of finely chopped cooked spinach on rice, topped with a poached egg."

Mom and I opted for the poached eggs Florentine, which I also ordered for Trixie, but Holmes ordered hash browns, two fried eggs, and country sausage.

When Shelley left to place our orders, we spoke in hushed tones about how to best handle the situation.

"If Shelley has already heard about it, then it won't be long before everyone knows," said Holmes.

Mom reached for a blueberry muffin from the bread basket. "I'll hunt down Margaret as soon as we're done eating."

Mr. Huckle hurried toward us. "May I join you? I like a second cuppa at this time of day."

"Of course," Mom and I chimed.

The last of the guests paid their check and left.

Shelley carried a giant tray from the kitchen and placed beautifully plated breakfasts before us. Trixie danced on her hind legs until Shelley placed her bowl on the floor.

"Do you mind if I join you?" asked Shelley. "I usually eat during the lull before lunch."

"Please do," I said.

In a matter of minutes, Shelley sat down with a plate of praline French toast that made me rethink my healthier egg choice.

"I don't see Radar. Did you locate him?" Mr. Huckle chose a bagel from the bread basket.

"They're going to hear about it sooner or later," I said to Mom and Holmes.

Holmes and I told them what had happened.

"Carole?" Mr. Huckle frowned. "The woman who hoped to marry your father?"

Mom choked and quickly drank coffee.

"Marry him?" That surprised me.

"Oh, yes. Didn't she tell you? She dated a string of rather coarse men. I'm not quite clear whether they were simply juvenile or ignorant. In any event, she met your father when he was buying a gift for Lucy. She worked in a nice high-end store and assisted him with his purchase. He impressed her with his manners and friendly nature. So she asked him out. Quite daring on her part, I think."

Listening to him, I felt guilty for not spending more time with Carole. My dad was the wrong choice for her, of course, but I suspected I would have liked her under other circumstances.

"Call me old-fashioned," said Mom, "but I don't think I would have the guts to ask a man to dinner or a show."

"It wasn't dinner," said Mr. Huckle. "Sam bought her

an ice cream cone and told her about the inn and his mother
having a big birthday. And that was all it took for her to
be convinced he was the one."

"Sounds like what she really wanted was a father figure." Holmes glanced at his watch.

"In a hurry?" asked Shelley.

"I should probably get to work sometime today."

At that moment, the sound of boots in the lobby drew
my attention.

Twenty-Two

❖ ❖ ❖ ❖

Trixie barked and raced into the lobby.

I jumped up from my seat and hurried after her. No less than eight cops stood before me, one of whom was Sergeant Hayward.

He boomed, "Anderson and Haynes, take the second floor. Fuentes and Kowalski, you take the third floor."

"Hold it! Stop! Everyone, stop!" I yelled. "What is going on here?"

"We're searching the premises for two fugitives. One Joshua Miller and one Dana Carrington."

The cops resumed their trek up the stairs. A handful of guests had ventured from their rooms and were looking down the stairwell to see what was happening, including Aunt Margaret.

"Stop!" I shouted as loud as I could, and I had a voice that carried well. In a more civilized tone, I asked sweetly, "Do you have a warrant to search this property?"

The boots clattered down the stairs at a relaxed pace

and I knew the answer. The sergeant meant to intimidate me so I would do what he wanted.

Aunt Margaret made her way down the stairs between them.

"In that case, you have disturbed our guests enough and I would ask you to kindly leave the inn."

"Don't think I won't book you for harboring a fugitive."

"I don't think you will because they're not here. Besides, they aren't fugitives. They are out on bond."

"Maybe you ought to talk with your aunt. One of those bonds has been revoked and don't think we won't book them for a second murder. You won't have enough money to bond them out now that they have committed a second crime."

My heart pounded in my chest. I hoped my state of agitation wasn't obvious to him. I took a deep breath and marched over to the door. My hand was shaking, so I gripped the handle harder and opened the door as a sign they should leave.

When they were out on the front porch, I was tempted to slam the door behind them, but the lobby had filled with guests and family, so I collected myself and tried to appear unconcerned when I was actually shaken. I closed the door, turned the lock, and stood with my back to the door.

My entire body quivered with adrenaline and panic. Holmes rushed over and hugged me to him. A smattering of applause broke out. But I also heard people asking if fugitives were staying at the inn. Oh boy. They would be checking out like lemmings.

Aunt Margaret tented her hands over her nose and mouth. "What have I done? This is all my fault. I didn't realize that revoking Dana's bond would lead to anything like this."

I looked at Mom. "Maybe you two can talk in the library?"

Mom nodded and beckoned to Aunt Margaret.

Oma frowned. "What happened?"

I nodded at her. Raising my voice, bolstered by one of Holmes's arms still around me, I said, "I apologize for the disruption of your day. There are no fugitives here. Everything is fine." I looked up at Holmes. "Go ahead to work. I don't think they'll be back and even if they get a warrant, it will take hours."

"Are you sure you're okay?"

I kissed him. "I'm fine. Nothing a cup of hot tea won't cure."

"Call me if you need me. I'll be at the Davis house. I can be here in minutes. Okay?"

I smiled at him, hoping I looked braver than I felt. "I'll hold you to that."

"Let me know if there are any developments."

"I promise."

He loped down the hallway. Part of me wished he w stay, but that was silly. If Sergeant Hayward returne a warrant, there wouldn't be a thing Holmes or any could do about it.

Oma patted my back. "I never dreamed any this would happen. What has Joshua gotten hi

As we walked to the inn office, I told her Oma was horrified. "Joshua would not do su barely knew her, if at all. It makes no sen

"I totally agree. But why was Radar's why are they hiding?"

Oma sighed. "Maybe they are gone away." She sounded hopeful and sad

I doubted that they had left the sure, I'm going to search the attic ment of the inn."

Oma nodded. "If they were seen them. I know Casey falls

have heard them if they went to the magic refrigerator for food. Holly, we have another problem as well. Some of the Cat Fest people are arriving early. Tomorrow and Thursday. We will need to shuffle some rooms. Margaret will go to stay with your mother."

"Lucy can bunk with me." I met her gaze. "And the Ben if need be."

"Yes. I think this is the wisest course."

Keys in hand, I ventured into the basement first. Trixie and Twinkletoes dashed down the stairs. They didn't get to snoop around the basement often. Like many very old basements, it was a little bit creepy. We kept stanchions there, along with additional chairs, folding chairs for outdoor events, signs, and decorations. Unlike the attic storage room, it was actually pretty well organized. It also housed furnaces and a mechanical room for hot water boilers. I passed a line of lanterns that we used when the power went out. Most were battery operated, but Oma liked to keep candles on hand as a backup.

But there was no sign of anyone living there. I looked for crumbs or blankets. Nothing was amiss.

I took a luggage rack up to Josh and Dana's room. I slid the key into the lock, but it wasn't locked. I tried the handle and the door swung open easily. I tried to remember when I had last unlocked the door. Was it when I brought h upstairs to the room? I stepped inside warily. "Josh?" lled. "Dana?"

quick check of the closet and bathroom confirmed o one was there. Maybe they had forgotten to lock om. Or maybe they had come back? Aunt Margaret e had slept there in case they returned. I relaxed. st be the one who forgot to lock up.

ded their belongings on the luggage rack. They ve much. The pricey dress that Dana had worn to rthday party. A couple of suitcases, with contents

in disarray. I didn't poke around in them, but they were a mess. Conventional toiletries like toothbrushes. They must miss those things. Or had they restocked in town? I would hate going without a toothbrush for more than a day. I didn't see any phones or laptops. But that prompted me to text Josh.

Josh, the police were here. We know about Carole. Please come to the inn. Ben can go with you to the police to straighten this out. We're all worried about you. Don't make your mom and Oma go through this agony.

I didn't expect a response. But if he read it, maybe it would put a seed in his head and he would realize that he had to come back. If not for them, then for everyone else, especially Aunt Margaret.

I rolled the luggage rack to the first-floor storage room where I had stashed the goodies for the cat baskets.

After taking care to lock up the storage room, I asked Marina to clean Josh and Dana's room and Zelda assigned it to a Cat Fest guest.

I ventured up to the third floor with Trixie and Twinkletoes. Across the hall from my apartment was an enormous attic storage room. If I were hiding, that's where I would go. Big dormer windows filled the room with sunlight. And it was where we stored bed frames, mattresses, lamps, and miscellaneous furniture, among other things, making it far more comfortable than the basement.

I placed my ear against the door and listened. I didn't hear anything. Taking a big breath, I unlocked the door. The loud click made me shiver. It would have warned them if they were inside. I swung the door open and listened again. There wasn't anything inherently spooky about the huge expanse. I'd been in it many times. And yet there was a fear in the back of my mind that I might actually find them there. I made my way past the old bedposts and dressers, chairs that reflected interior fashions through the decades, and boxes upon boxes stacked with old receipt books, extra salt and pepper shakers, holiday decorations, and other paraphernalia that an inn needed.

Making my way to the back, I breathed easier. I hadn't lied when I said that Josh and Dana weren't in the inn. There was no sign of them.

That done, I took the keys back to the inn office, where my dad sat on the sofa between Mom and Aunt Margaret. I had never seen Dad cry before. At the sight of me, he jumped to his feet. "Holly! At least you're okay." He wrapped his arms around me.

"Dad?" I glanced around. Oma blew her nose. Margaret wiped her eyes. "Did they find Josh?"

Oma shook her head.

Dad released me but held on to my hands. "It's my fault that Carole came here. I was so busy that I ignored her entirely. I even avoided her! And now she's dead."

"Dad," I said softly. "You didn't invite her. She came on her own. She could have gone home any time. You had nothing to do with her demise."

"That's what Nell said."

"Listen to Mom. She's right. It's a horrible tragedy, but it wasn't your fault."

"Sit down, Hollypop."

Dad returned to his spot between Mom and Aunt Margaret. "I don't want anything to happen to you. Honey, I want you to marry Ben. I'm not around here to look after you. You can move back to Washington and live a normal life."

"Dad, I don't think this is the right time for this conversation."

"It's exactly the right time. I don't want what happened to Carole to happen to you."

"In the first place, we don't know what happened to Carole. In the second place, I have Holmes. I ditched Ben a long time ago."

"Holmes," he snorted. "What kind of man gives up a good career in architecture to come back to Wagtail? He's a local boy, honey. I want more for you. Ben has a good job and can take care of you."

I looked over at Oma, who rolled her eyes and shook her head like she thought Dad was nuts.

"Dad, in the first place, that's horrendously old-fashioned. I'm supporting myself. I don't *need* a man to do that. And second, just because you don't want to live in Wagtail doesn't mean it's not the right place for me. I love my life here. It's exactly where I want to be. And if all that isn't enough, I'm in love with Holmes."

Mom smiled at me. "Have you forgotten what that's like, Sam?"

He shot her a look.

Mom was not deterred. "Holmes is as good and honest as they come. He's the first to pitch in to help anyone in town. If you would take the time to get to know him, I think you would like him."

Zelda rapped on the door and cleared her throat. "Sergeant Hayward would like to see Sam."

"Me? What for?"

I winced. "Because Carole came here to see you," I whispered.

Sergeant Hayward appeared in the doorway. "We can do this here or at the police station in Snowball."

Dad rose and faced Hayward. "Here will be fine."

Sergeant Hayward gazed around. "Where did Dave interview suspects?"

Mom gasped and held a hand at her throat.

Oma responded in a calm voice. "Usually here in the inn office. However, given the circumstances, I'm afraid

I cannot allow that. You will have to find an alternative site. Perhaps the inn library would suit you?"

Good move, Oma! The library didn't have a door that could be closed. We could listen from the lobby.

A red blush of anger crept up Hayward's throat to his jaw. "Maybe Dave never told you this, but a little cooperation with the police can pay off."

Oma didn't back down. "I will not be bribed, Sergeant Hayward."

Great. Now he hated all of us. Oma was right, of course, but it wasn't going to make things any easier.

Hayward beckoned to my father. "Show me to the library."

Dad left the office.

"I hate to say this after the previous conversation, but I think we'd better get Ben down here." Mom gazed at me. "Can you call him, Holly?"

Oma looked at the watch. "Four minutes more."

Aunt Margaret frowned. "What happens then?"

"We follow them to listen."

Twenty-Three

❧ ❀ ❧ ❀ ❧

"Mom!" squealed Margaret.

"Really, Margaret, did you think we would let Sam go with him alone?" asked Oma.

"We won't be able to help Sam," said Aunt Margaret.

"Margaret! Of course we can when we know what that odious policeman wants with him." Oma checked the time again.

I texted Ben to let him know what was going on and asked him to come to the lobby. Where was he anyway?

The four of us left Zelda manning the registration desk and walked through the hallway to the main lobby. Oma walked straight to the desk in the main lobby, which was usually where Mr. Huckle stationed himself in between jobs. He confirmed having seen Dad with Sergeant Hayward.

The inn library was a small three-sided room that connected the main building to the newer cat wing. The missing fourth wall was open to what became the hallway through the cat wing. It had a lovely fireplace and a big cushy window seat for curling up with a book. Oma and I were big mystery fans, so that genre was well represented. There was also a small take-one leave-one shelf for visitors.

We drifted closer to the open side of the library, straining to hear the conversation yet remain out of view.

"How did you know Carole Hobson?" asked Hayward.

We knew all that. Dad explained how he met her when shopping for Lucy.

"And then you dated her."

"Not really. I never asked her out or anything. I bought her an ice cream cone because she'd been so nice when she helped me. I don't know what's popular with young women. I'd hardly call that a date."

"You must have seen her again."

"I may have passed her on the street and said hi."

"I find it interesting that you now want to claim that you barely knew her when in reality you invited her to come to Wagtail for your mother's celebration."

"I did not invite her. She showed up on her own."

"Come on now. You expect me to believe that a pretty woman much younger than you came here just to be with you. Did you or did you not take her to your mother's celebration?"

"Well, yes. I did. It seemed like the kind thing to do at the time."

"Isn't it true that you invited Carole here to flaunt her in front of your ex-wife?"

"No! That's ridiculous! Your entire line of questioning is absurd. I'm not going to say anything else. I'm done. I had nothing to do with Carole's murder. Nothing!"

"You can't just walk away."

"Yes, I can. Do you think I'm an idiot? I have a right

to cease answering questions and to consult with an attorney. And you can't do a thing about that."

"Where is your nephew, Sam?"

"I wish I knew."

Dad walked around the corner, surprised to see us leaning in to listen.

I hugged him. "Well done!"

Ben finally made an appearance. "This family needs a lot of lawyers. Sorry, Sam, it would be a conflict of interest for me to represent you. I can recommend someone else, though."

"Thanks, Ben," said Dad. "I'd better have one lined up. Though to be honest, I don't even know where Carole was killed."

"You also have an alibi," said Ben. "Oma can testify that you slept in her apartment."

Oma and Dad exchanged a look that made me very uncomfortable.

Oma must have been uneasy too, because she clapped her hands together and said, "I must get back to work."

I spent the next few hours preparing the gift baskets for the Cat Fest people. They were darling. Everything a cat person could want plus a bottle of locally produced wine, cheeses, crackers, and chocolate for the cats' people.

It was a mindless task, though, and I couldn't help feeling guilty for not having paid more attention to Carole. I could have taken her to lunch or invited her to have dinner. But I had been so absorbed in Josh's problems that I didn't make time for Carole. I had sent her off shopping.

"Holly?"

I recognized Ben's voice. "In here."

"What are you doing?"

"Getting ready for the next wave of guests."

"Already?"

"The first ones will be arriving tomorrow and Thursday. The Cat Fest begins on Friday."

"Oh yeah. I've seen notices about it around town." Ben scooted closer to me. "So what's on tap for today?"

"What are you doing here, Ben?" I knew it sounded rude, but seriously, we were over a long time ago!

"Maybe we could take Trixie for a walk this afternoon."

He wasn't fooling me. He didn't much care for dogs or cats. He was dodging my question. "What's going on?"

He reached for my hand. I snatched it back before he made contact.

"I miss you, Holly."

"Oh, Ben. You know that's not true. Did you break up with someone?"

He scowled at me. "See how well you know me?"

"That's not the same thing as missing someone."

"We used to have so much fun together."

"I won't deny that we had some good times. But Ben, that was ages ago."

He leaned against shelving, looking like a lost kid.

"Could it be that you miss Wagtail?" I asked.

He straightened his glasses. "Nah. All these cats and dogs running around?"

"Maybe you like it because it's a small tightly knit community. I loved living inside the Washington Beltway, but there's a certain comfort in knowing most of the local people. Washington runs at a faster speed and there are a lot of transients."

A ding sounded on his phone. He pulled it out of a pocket and looked at the screen. "Bad news. They found Josh's and Dana's fingerprints in the cabin where Carole was murdered."

I staggered backward a little bit. That was about the worst news I could imagine. On the bright side, though, it took pressure off Dad. "They'll be back with a warrant any time now, I guess."

Ben tilted his head. "Is Josh here?"

"No. I searched everywhere I could think of after the police left earlier. If Josh or Dana is here, I don't know about it."

"Holly, is there anyone else who could have murdered Frank or Carole?"

"What are you getting at?"

"What about that guy who went out with Zelda?"

"Nate. If he were going to kill someone, I think it would be Dana."

Ben shook his head. "If we can believe what Nate told you, and Dana has his flash drive, she's safe from him. He wants it back! If she's dead, chances are good that Nate will never know where it is."

Done with the baskets, Ben and I stepped out of the storage room, and I locked it. He followed me to the office, where I picked up all the keys I thought I might need.

The police arrived at six o'clock. Luckily, the very time when most guests were out eating dinner. Trixie barked at Sergeant Hayward when he marched up to me in the lobby and rather rudely thrust a search warrant in my face.

I handed it to Ben and walked up the stairs, with Twinkletoes, Trixie, Hayward, and eight uniformed policemen behind me.

Ben trailed along. When he caught up to me, he said, "It includes the room Josh and Dana occupied, Oma's apartment, and yours, and all other public rooms.

I unlocked the room Josh and Dana had used. "They never slept here. They left after a couple of hours."

"Where are their things?" asked one of the cops.

"In the storage room downstairs."

From there, I led them up to the third floor. "This attic storage room is not on the warrant, but I'm happy to show you anyway." I unlocked the storage room and they burst into it. Of course, Josh and Dana weren't there, either. Next, they roamed through my apartment. We returned to the second floor, where they barged into Oma's apartment.

"Technically, I think that's all, but I'm happy to unlock the basement for you." I led the way, with Twinkletoes and Trixie running ahead. The cops panned out through the huge basement, which had plenty of places to hide. When we returned to the main floor, I unlocked the storage room and two of the cops removed Dana's expensive dress, which I had left on a hanger, and the two rolling suitcases.

"There's not much here," said one of the police officers.

I shrugged. "That's all they brought."

After that, I showed them to the front door.

Hayward looked from me to Ben and back to me, again. "You are a piece of work. You could have them in any of the other rooms, holding their stinky breath, and hoping we won't think of that."

I spoke in the calmest voice I could muster. "Sergeant Hayward, the other rooms are rented out to people. I think we both know that a hotel room is like a home where warrants are concerned. You would need warrants for each of those guests to enter their rooms. But I'll be honest with you and make this easier. None of the Millers have seen them since they left the inn."

When the door closed behind them, I felt an enormous sense of relief. Dad had taken Oma and everyone else in the family out to dinner to spare them the unpleasantness of the search. "Didn't Dad ask you to go to dinner with them?" I asked Ben.

"Quite the opposite. He wanted me to stay here in case you needed legal help."

"Thanks for passing up on dinner. I appreciate your

assistance." I was thankful that he'd been there to back me up, but I also suspected it was one of Dad's efforts to throw us together again. Poor Dad. He was simply going to have to get over his affection for Ben because as far as I was concerned, Ben was just an old friend. And that was not going to change. "How about I buy you dinner tonight if Mr. Huckle will watch the inn?"

"Great! But this time, promise you won't take off before we've eaten?"

"We're not following Zelda tonight. Where would you like to go?"

"How about Hot Hog?"

At the mention of her favorite restaurant, Trixie yelped and ran in dizzying circles.

I laughed, but Ben frowned at her. I texted an invitation to Holmes but didn't hear back from him.

Mr. Huckle arrived in half an hour, pleased that he could be helpful. He settled at the desk. "I hope Mrs. Davis will come through. She's such a delightful woman."

"If you see Josh or Dana, let me know immediately."

The four of us walked over to Hot Hog, with Trixie and Twinkletoes leading the way. They even chose a table before Ben and I arrived. They sat on a bench waiting for us at a table on the outdoor porch. Holmes arrived five minutes later.

He pecked me on the cheek and pulled up a chair.

"Didn't know you were coming, Holmes," said Ben.

Holmes looked surprised. "I appreciate the invitation. It's been a long day."

"You, uh, were with Holly this morning when you found Carole?"

"Holmes drove us in his off-road vehicle. We weren't sure there was a road," I explained.

"There was," said Holmes, "but it was dirt. On snowy or wet days, it might be a challenge."

The server arrived. "Pulled chicken dinners for Trixie and Twinkletoes?"

I probably should have been embarrassed that Trixie and Twinkletoes had favorite meals known by the staff of the restaurant. I nodded and ordered my own favorite, pulled pork. Ben and Holmes opted for ribs.

When the server had brought drinks and water bowls, Ben lowered his voice and told Holmes about the police searching the inn. "C'mon, Holmes, you know every inch of Wagtail, where do you think Josh and Dana are hiding out?"

"If I had any clue, I would have gone there and tried to talk them into turning themselves in."

"It must be hard," I mused. "They have nothing with them. I don't know where they're getting food. How long can they last like that?"

Holmes grimaced. "You'd be surprised by the number of people who live off the land. Some people build houses out of cast-off materials. They use glass bottles, discarded tires, even straw bales."

"Straw bales? Don't they catch fire?" asked Ben.

"I'm told that the bales are so tightly packed that oxygen can't get in for a fire to take hold," Holmes replied.

When our dinners arrived, Ben and Holmes chowed down, but I was still thinking about Josh. "When we were kids, you and Josh hung out together. But weren't there other boys that you played with?"

"Well, sure." Holmes sipped his iced tea. "There were local kids that we knew. I've talked to a few of them, but no one has seen Josh."

"They might not recognize him when he grows that beard again," I mused.

Holmes clutched my hand when we walked back to the inn. The spring evening was mild and held the promise of summer. Honeysuckle already perfumed the air. The five of us walked down to the lake and looked up at the twinkling stars. I couldn't help thinking that Josh and Dana were probably looking at the same sky, maybe not even very far away from us. And yet we couldn't find them.

As we turned to leave, I glanced at the boat and cried out, "There are two of them!"

Twenty-Four

※ ※ ※ ※

Holmes and Ben studied the boats.

"Don't you see? This one isn't an inn skiff. This is the boat that Frank took out the night he was murdered."

"Are you sure?" asked Ben. "They all look alike."

Holmes chuckled. "You're not a boating kind of guy, are you, Ben?"

I walked closer to it. "Someone brought it back and docked it. Why wouldn't they have said something?" I pulled out my phone and texted Dave about the boat.

My phone rang. It was Dave calling. "Don't let anyone touch it. I'm on my way."

"We need to guard the boat until Dave gets here. He doesn't want anyone touching it."

To my surprise, Dad strolled toward us carrying a tray of green drinks. "Good evening, all. I saw you from the window and thought I'd join you. Margaret, Nell, and Oma are having after-dinner drinks, so I brought some for you.

They're called a Japanese Slipper. Don't ask me why because I have no idea."

"That was nice of you." I took a drink and pointed at the boat. "Frank's boat is back."

"No kidding." Dad gazed at it. "The person who docked it knew what he was doing. Boat fenders are out. It's docked properly. Looks like it's in pretty good shape. I don't see any trash inside, no apparent damage."

"That's peculiar, isn't it? Who could have brought back Frank's boat?"

"Josh," said Holmes.

Everyone spoke at once.

"Hey!" shouted Dave. "What's going on?"

"We think Josh might have brought back the boat. That would explain why no one could find him. They've been on the move on the lake."

Dave shooed us all away so we wouldn't contaminate anything.

Before I went to sleep that night, I went out on my terrace to see what was going on. Lights had been set up on the dock and a couple of officers were collecting evidence from the boat. I was glad I could go to bed.

My inn phone rang at a disturbingly early hour the next morning. I knew it couldn't possibly be good news. I fumbled for the phone in the dark. "Hello?"

"Sorry to wake you, Holly. This is Cook. Shelley hasn't turned up for work this morning. I made coffee for some early birds, but I can't cook and serve breakfast when it gets busy."

"I'll be down in a few minutes." I hung up the phone. That wasn't like Shelley. I hoped she was okay. I phoned her from my cell phone while I threw on a long-sleeve white shirt and a navy blue skirt. No one answered. I slipped into soft shoes with rubber soles and good padding, then brushed my hair back into a ponytail and added tiny earrings.

Twinkletoes yawned and turned around like she planned to curl up again.

"Okay, let's go. I have work to do."

Trixie and Twinkletoes grudgingly jumped off the bed. I locked my apartment behind us and led them downstairs through the registration lobby to let Trixie out. It was still dark outside. It was as if she understood that we had an emergency on our hands because she didn't take long and ran back inside.

"No begging while I'm serving. Got that?" I asked.

Trixie wagged her tail, but I had my doubts that she listened.

Judy Davis was already at a table drinking a cup of coffee. Her cats lounged comfortably at her feet. "Good morning, Judy! Has Cook taken your order yet?"

"You're serving today? Where's Shelley?"

"I'm not sure." I left it at that.

"I certainly hope she's okay."

"So do I. Do you know what you'd like, or should I find out what the specials are today?"

"I need something fortifying. They're installing kitchen cabinets today and I plan to be there to make sure the kitchen is the way I want it."

"That's exciting!"

"What do you think? Pancakes or fried eggs with hash browns?" she asked.

"The protein in the eggs might hold you longer."

"I think you're right. Another cup of coffee, please, and two trout breakfasts for Sassy and Patience."

"I'll get right on it."

I marched into the commercial kitchen and told Cook

what Judy had ordered. "I called Shelley, but no one answered. Did she say anything about needing today off?"

"Not a word."

"I'm going to call Dave. Someone needs to check on her."

From the raspy sound of Dave's voice, I gathered that the ringing phone had awakened him. "Sorry to get you up so early, but Shelley didn't show up for work this morning."

Suddenly Dave sounded wide awake. "What? That's not like her at all."

"I know! Would you mind doing a wellness check on her?"

"On my way." He disconnected the call.

I felt a little bit better knowing that he would go to Shelley's house. She could be sick or have fallen. At least she would be in good hands now. But if, heaven forbid, something had happened, she wouldn't be coming in to work. I phoned Amelia Sanchez, who worked on Shelley's days off. She answered my call sounding awake and chipper. I explained that Shelley hadn't arrived for work and asked if she could fill in that day. Amelia said she could use the extra income because she was saving for her son's braces, and she would be glad to come.

That was a huge relief. I would cover until she arrived.

Cook started barking things at me. "Fill the bread baskets. Place salt and pepper on the tables. See if anyone else has arrived. Make a round pouring coffee."

"What are today's specials?"

"Smoked salmon eggs Benedict with avocado hollandaise, lemon ricotta pancakes, and fruit and nut granola made here at the inn."

Just listening to those dishes made me hungry. I emerged from the kitchen and refilled Judy's coffee cup.

Paul Mellor had arrived. "Any muffins this morning?"

"Coming right up." I retrieved a bread basket for him,

but when I stepped into the dining area, I paused for a moment and watched him.

Paul waited outside on the terrace, looking in the door. It seemed to me he was anxious.

I pushed the door open. "It's a beautiful morning to watch the sun rise."

"Hmm?" Paul took the basket from me.

"Would you like some coffee?"

"Oh, yes!"

"Choose a table. I'll bring it out here to you. Do you know what you'd like for breakfast or should I bring you a menu?"

"Out here? You mean I could eat out here?"

"Sure! It's a little chilly because the sun is just coming up, but it's also very peaceful."

"Yes, it is." He gazed around. "I'd like to eat here."

I told him the specials, but he asked for scrambled eggs with toast and a double rasher of bacon.

When I went inside, it seemed the dining room had filled up. Yikes! I made a quick round pouring coffee and tea, then fetched bread baskets so people could enjoy muffins and croissants while I took their orders. To my surprise, Lucy showed up and started making rounds with coffee.

"Thank you so much for pitching in!" I kissed her cheek.

"Dad always says it's a family inn. And it's not like I have anything else to do."

Lucy-the-dog had settled by the fireplace with Trixie and Twinkletoes. I wondered why they were being so patient about being served their breakfasts. It wasn't until Amelia arrived that I realized they were waiting for her or Shelley to show up.

I took off my server apron and told Amelia, "I have never been so glad to see you."

Amelia smiled. "Waiting tables isn't for everyone." She surveyed the situation.

"We have two people eating on the terrace."

"Okay. No problem." She swept into the kitchen and reappeared with a huge tray. "This is for Oma's table, I think?"

I confirmed that.

Lucy and I collapsed at Oma's table, where Dad and Margaret also sat. Amelia served their breakfasts and asked Lucy and me what we wanted.

"I can get it," I said to Amelia.

"No, thanks. You'll only be underfoot." She winked at Lucy.

"In that case, I'll try the salmon eggs Benedict with avocado hollandaise. Trixie will have a turkey omelet for dogs, and of course, Twinkletoes always likes salmon."

Lucy ordered the granola and the turkey omelet for Lucy-the-dog.

"I see that Lucy will be coming to Wagtail more often. Well done, my dear." Oma smiled at her. "But I am quite concerned about Shelley. Do you think she is sick?"

"I have no idea. I asked Dave to check on her, but I haven't heard back from him." I checked my phone. Dave left a text about half an hour ago. I read out loud. "'No sign of anything wrong at Shelley's house but she's not here. On my way to her mom's place.'"

"Shelley always calls when she cannot work," said Oma. "She is extremely reliable. I don't like this at all."

I felt the same way. I could count the number of times Shelley had been sick. She always let us know. Sometimes even the night before.

"Forgive me for interrupting."

I looked up to see Judy Davis.

"There's nothing to forgive. What can we do for you?"

"I'm just wondering if it's safe to leave my cats in my room while I'm at the house this morning. I usually take them to the Cat Sitter, but they aren't open this early."

"They will be very safe in your room," said Oma. "The cat wing was designed with them in mind."

"If you don't want Marina to open the door and clean today, you can hang the sign out, but she's great with cats. I've seen her trick some very spunky felines who thought they had an opportunity to escape."

"Well, that makes me feel much better. Thank you." Judy headed to the cat wing, with Sassy and Patience walking on their leashes with the calm of cats who'd been doing it all their lives.

After breakfast, Oma had plans with Dad, Margaret, and Mom again. She made me promise to let her know the minute we found Shelley. I planned to dash upstairs to change clothes and brush my teeth but stopped by the registration desk first. The lobby was empty save for Casey snoozing on the love seat. Perfect, I thought. I would have a minute to check the day's schedule.

Trixie ran around to the back of the counter and Twinkletoes jumped up on top of it. I followed Trixie and screamed.

Twenty-Five

❖ ❖ ❖ ❖

The crouching man leaped at me and pressed his hand over my mouth. "Hush, Holly. It's just me, Josh."

I turned toward Casey. He mumbled and shifted away, still asleep! Trying to catch my breath, I faced the man beside me. It was Josh all right. His cheeks were flushed, probably from worry that someone would spot him. His clothes smelled rank. His chin sported the beginnings of a beard.

"Where have you been?" I asked as he rubbed Trixie's ears.

"Never mind that. Is Radar with you?" he asked, a hopeful lilt in his tone.

"No. I haven't seen him since he ran out the door with Dana and you."

Josh's head sagged. "They have him, Holly. Can you show me how to find him on the GPS collar app?"

My heart sank. "Who is *they*?"

"I don't know for sure. Dana's husband, I think."

"Josh, she doesn't have a husband." I knew I sounded a little bit whiny, but really, what would it take for him to realize she wasn't the poor abused woman she claimed to be?

"Please, Holly, this is not the time to argue about whether Dana is lying."

"Nate. His name is Nate and they never married. Josh, Dana has bamboozled you. She has sucked you in and taken advantage of you."

"I didn't come to argue with you. I know you love Radar. Can't you just show me where he is?"

"You took the collar off him." Wouldn't he remember that?

"No, I didn't."

I pulled out my phone and opened the GPS collar app. "See this one? Guest #5. That's the one Radar was wearing."

"Great. So where is it?"

I took a deep breath and zeroed in on it, enlarging the image on the screen several times.

"Wait, where is that?"

"See this building?"

"Yeah."

"That's the police station in Snowball."

Josh's eyes widened. "Is that a dog shelter? Can you spring him?"

"It's not a dog shelter, Josh. It's the police station. They collected the collar as evidence."

"Why? Why would they do that? We're legitimately out on bond."

Now I was confused. "You do know that your mom revoked Dana's bond?"

"She what?" The flushed cheeks drained of color. "What . . . why? Why would she do that?"

"Because Dana has been lying to you all along. And,

of course, she lied to Aunt Margaret. After Dana took off and we didn't know where you two were, Aunt Margaret had to reconsider. The bond means she'll get Dana to court. How could she do that if Dana is going to run off and no one knows where she is?"

"I have spent over three months with Dana, twenty-four hours a day. Who do you think can make a better assessment of her character? My family, who has spent a collective couple of hours with her, or me?"

Of course, when he put it that way, the logical response was that Josh would know her best. And why would I believe Nate, a complete stranger, over my own cousin? "Come into the office with me."

Josh glanced around nervously. "Make it quick."

I unlocked the office door and switched on the computer. Much as I had before, I Googled Nate and found the photograph of him with Dana. The caption still read *Nate Carrington breaks off his engagement to Phoebe Philips.*

I heard a sharp intake of breath from Josh. "They must have reconciled and married after this photo was taken. Phoebe Philips?" Josh leaned over the keyboard and typed *Phoebe Philips.*

There were a lot of women by that name. A model, several artists, authors, and countless others. The woman calling herself Dana Carrington must have fallen to the end of the line. There were only a smattering of pictures of her with Nate and they were all old. Josh typed in *Mrs. Nate Carrington.* A lot of images showed up, but none were of Dana.

"This doesn't mean anything. She tries to stay off social media so her husband can't locate her." But Josh no longer sounded as certain as he had before. "And what kind of police would confiscate a dog collar as evidence?"

He still wasn't getting it. "Carole. Don't you remember

Carole? When they went to the murder scene, they found Radar's collar."

"Carole?"

Honestly, I didn't recall him being so dense as a kid. "You don't remember murdering Carole?"

"I have never murdered anyone in my entire life."

"Didn't you spend time in a cute little cabin? The keys were in a frog?"

A hint of a smile finally appeared. "I remember the frog."

I figured as much. Not many people hid keys in a frog. They must have stumbled upon it. "That's where we found Radar's collar." I swallowed hard. I hated to accuse him of murder, but someone had killed her, and he'd already admitted to being there. "That's also where we found Carole."

He frowned at me. "Your dad's date? Was her name Carole?"

I nodded grimly.

He gazed at the floor. "Yeah. Dana was upset. She thought her husband was in the woods, spying on us. We left in a big hurry."

"Such a big hurry that you forgot to lock the door."

He shrugged. "Could be. Radar went with us."

"Someone must have removed his collar. We found it under a cushion."

"Are you sure it wasn't another dog's collar? I'm certain I didn't take it off. I thought the idea was really cool and that I should buy one for Radar. It would work all over the earth, no matter where we went."

"There were two of you present."

"I know you don't like Dana, but why would she take Radar's collar off?"

"So you couldn't be found?"

He gave me a somber look as if that hadn't occurred to

him. "Look, if I were Dana or Phoebe and I was running from a guy who followed me across the world, I'd use a fake name, too. That guy Nate must have been very cruel to her."

"I could call him so you can meet him."

"You've seen and spoken to him? Is he staying at the inn?"

"You're safe. He's not a guest of the inn. But Josh, he seems like a nice guy. Dave spoke with him. Dana stole a flash drive from him and that's all he wants."

Josh took a step back. "I don't believe that."

"He was in Paris for a conference and she nabbed it from his hotel room. Josh, there are too many coincidences."

"There aren't any coincidences. You're the one who fell for this guy. Oh my gosh, Holly! You were beginning to make me doubt Dana. But he's the one who's lying. He must have murdered Frank! I can't believe you bought his story." Josh turned toward the door. He stopped and looked back. "Dana said he was a liar and a pro at convincing people that he was telling the truth. She was right all along! He must be the one who has Radar!"

"You'd be lucky if he did. He likes dogs. How do you know that someone has Radar? He could be running around the mountain somewhere."

"It's not like him. He's rarely more than a few feet away from me."

"Josh, he crossed the lake and wound up in my bed two days in a row."

"I never figured that out. It wasn't like him at all."

"I can post an ad for a missing dog on the Wagtail social media group."

Poor Josh looked as if all the air had drained out of him. He nodded. "I'd appreciate that."

"Would you like some food?"

"Actually, Dana would like her stuff."

"Then she'll have to go to the police department to get it."

Josh stared at me wide-eyed. "You turned it over to the cops?"

"I didn't turn anything over. They brought a warrant and collected your belongings. You've been charged with murder, Josh! You were unbelievably lucky to get out on bond, and now that there's been a second murder, there's no hope of that happening again."

I moved closer to him and spoke softly. "I know you don't want to go to jail. But if you're right and Dana isn't lying, then that might be the safest place for her to be. You need to be realistic. Oma is the mayor here. I'm not saying she can get you off these charges, but if you leave here and the police catch up with you somewhere else, you won't have anyone on your side."

"She's so afraid. I can't let anyone hurt Dana. She's so delicate. She wouldn't survive being in jail. I have to go." Josh left the office in a hurry.

He paused before bolting out the sliding glass doors. I wondered if he was reconsidering what he believed about Dana.

I ran over to Casey and shook him. "Watch the inn!"

He groaned and rubbed his head.

"Stay here until Zelda comes."

I dashed to the sliding glass doors. They slid open and I ran outside. My hope faded. I didn't see Josh anywhere.

But Trixie did. She trotted toward the Green and I followed her.

In broad daylight, it wasn't hard to follow Josh through the Green even though he kept off the walking trails. I had to duck behind trees a couple of times. I hoped that he didn't notice Trixie sniffing the ground.

He turned right abruptly, left the Green, and slowed down as he entered a popular neighborhood. At the end of the street, he crossed a road and started up a mountain trail.

I lagged behind. If he turned around, he would see me for sure. I felt like a rat, hunched over and darting along the trail to see where he had gone. And I was a rat, spying on my own cousin. He made a left turn. I hung back and motioned to Trixie to come by holding my right arm up and bending my elbow, so my hand moved toward my chest.

She wagged her little tail and came running.

I picked her up and slowly walked farther, keeping an eye on the left side of the trail. Sure enough, an A-frame cabin came into view behind the trees. Another empty cabin, I guessed. They had probably gotten lucky with an unlocked window or an extra key that hadn't been well hidden. I didn't dare go closer for fear that they would see me and take off again. I set Trixie down and whispered, "Let's go."

Walking home, I debated what to do now that I knew where they were staying. I didn't really want to tell the police. Josh *was* my cousin. My only cousin, actually, and I was having trouble wrapping my head around the possibility that he had murdered two people. And why? Because he mistakenly thought Frank was Dana's vile husband? That didn't explain why they would have murdered Carole.

I knew the right thing to do, though. I decided I would consult with Oma and Dad as soon as I could reach them. Margaret would be too emotional. She would never turn in her own son. I couldn't blame her for that.

When I reached the inn, Casey had left, and Zelda was behind the registration desk. "Is Oma still here?"

"I haven't seen her. Is it true that Shelley is missing?"

I nodded. "Do you know where she might be? Did she

say anything about a sick relative or plans to go somewhere?"

"No. She said she was going home to work on piecing
together the quilt she's making for her mom's birthday."

"Was anyone going to help her? Was she going to stop
to pick up dinner? Anything like that?"

"No. I don't think so."

"Thanks, Zelda. Maybe you could call some of her
friends and ask if they've seen her?"

"Good idea."

I walked up the stairs and knocked on the door to Oma's
apartment.

Dad opened the door.

"Oh good! You're still here." I walked in and Dad closed
the door behind me. Lucy and Lucy-the-dog sat on Oma's
sofa.

"We're a little down," Dad said. "What with Carole's
murder, Josh having disappeared, and now Shelley missing, none of us feel right having fun. It's hanging over our
heads. If only there were something we could do."

Lucy scowled. "Dad has forbidden me to go anywhere
on my own today."

I looked at Dad.

"One woman is missing and another one is dead, Holly.
You shouldn't be wandering around town by yourself, either."

Oma poured me a cup of tea. "It is all very troubling.
And worse because Joshua is involved."

"Josh was here this morning," I blurted.

"Is he all right?" asked Oma.

"A little grubby, but he's okay. Trixie and I followed
him—"

"See?" said Dad. "That's exactly what I mean. You
shouldn't be doing things like that."

"Dad, this is Josh we're talking about."

"Holly, I love Josh, too. But something is very wrong. You can't deny that Frank and Carole are dead, and Josh fled from both crime scenes."

"What did he want?" asked Oma. "Food?"

"Radar is missing. He thought I could find him through the GPS collar. We found it at the cabin where Carole was murdered and now it's in the police station. They must have taken it as evidence after Carole's murder. It was odd, though, when I spoke with him. He didn't seem to realize that Carole had been killed."

"You think he has some kind of brain injury?" asked Oma.

"That would explain a lot," grumbled Dad.

"You know, it *is* possible that he left before someone else murdered her," said Lucy.

"He denied ever having murdered anyone."

Oma spoke firmly. "I have been giving this a great deal of thought. While I would not wish to defend the heinous actions of a family member, I also think that as his family, we should believe Josh. He does not have a history of lying. He was a fun boy, but not a cruel or reckless one. We should stand behind him."

"That's what family does, isn't it?" asked Lucy.

"I showed him the photos of Nate with Dana as Phoebe Philips."

"That's a major step forward," said Dad. "How did he take it?"

"He rationalized and said he would use a different name, too, if a dangerous person were trying to find him. I don't know what to do. On the one hand, I certainly don't want to see anyone else murdered. But I feel like telling the police where they are is—"

"Betrayal," Lucy said simply.

We fell silent. I assumed they felt the same way. "What does a family do in a case like this?"

"We do what is right," said Oma. "Not what we want. Not what we wish or desire. We do the correct thing, and we all know what that is."

All eyes were on her.

"Margaret will never forgive us," I said.

"We have had this conversation. Margaret is aware that Joshua has placed himself in this terrible position." Oma looked stern.

"Is that why she's not here?" I asked.

"She is with your mother," said Oma. "Nell is good at comforting her. Margaret is having difficulty accepting that her beloved son could have done something this heinous."

Well, sure. Who wouldn't? "So I should call the police and tell them where Josh and Dana are?"

Oma nodded. "It is not betrayal to do so. It would be far worse if they try to avoid capture and someone is injured—or killed."

I looked to my dad, who said, "I think Oma is right."

With a heavy heart, I pulled out my phone and called Dave.

Twenty-Six

❖ ❖ ❖ ❖

Dave answered his phone immediately. "Did she turn up?"

"You still haven't found Shelley?"

"She vanished, Holly." He sounded frustrated.

I took a deep breath and blurted, "I know where Josh is."

There was a long pause. "Are you sure?"

"Pretty sure. I followed him there."

"Okay. What's the address?" he asked.

"I don't know. It's a little cabin just outside Wagtail proper. I followed him on a trail through the woods."

"You're sure he didn't see you?"

"I don't think he did, but there's no way to know for sure."

"I don't want to wait for a team from Snowball. And it might go better if we take a small crew instead of rushing them. What's the closest street?"

"Hickory."

"Meet me there in fifteen minutes." The connection went dead.

I relayed the conversation to Oma, Dad, and Lucy.

"I'll go with you," said Dad. "Lucy, you stay here with Oma. And maybe we should avoid mentioning this to Margaret until they're in custody."

Dad nodded at me, and we left. Downstairs, I grabbed the keys to a Sugar Maple Inn golf cart and a halter and leash for Trixie. I suited her up. "No running off or barking. Got it?"

Trixie wagged her tail, which I knew meant she was glad to be involved but would do what she wanted anyway. Dogs always thought they knew best.

The three of us boarded the golf cart and headed across town to Hickory Street. Dave and two officers whom I'd seen around before arrived at the same time. We left our golf carts, crossed the street, and started up the trail. No one said a word.

As soon as I saw the A-frame, I pointed at it.

"Stay here," whispered Dave.

I winced at the thought of him using his crutches to navigate through the woods to the house. There was no way he wouldn't make noise snapping twigs or falling.

Dad placed his arm around my shoulders. We watched as they checked out the house. It was so quiet that we heard birds chirping.

And then a window creaked open. A bleached-blond Dana jumped out of it and landed on the ground in a heap. She struggled to her feet and took off running, but she was no match for the officer who'd been waiting for her outside. He tackled her to the ground and handcuffed her.

Dave and the other officer accompanied Josh, who was similarly handcuffed.

"I knew you couldn't be trusted," Dana shrieked. "Josh,

look who's here. Your helpful relatives! And you believed them instead of me? Liars!"

Josh gave me such a woeful look that it was all I could do to not shed a tear.

"I'm sorry," I whispered as he passed me.

"I thought I could trust you." He met my eyes and jerked his head a tiny bit as though he was trying to tell me something.

In that moment, I saw past the stubble on his chin, past the clothes in need of a wash, and all I saw was the Josh I had known when we were kids and the two of us ganged up to tease Holmes. That subtle jerk of his head used to mean he was up to something. But what did it mean now? It suddenly dawned on me that maybe he'd wanted to be caught. If he couldn't convince Dana to turn herself in— and from her mad dash for freedom, I suspected that was the case—then maybe this was the only means he had to stop running and make sure they were in a safe place.

As he moved ahead, Dad and I brought up the rear and I realized that Josh held something in his fingers.

Trying to be subtle, I walked faster and caught up to Josh. "You'll be safe now." I reached for his cuffed hand behind his back and took the paper he held in it.

"Gee, thanks," he said in a snotty tone.

I fell back with Dad and crammed the little slip of paper into my pocket. As far as I could tell, no one had noticed. Except maybe Dad.

Back at the golf carts, Josh called out to me. "Holly, find Radar. Just please find Radar and take care of him."

It sounded as if he thought he was going away for a long time. That worried me.

As I drove the inn golf cart home, Dad placed his hand over mine. "I hope that's the worst thing you ever have to do in your life, sweetheart. I know how hard it was."

"Facing Aunt Margaret might be worse."

"She'll be miffed at first, but I have to give Margaret credit for always being reasonable. She may not like it, but she'll come around."

When we arrived at the inn, it seemed like my entire family, including Margaret and Mom, had gathered in the reception lobby. I was relieved that Dad told them what had happened.

"Except for Dana trying to vault out of a back window to try to escape, it was anticlimactic. She had a few choice words for us, of course. But that was the highlight."

"What did Josh say?" Aunt Margaret clutched a tissue.

"Not much, actually. He was quite cooperative. Almost as though he was glad it was over. Resigned, I would say." I thought of the paper he'd given me but decided it might be better if I looked at it in private.

"It can't be easy to be on the run all the time," said Lucy. "Cheer up, Auntie Margaret, at least we know where he is now."

"In a cold dank jail cell," said Margaret glumly. "How did this happen? He was such a smart little boy. Where did I go wrong?"

Dad hugged his sister. "This isn't your fault. He fell for the wrong woman."

"Do you think they'll let me bond him out again?" Margaret looked like she might burst into tears.

Dad shook his head. "Highly unlikely."

"If there's a shred of a chance, then I'm driving over there right now."

"I'll drive you, Margaret," Dad offered.

"We will all go," said Oma. "It is past lunchtime. I know a cute little place where we can get some lunch. Yes? You, too, Lucy?"

I told Zelda I would cover for her while she got some

lunch. As soon as everyone cleared out, I unfolded the slip of paper. It was handwritten in block letters.

I HAVE THE GIRL. SHE WILL BE RELEASED WHEN YOU TURN OVER THE FLASH DRIVE TO ME. GIVE IT TO HOLLY AT THE SUGAR MAPLE INN. NO COPS OR NO DEAL.

Twenty-Seven

I could barely breathe. I needed to talk to Josh.

Did he write this? Was Josh with Dana because *he* wanted the flash drive and the money? No, that didn't make sense. Not unless he had intended to give the note to Dana. But would she know who "the girl" was? Would she care? So far it seemed to me that she was only interested in herself.

The only other option I could think of was that he or Dana had received the note from someone else. But why not let the police see it? Why had he taken it with him? Why had he passed it along to me?

I couldn't imagine not showing it to Dave. What was I supposed to do with the flash drive anyway?

I read the note again. "The girl" had to be Shelley. I hadn't heard of anyone else who was missing. I checked the online social group for Wagtail. No mention of a missing person, not even Shelley! The only thing that came up under the word "missing" was the post about Radar that I had added.

Zelda returned from lunch, and I tucked the note in my pocket again.

She reached out her arms and hugged me. "You look so upset. I would be, too, if my cousin had been arrested for two murders. But he's safely in prison now. You have nothing to fear."

I nodded. If she only knew! "I'm going upstairs to grab a quick shower. I'll have my phone with me, so just call if anything pops up."

"A long hot shower is exactly what you need!"

I trudged up the stairs and peered down the hallway before continuing just to be sure no one was lurking there. Part of me wished Josh had written that message. I was on my way up to my apartment when I realized what should have been obvious. The note had to be from Nate. He had been completely open about wanting the flash drive back. Of course! I had pegged him all wrong. And I had thought I was a pretty good judge of character.

Shame swept over me. Dana had been right all along. Okay, so he wasn't her husband, but he was after her because he wanted his flash drive back. One couldn't really blame him for that. She shouldn't have stolen it in the first place. But he had gone too far. I didn't understand why he would have murdered Frank. He admitted that he had hired Frank! And Carole. Poor, poor Carole. Had she been in the wrong place at the wrong time? I could only hope Shelley wouldn't end up like Carole had.

I unlocked my door and swung it open. Trixie scampered inside and stopped to smell something. My blood ran cold.

It was only an envelope. Plain white, completely ordinary. The kind you might send with a greeting card in it. But chills ran through me. On the top, handwritten in block letters was my name. **HOLLY MILLER**.

I closed the door and locked it. Had the person worn

gloves when writing? Could the police find fingerprints on it?

Just in case, I hurried to my kitchen and retrieved a pair of non-latex gloves from a box I kept under the sink. I slid them onto my hands, and only then did I pick up the envelope. Holding it gingerly so I wouldn't smudge any potential fingerprints, I examined it. There wasn't a single thing about it that I found remarkable or in any way unusual. The flap was gummed shut. In case the sender had licked it, I fetched a pair of scissors and sliced it open to preserve any DNA that might be under the flap. Inside lay a small note that looked exactly like the one Josh had passed off to me. I extracted it, unfolded it, and read.

> PLACE THE FLASH DRIVE INSIDE A BAG OF DOG TREATS
> AND LEAVE IT ON THE BENCH OUTSIDE OF FARM AND
> FORK ON THURSDAY AT NINE PM. FOLLOW THESE IN-
> STRUCTIONS CAREFULLY IF YOU WANT TO SEE THE GIRL.
> NO COPS OR THE DEAL IS OFF.

I sank onto my sofa. How was I supposed to do that when I didn't know where the flash drive was? Even worse, wouldn't the police be searching the cabin where Josh and Dana had been hiding? If they found a flash drive, wouldn't they have taken it as evidence?

Oh, Shelley! We were in a pickle!

I dragged myself to the shower, my head in a whirl over how this could possibly be accomplished. I had to get a grip. The first thing I had to do was tell Dave. Preferably in a private area where we couldn't be seen in case I was being watched. Perhaps more importantly, I needed to find the flash drive. Nate had shown us a photo. It hadn't looked very special. And it was so small that Dana might have it on her. The police would place it in storage as one of her possessions and the whole thing would begin again when she was released.

I needed coffee. Strong coffee. I pulled on jeans and a pink cotton shirt, then wandered into the kitchen to make coffee. While the water boiled, I picked up my cell phone to call Dave. I gazed at my phone with new terror. Could someone track my calls or listen to them? Would they know I had phoned the police? I decided the old-fashioned landline of the inn phone system might be safer.

I phoned Dave, planning to be careful about what I said. When he answered, I tried to sound cheerful in case anyone was listening. "Hi! Just checking in with you. How's it going?"

"Most of your family is here, along with Ben, who is trying to get Josh released with an ankle bracelet."

Oh, wouldn't that look great to inn guests! I wanted Josh to be released, but if he stayed at the inn, it would be the equivalent of hanging a sign on the door that said *Accused Murderer Within. Enter at your own risk.* Nope. We would have to find him a place to rent.

"When will you be back?"

"Not sure."

To throw anyone off who might be listening, I added, "I miss you. We need to talk."

A long silence followed. "Okaaay . . . Dinner tonight?"

I could tell he was confused. I stifled a giggle. "As soon as you can get here." I hung up the phone, added milk to my coffee, and sipped it.

There was one alternative to handing the flash drive over to a murderer, but it meant finding Shelley by nine o'clock tomorrow night. We didn't have time to wait for the slow wheels of justice to turn. Dave might not be back until late. We couldn't waste an entire afternoon of daylight.

At that moment, someone knocked on my door. Trixie jumped up and barked.

"Who is it?"

"Shadow."

I recognized the voice of our handyman and opened the door.

"Weren't you expecting me? Holmes said to come up here." His bloodhound, Elvis, looked up at me, then romped inside to play with Trixie.

We heard the dull thud of heavy footsteps running up the stairs. Holmes joined us on the landing, breathing heavily. "Oh good. You're here."

They entered my apartment, and I closed the door behind them.

Holmes caught his breath. "Hi, Holly." He planted a smooch on me. "Dave called me half an hour ago. A couple of years back Shadow and I and a handful of other Wagtailites were deputized to assist in case of emergencies. Dave is stuck in Snowball, but he's worried about Shelley, who is still missing, so he'd like us to take our four-wheelers and look around up the mountain. She might have taken a hike or a walk and fallen. She could have broken a leg or something. We're supposed to look for anything that seems out of the ordinary. It still gets pretty cold at night. We need to locate her. I've called six other people. Here's a map. This is your zone, Shadow, so we won't be duplicating efforts."

I was glad they were going to look for Shelley, but now I didn't know what to do. Dave didn't know the entire situation.

"What's wrong, Holly?" asked Holmes.

I sucked in a deep breath. I knew they were trustworthy. "Shelley isn't lying out on a trail." I retrieved my gloves and the slip of paper to show them. "We still need to find her. But I think it's more likely that she's in a cabin or a shed."

"What flash drive?" asked Shadow.

I told them about Nate and the flash drive that Dana had allegedly stolen from him.

"Then that's who has Shelley," said Holmes.

"Maybe. We can't exclude him. But I was there when Dave spoke with him, and he seemed like a nice guy. He wants the flash drive back, but I'm not sure he'd go to these lengths. And there's the weird fact that he hired Frank to find Dana. So why would he murder him?" I cringed as I said it. I went back and forth about Nate. Part of me wanted to think he was a good guy, but who would want the flash drive back more than Nate? Maybe he was the evil man that Dana claimed.

"It says 'the girl'; how do we know it means Shelley?" asked Shadow.

"I'm not aware of any other missing women. Only Josh's dog, Radar," I said. "I think we should still look for her, but one of the searchers is liable to get hurt or mishandle the situation." There was a catch in my voice when I added, "Or he might kill Shelley if he's spooked."

"So we'll spread out and look around. A lot of the cabins are still empty right now," said Shadow. "We can look for tire tracks or smoke coming out of chimneys. Things like that."

"Shadow, you and I can split this zone and I'll get someone to tail this Nate fellow." Holmes pointed at the map.

"There's something else. Two brothers have been staying with us, Paul and Ted Mellor," I said. "They seem nice enough, but they've been kind of weird. Skittish. Like they don't want to be seen. Maybe someone should tail them, too."

Holmes nodded. "I don't suppose you have photographs of them or Nate?"

I pulled up the photo of Nate on my phone and showed it to them.

"Nate Carrington!" exclaimed Shadow. "I thought that name sounded familiar. He's a big shot! No way would he kill anyone."

"You've heard of him?" I asked.

"Sure. Everyone has." He gazed at Holmes and me. "Except for you two, apparently. He's like a gaming genius. He sold his company for a lot of money."

"How do you know that?" I asked. "I thought you were into woodworking."

Shadow laughed at me. "It's not the only thing I do. I dabble a little in some of the games."

"Let's get going. I need to round up the other guys." Holmes opened the door to leave.

"I'll look around Wagtail a little bit," I said.

The two of them took off. I placed the notes in a plastic bag and took it along in a purse in case Dave came back sooner than I expected. And I didn't want anyone making off with them!

Trixie and Twinkletoes followed me downstairs, where I took a key to a golf cart. "Zelda, I have a few things to do in Wagtail. Call me if you need anything."

She nodded and answered a ringing phone. "Sugar Maple Inn."

Trixie and Twinkletoes jumped onto the front seat of the golf cart. "We're going to look for Shelley and Radar."

Trixie's tail wagged furiously at the mention of Shelley's name. There was no question in my mind that she knew who Shelley and Radar were. I started the quiet electric engine and drove toward Mom's house. We coasted along residential streets. Birds chirped and flew overhead. We waved at people on the sidewalks as we passed them. It would have helped if I had known what we were looking for. An hour later, we passed the church, and I recognized a Sugar Maple Inn golf cart in the parking lot. I pulled up next to it and looked around. I peered inside the church, which was silent and empty. Trixie ran toward the woods in the back of the graveyard. Uh-oh. Maybe she was on the trail of someone. I hurried behind her.

Paul and Ted were in the woods.

"Trixie!" I hissed, hoping they wouldn't hear me.

She looked back at me, and I gave her the come signal with my hand. But it was too late. Paul saw me.

His expression worried me. It was a mixture of horror and fear. "Holly," he choked.

"Hi!" I tried to sound chipper. "I just saw the golf cart in the church parking lot." That was a lousy reason to have stopped and wandered into the woods. I sought something, anything, to say that didn't involve Shelley. "I'm out looking for Radar. Looks like a border collie but he's golden and white?"

Ted held a shovel, which worried me. "We're geocaching." He said it as though he had practiced it. Stiff and odd.

"That's fun!" I forced a smile. "Well, let me know if you see Radar."

Paul sounded less tense than his brother. "We will do that," he said very precisely, as if he were being formal.

No one spoke that way. It was as if they were trying too hard to act natural.

They stood frozen, watching me. I waved at them and left the woods, worried about what they were really doing and why they had a shovel. Geocaching was popular on Wagtail Mountain. People loved to find the things other people had left behind for them to locate. But one of the main tenets of geocaching was that items were not supposed to be buried unless it was with the express permission of the landowner. Few people wanted their land pockmarked with holes just so someone could find a whistle or a few foreign coins.

Something was up with those two and I didn't like it. Back in the golf cart, I phoned Holmes and let him know where the Mellor brothers were so someone could follow them.

After driving through alleys and streets, knocking on the walls of sheds, and peering through basement windows of houses I knew to be unoccupied, I had accomplished nothing. There was absolutely no sign of Shelley.

Zelda's shift was coming to an end, so I headed back to the inn to man the desk for another hour.

"Do you have plans tonight?" I asked, remembering her date with Nate.

"Nope. Just a cozy evening at home with my kitties."

"Um, I don't really know how to say this, but please don't go out with anyone tonight. Especially not Nate."

Her brow furrowed. "What's going on?"

I couldn't tell her. I loved Zelda, but discretion was not one of her virtues. "Well, you know, we can't find Shelley."

"You think Nate is involved? I would hate that. I like him!"

"Yeah. He seems very nice. Just stay home tonight. Okay?"

"I should be so lucky to have a date. See you tomorrow!"

The daily pet parade that took place on the plaza in front of the inn was starting. Watching it through a window in the reception lobby, I couldn't help thinking of Shelley, who always got a big kick out of the costumed animals. The Chihuahua in a tutu and a blond wig cheered me up a little. She pranced as if she knew she was the star of the show. Even the adorable bulldog in a pirate costume didn't come close. I was surprised to see Lucy-the-dog dressed like a bee. That meant they were back from Snowball.

Had they been able to get Josh out of jail? With high hopes, I checked to see which room Josh was in, but he wasn't registered. He must still be in the slammer.

Dave barreled into the reception lobby just before I locked the doors. "Any news on Shelley?"

"Maybe we should speak in private, so we won't be seen together."

"Is Holmes jealous?" Dave teased.

"Ha ha," I said drolly, leading the way into the inn office. I closed the door and the curtains.

"Holly? Now you're scaring me."

I handed him gloves and then both of the notes.

Dave's complexion went completely white when he read them. "Where did you get these?"

"Josh handed me the first one. The second one had been shoved under my door."

"This changes everything."

I nodded. "I drove through town today knocking on sheds and checking unoccupied houses."

He ran a hand over his face. "Wow. It confirms what Nate told us, doesn't it?"

"And it points at Nate. Holmes was going to get someone to tail him. He'll have to check on Shelley or bring her food, right?"

"One would hope so." Dave picked up the landline and phoned someone. "Hi! Could you give me the address of the house you rented to Nate Carrington?"

Dave scribbled something on a notepad. "Thanks. I owe you one." He hung up the phone. "I'm going there now to scope it out."

Twenty-Eight

❀ ❀ ❀

"Not alone, I hope?"

A faint glimmer of a smile crossed Dave's mouth. "Thanks for worrying about me, Holly. I'll get one of my officers to go with me."

He swung toward the doors with ease.

I unlocked them for him. "You've conquered those crutches."

He grinned. "I think I've gotten the hang of it. Can't wait until I'm done with them, though." He continued on his way toward the doors.

"Be careful. And let me know what happens. Uh, Dave?"

He stopped. "Yeah?"

I lowered my voice and told him about Paul and Ted in the woods with a shovel. "It was very strange. When they checked in, they paid in cash. No one does that anymore. And they asked that the people answering the phone not confirm that they were staying here. I thought it was an unusual request. Some famous guests have asked that they be registered under another name so that fans won't hang around waiting for a chance to see them. I can't blame them. I once had a stranger bring a tray of food to a well-known singer who was a guest. The stranger tried to pass herself off as inn staff, but obviously I know who works here and who doesn't. I don't know what's up with Paul and Ted. But I didn't see any sign of Shelley at all."

Dave took a deep breath. "Nate first. He's our best bet. Then I'll come back and see if I can figure out what's up with Paul and Ted."

"Keep me posted."

"Will do."

As soon as he left the inn, I locked the sliding glass doors again.

"There you are!"

I turned around to find Judy Davis in the lobby. She smiled brightly at me. "I just wanted to be sure you found the note I slid under your door."

The hairs on my arms stood up, and I could hardly breathe. "*You* slid the note under my door?"

"Yes. We wouldn't want anyone else to read it, would we?"

Had she seen Dave leaving? Probably. I tried very hard to stay calm, but my breath came ragged. Was I supposed to thank her? Tell her we were looking for the flash drive? I stared at her. She couldn't possibly be involved in the race to get the flash drive. Could she? No, that was crazy. She'd been to the inn many times before. I should test her with a question. "Did you know that Dana is in jail?"

"Again?" She shook her head. "She should have stayed here at the inn instead of running off. Josh adores her, but she doesn't seem to appreciate it. When you find the right fellow, like my John, you need to stick by him. Was that Officer Dave who just left?"

Ohh. She worked that in very smoothly. To lie or not to lie? I should tell the truth because she'd obviously seen him. But I needed a good excuse. Something that made it sound like he wasn't here to discuss the note. "Yes, it was. He was looking for Oma. Something about the Cat Fest that begins on Friday."

"Your grandmother is such a remarkable woman. And so kind. Will Shelley be back to work soon?"

Once again, I didn't know what to say. Was she testing me? "I hope so."

She smiled at me. "I do, too. Have a good evening."

She turned and walked along the hallway toward the main lobby.

My heart pounded. I didn't move until the sound of her shoes clicking on the floor had faded. It didn't make any sense. Judy and her husband were building a house in Wagtail. They couldn't possibly be involved with Nate or Dana. Could they?

I picked up the phone and called Dave to let him know about Judy and the ransom note.

"Judy? You have to be kidding me. I've spoken with her several times. She's very nice."

"I was surprised, too."

"I'll post someone to watch the inn tonight and follow her if she leaves."

I thought that was an excellent idea. Anything to find poor Shelley.

Twinkletoes jolted me out of my thoughts by rubbing around my legs. I swung her up in my arms. "You're not fooling me. You think it's time for dinner, don't you?"

She purred affirmatively.

I set her on the floor. She scampered to the hallway that

led to the main lobby, then stopped and looked back at me as if she was wondering why I wasn't following her.

"Okay. I got your message." I called Trixie, who joined Twinkletoes in running along the hallway.

I found my family in the private kitchen. Only my half siblings and Lucy-the-dog were missing. I couldn't blame them. They were probably out on the town enjoying life. But Josh was back! "Josh!" I cried. "I'm so glad to see you!"

Everyone chattered cheerfully—except for Josh. His eyes met mine and I could tell he was angry.

"Hi, sweetheart," Mom called out. "There's a lovely spring salad with walnuts and maple-balsamic vinaigrette, delicious crab cakes, and I heated up a veggie pasta dish that I think you'd like."

"Thanks, Mom." I grabbed a plate and helped myself. Mom hadn't covered half of the food options on the island. I checked the refrigerator for dog and cat food that had been prepared by Cook and served Twinkletoes tuna and shrimp in aspic. I suspected Trixie would like the cod and macaroni dinner.

When they were happily eating, I sat down at the table. Under normal circumstances, I would have welcomed Josh home, but from the looks he gave me I had a bad feeling that no matter what I said to him, his response would not be pleasant.

Aunt Margaret smiled at him like she was relieved to have her baby safely home.

Oma, Mom, and Dad talked nonstop about the inn, the upcoming Cat Fest, and their plans for the next day.

"How can you be so cheerful?" demanded Josh. "I'm grateful that you sprang me, but Dana is eating garbage and sleeping in a cold cell."

Silence floated over everyone. Aunt Margaret finally

spoke. "We've been over this, Josh. I am not putting that much money at risk for someone I barely know. Dana's previous abrupt departure from the inn does not inspire confidence in her. If she needs bail money, maybe she can call her own family."

"She doesn't have one. She doesn't have anyone but us!"

"Well then, she should have considered her actions before she left me in the lurch not knowing if she would show up for court or if I would lose my money. I'm sorry, honey. Dana has lied to us and is completely undependable. She has no one to blame but herself, Josh. We offered her a lovely hotel room but she fled and we had no idea where you two were. As it is, I had to pay a huge bond because you're a flight risk, too."

"Flight risk," joked Dad. "Josh is the only person I know who could literally fly away."

"I'd like to do that. I never imagined that coming back to Wagtail would be such a nightmare. I thought I could trust my family."

Oma's tone was a little bit sharp. "You *can* trust us, Josh. We have done everything in our power to help you. But we have not been able to trust *you*."

Josh recoiled as if that had never occurred to him, and he had thought the trust factor only went in one direction.

After dinner, I excused myself and phoned Dave hoping for news about Shelley.

It had been nice to spend the evening with Mom, Dad, and Aunt Margaret. But the entire time, I was thinking about Shelley. Wherever she was, she might be suffering. She weighed heavily on my mind. I hoped she would be all right. And I couldn't get Josh out of my mind. I loved my cousin. He had always been so carefree and fun. And now he was in so much trouble. I went up to my quarters around eleven, exhausted. More from anxiety and worry than from anything physical.

I collapsed on the sofa. Twinkletoes jumped into my lap and Trixie hopped up next to me. She rested her head on her front paws. My feet up on the ottoman, I thought I really should go to bed. Instead, I couldn't get Shelley out of my mind. Was she cold or hungry—or alive? I thought about Judy, who had seemed so nice. But she had come right out and told me that she slid the note under my door. She even tracked me down to be certain I had found it. And I thought about Nate, who was at the heart of this mess. He had sounded reasonable and calm yet rightly upset about the possibility of losing a lot of money. And then my thoughts drifted to Paul and Ted. I didn't want to imagine that they were preparing to bury something—or someone.

A dog barked in the distance, a regular occurrence in Wagtail, where there were so many dogs and an equal number of squirrels, rabbits, raccoons, and possums.

But Trixie raised her head. Her ears perked and she seemed to be concentrating.

"It's just a pup, Trixie."

The dog barked again. Several barks this time.

Trixie whined.

"Do you know that dog, Trixie?" I patted her. "Don't worry. He or she probably wants to go inside the house."

But Trixie didn't relax. She kept her Sphinx-like position, remaining alert and waiting to hear more.

I grinned at her. Sort of like me waiting for a phone call.

There was a soft knock at the door. "Holly?"

"Dave?" I picked up Twinkletoes, relinquished my comfy position, and opened the door.

Dave rushed in and closed it behind him.

"Is someone chasing you?"

"No. I just didn't want anyone to notice me here. I'm

not taking chances with Shelley's life on the line. I wish it didn't take me so long to get around on these stupid crutches."

Trixie ran to the French doors that led to the terrace and scratched on them.

"What's with her?" asked Dave.

"We heard a dog barking outside." I opened the door for her.

Trixie jumped onto a chair and looked out at the dark lake. The dog in the distance barked again. Trixie barked back at it.

"Hush! You'll wake all the guests."

"Have you got binoculars?"

I retrieved them from the living room and handed them to Dave. "You won't be able to see much. There aren't any lights on the shore across from us."

Dave looked up at the moon before peering through the binoculars. "I can make out the dog. I could use a little more light, but it looks like that could be the dog who's barking. He's running back and forth on the pier. Oops! He jumped into the water."

I grabbed the binoculars from him and peered through them. "It looks like he's trying to swim this way. Poor little guy." I couldn't make out the dog very well, but the shape of his head reminded me of Radar! "Come on."

I tossed my keys to Dave and ran out, with Trixie and Twinkletoes way ahead of me. Once downstairs, I opened the sliding glass doors and took the key with me. As we dashed outside, we ran into Dad.

"Where are you going in such a rush?" he asked.

"There's a dog in the water. It could be Radar. Looks like he means to swim across."

"I'll come with you. You might need some extra hands."

We hurried down to the dock and suited up Trixie and

Twinkletoes in life vests. I threw an extra one in the boat for the other dog and hopped in.

"Wait! Wait!"

I looked back to see poor Dave hobbling down to the water as fast as he could go on his crutches.

"You can't go," I said. "What if we capsize? Your cast would take you under."

"No problem. Hand me three life vests."

Dad helped him into the boat. Meanwhile, I was frantically searching for any sign of the dog's head.

Dave pulled on a life vest and wrapped two around his leg. Some people were just hardheaded.

We took off. "Everyone look for the dog!" I shouted. Fortunately, the water was calm and peaceful. But it was still way too cold for swimming. "Does anyone see him?"

"There he is." Dad pointed ahead.

The poor little guy seemed to be swimming toward us.

"I think you're right," shouted Dad. "Looks like that's Radar."

I hoped he would stay afloat until we reached him. When we were twenty feet away, he turned around and swam back to the pier on the other side. Oh no! He must have been getting tired. I kept going and so did he.

"Why is he turning back?" shouted Dad.

"Maybe he's afraid of the boat," Dave responded.

Happily, Radar made it back to shore. We were close enough to see him shake the water off his fur. Then he trotted out on the pier and seemed to wait for us.

"Crazy dog!" Dad shook his head. "Did you bring a leash? We might need one."

I slowed the engine to idle and smoothly brought the boat alongside the pier. "Didn't even stop to think about it. We can probably rig one up."

Radar barked at us and trotted away.

Trixie and Twinkletoes jumped out of the boat onto the pier.

Radar barked again and the three of them scampered into the woods.

"Oh great," Dad groaned. "I thought this would be a quick rescue mission of one dog, and now three animals are on the loose in the woods."

We docked the boat. I called each of them, but not one of them came to us.

"Swell. And no flashlights, either."

Dave and I immediately took out our phones and turned on the flashlights.

Dad looked a little sheepish. "Oh yeah. I always forget about that."

But I was worried about something else; I hoped we wouldn't hear Trixie's melancholy howl that meant someone was dead.

"Trixie!" I called. "Trixie, come!"

She trotted back toward us, but when I kneeled and put my arms out, she turned around and ran a few feet back.

Aargh. I followed her and she ran deeper into the woods. I continued behind her until we reached a door. I stopped short. There wasn't a building, only a faded green door. It looked to me like a Dutch door, the kind where the top could be opened while the bottom was still closed. It was definitely old, except for a shiny new padlock. I shined my light around in search of a building and finally realized that whatever was on the other side had been built back into the hill. Brush had grown over the top.

Radar and Trixie scratched at the door, scraping off paint with their claws. Twinkletoes perched in the brush over the door and looked down.

"Holly?" It was Dad's voice.

"Over here." I shined my phone flashlight in the direction I had come. I could hear Dave lurching through the uneven terrain of the woods.

I turned and aimed my light at the door again.

Dave was breathing hard when he arrived with Dad. "Good grief. What is that?"

"Must have been here a long time." Dad jiggled the padlock. "Someone is still using it."

"It's like a hobbit house," said Dave. "I heard some people are building houses like this. They stay the same temperature year round."

"Okay. It's late and I'm tired," Dad grumbled. "These rascals have taken us on a wild-goose chase. Holly, if you grab Trixie and I pick up Radar, will Twinkletoes follow us back to the boat?"

"Maybe." I was more concerned about the fact that the dogs were so determined to get inside. And then we heard a pitiful mew. "Where *is* Twinkletoes?"

The mew came again, but louder. I thought for sure that it came from inside the door. "Oh no! She's inside! Twinkletoes?"

"Rowww!"

I seized the padlock and tried to open it. When that didn't work, I kicked the door. It was old. Maybe it would give.

"Stop, Holly." Dave handed me one of his crutches and pulled a Swiss Army knife out of a pocket. "This isn't the easiest way to unlock a padlock, but since we have no other tools, it will have to do. Both of you will have to spell me on this. It takes a while." He flicked out a blade and, putting most of his weight on his uninjured leg, he began to saw at the shank.

"Where did you learn that?" asked Dad.

"Aww, you pick up things. I learned some hacks when I was in the Navy. People get themselves in all kinds of situations, so it's good for a cop to know some tricks."

"This will take forever. Maybe I should look around on top. The hole she fell through might be large enough for me to jump in and get her out."

"No way. Maybe in daylight," said Dad. "But we could fall into some other hole."

He had a good point.

The three of us took turns sawing the shank until it finally broke loose. The second Dave lifted it off the latch, I pushed the door like a mama bear. It swung open.

Twenty-Nine

❖ ❖ ❖ ❖

All three of us aimed our phone flashlights inside. Twinkletoes's white fur stood out prominently against the dirt floor and dark beams of the structure.

I shot toward her. "Twinkletoes! Are you hurt?" But when I bent to pick her up, I realized that she was curled up on a body. I shifted my light to the face. "It's Shelley!"

Dave hobbled in without his crutches. He bent his good knee and fell over.

"Dave!"

He moaned, "Aargh. I'm not good at having a bum leg. Can you hand me my phone? Shelley! Can you hear me? Shelley!"

I flashed my light around in search of his phone. It had toppled several feet away. When I handed it to him, I could see from his pained expression that he wasn't fine. But part of that might have also been worry about Shelley.

I kneeled on the other side of her and took Twinkletoes

into my arms. "She's breathing. It's shallow, but I can see her chest rising ever so slightly. Shelley?" I picked up her hand and held it in mine. "Shelley? Can you wake up?"

"Not yet, Mom," she slurred.

"I'm calling an ambulance. Where are we?" asked Dad. "I don't know where to tell them to come."

Dave raised his hand for Dad's phone. "Sergeant Quinlan here. Hi, Sheila. Are you looking at the map? We're across the lake from the Sugar Maple Inn. My best guess is we walked southwest and must be getting close to the old Rumford farm." There was a pause. He handed the phone to Dad and said, "Stay on the line with her." He looked at his watch. "Maybe it's a good thing that we found her in the middle of the night. Unless her abductor is very close by, he won't hear the commotion and know she's been found. Maybe we can set a trap for him."

"I think she's been drugged."

Dave nodded. "Unquestionably. But she's still alive and that's what matters."

In the light of my phone, I could see that he held on to her other hand and looked at her tenderly. "You're going to have to ask her out, you know."

"What are you talking about?" Dave asked.

"I mean that you have to do things together away from the inn. Not just when she's trapped at work."

He scowled at me. "Did she tell you that?"

She had, but I thought I'd better take the heat for what I was saying. "Everyone can see the way you two look at each other. You just need to get together on your days off and do fun things."

In a dry tone, he said, "I will keep your advice in mind."

Half an hour later, we heard voices calling to us. Dad stepped outside and shouted to guide them to us.

The first emergency medical technician to step inside was a young man. "What is this place? A bunker?"

Dad snorted. "It's a root cellar. Back in the days when they didn't have refrigeration, this is where they stored their harvest to keep it cool."

I clutched Twinkletoes to me, called Trixie and Radar, and stepped outside to make room for the people who needed to attend to Shelley. I was very glad to be outside in the fresh air.

Before I knew it, they'd carried her out on a stretcher and fetched a second stretcher for Dave because he was in great pain. The police officer who had accompanied them gave Dad, me, the dogs, and Twinkletoes a ride to the Wagtail entrance, where we caught a Wagtail taxi back to the inn.

"What were you doing out so late?" I asked.

"I drove your mom home so she wouldn't have to walk alone in the dark."

"That was very considerate of you."

"I like the new Wagtail," he said. "I understand why you don't want to return to city life."

"In spite of two murders?"

Dad took a deep breath. "I'm very sad about them, especially Carole's death. I feel like I'm partly responsible for that."

"Why? You didn't have anything to do with it."

"Exactly. I didn't invite her. Never would have dated her, but she was here, and I should have been looking out for her."

"Dad, there's no way you could have anticipated what happened to her."

"I know. But it doesn't make me feel any less responsible."

At the inn, I made sure the sliding glass doors were securely locked behind us. We walked up the stairs to the second floor, but Dad didn't turn off to Oma's apartment.

"I think you missed your room," I teased in a soft voice.

"I graduated to a room of my own," he whispered. "Margaret and Oma decided Josh should stay in Oma's guest room. Margaret is sleeping on the sofa, hoping to catch him if he decides to leave."

"Do you think he will?"

"I doubt it. Not without Dana. And he knows that even if he managed to get over to Snowball, he wouldn't be able to spring her from the jail."

I gave Dad a kiss good night and headed back to Oma's apartment. As softly as I could, I rapped on the door. I didn't want to wake Margaret or Oma. Dad had said Margaret would be sleeping on the sofa, but I took a chance that Josh might be awake and hear me.

Fortunately, a sour-faced Josh answered the door. "I haven't left, Holly," he whispered in an irritated tone.

At that moment, Radar sprang toward him and placed his paws on Josh.

The transformation in Josh was remarkable. He picked up Radar and held him tight. "I was afraid I might not ever see you again, fella. Where have you been?" Just like that, Josh changed into the cousin I knew and loved.

I left without a word and proceeded up to my apartment, glad they hadn't put Josh in *my* guest room. Trixie and Twinkletoes scampered ahead of me as if they hadn't been up all night. How did they do it? I was exhausted and went straight to bed.

I woke at eleven on Thursday morning. The sun shone brightly outside as if summer would arrive any day. Mr. Huckle must have been there recently, because tea still steamed on the tray he'd left. I bit into a heavenly chocolate croissant and handed a breakfast cookie to Trixie. A small shark-shaped treat smelled like fish, and

Twinkletoes gobbled it up. I reached for the phone and called Dave.

He answered cheerfully, "Good morning, Holly!"

"Are you home?" I asked.

"Nope. I did a number on my leg last night. They cut off the cast and were able to get it back where it should be early this morning. I think they'll send me home later today."

"Any news on Shelley?"

"I'm with her right now. She's still groggy. They tell me her abductor doped her up with Rohypnol to keep her sedated. But they might release her later on today, too. Her mother is here with her."

"Did she tell you who abducted her?"

"She doesn't know. The doctors say that's not uncommon given the Rohypnol. It might come back to her, or it might not." He paused for a moment. "They found some fur in the root cellar that looks like it belongs to Radar. We'll be testing it to be certain."

"How did he get out?"

"Probably through the same hole Twinkletoes used to get in. They tell me there are claw marks where an animal dug recently. It's not on top like I thought, but on the side."

"Did they find anything that would give away the kidnapper?"

Dave sighed. "I don't know yet. Shelley is under police protection. There are two cops watching her at the hospital. They had some empty beds in intensive care and decided to put her there because it's harder for visitors to get into. Smaller, too, so anyone who doesn't belong stands out."

"How does she feel?"

"Groggy."

I asked him to keep me posted and ended the call. After a shower, I dressed in a short-sleeve white blouse and a blush flare skirt, added pretty blush sneakers, and headed downstairs. I took Trixie outside and when I opened the door to return, she raced through the inn to the dining area. She must have been as hungry as I was.

I poured myself a mug of tea and took it to a table outside on the terrace. A large round umbrella shaded us from the sun, and the air was a perfectly comfortable temperature. I leaned back in my chair, enjoying the day, which was all the better because Shelley was alive.

Across the lake, the inn skiff bobbed gently, still docked at the pier. Someone, probably me, had to go collect it. But the boat was the least of our problems. We had a kidnapper and a murderer on the loose. I assumed they were the same person but had no evidence of that.

"Hi. Mind if I join you?"

Radar nudged me with his nose. He was looking for affection. I scratched behind his ears.

Josh slid into the chair next to me and set a mug of coffee on the table. He was clean shaven and wore a shirt that was pressed so perfectly I suspected it came straight from a box and was brand new. I caught a whiff of a sandalwood aftershave.

"Please do. You look better. How do you feel?"

"Relieved. It's hard to be on the run all the time. I might have this stupid thing on my ankle, but I slept through the whole night, woke up to coffee and croissants, courtesy of Mr. Huckle, and . . ."

"And what?"

"It was nice being surrounded by people who care about me. That sounds so childish. I guess I'm glad this ordeal is coming to an end."

"What do you mean?"

"As cold as it sounds, I'm glad Dana is in a safe place. I feel guilty for thinking that way, but if she were here, she'd be running off somewhere, trying to hide. It's exhausting to be on alert all the time. I'm not happy that she's in jail, but at least I know that her husband, or that Nate guy, isn't going to hurt her there." He took a long swig of coffee. "I haven't killed anyone, Holly. Ever. You've seen Dana. I don't think she would have the strength to overpower a man and strangle him. I've heard about people who can do incredible things when they're under pressure, like lifting cars off babies, but I just don't think Dana would have the physical power to kill Frank Burton. She hasn't been out of my sight much and I haven't seen her attack anyone."

What he was saying made sense. I didn't want to burst his bubble, but I didn't think that would be sufficient to convince a jury. "Did Dana admit to being Phoebe Philips?"

Josh shook his head. "No."

"Did she admit to taking the flash drive?"

His eyes met mine. "No. She says she doesn't know anything about that."

"Do you believe her?"

Josh stared at his coffee mug. "I want to. But it's getting harder. That picture you showed me online is hard to overcome. But, Holly, someone *is* after her for something. She's hiding for a reason. Look what happened to get me into this mess. Two people were killed in places where we were staying, right after we left them. If that's not evidence of being pursued for something, I don't know what is."

He had a point.

"My biggest regret is that we came to Wagtail. I'll always be sorry that I brought this trouble to my family. Especially to Oma and Mom. They didn't deserve this."

His heart was in the right place. "Did you want me to follow you back to the A-frame yesterday?"

Josh grinned. "Was it that obvious?"

"It crossed my mind."

"I hadn't planned on it. But that note and the picture changed everything for me. Your clerk—the young guy?"

"Casey."

"He saw me trying to sneak into the inn to talk to you. He handed me the note. I thought it was from Mom or Oma, trying to convince me to turn myself in. I didn't even open it until I left the inn. It only referred to 'the girl.' At first, I thought it meant someone had Dana. I was scared out of my mind and burst into the house. But she was there. That was when I realized someone else was probably involved. I didn't tell Dana about it because she would have wanted to leave immediately. But I knew it had to come to an end."

"You could have just turned yourselves in."

He smiled sadly. "Dana would never have agreed. Never."

"Why didn't you hand the note over to the police?"

"I didn't trust them. They would have twisted it around and said I wrote the note or something. I knew I could trust you to do the right thing. For a minute there, when I was trying to get your attention, I thought I had blown it!"

"Radar led us to her last night."

"Radar? You're kidding!"

At the mention of his name, Radar jumped up and ambled over to Josh, who ruffled his fur.

"We think the kidnapper might have taken Radar, too. He found his way out, and last night, he stood right there—" I pointed at the shore across from us "—and barked. He even jumped in the water and tried to swim over here. I think he was glad when he saw the boat approaching because he turned around and swam back to shore. Which leads me to believe that he didn't swim over here the two nights he came by himself. Did you bring him and leave him here?"

"No. I don't have a clue how he got over here."

The door behind us banged open and Amelia bustled through carrying a huge tray.

She placed it on another table. "Cook sent these for you to try. They're pancakes made with healthy stuff." She placed a plate in front of each of us, along with a carafe of maple syrup. "He sent tuna for Twinkletoes and mini meatballs and scrambled eggs for Trixie and Radar. Is that okay? I can get you something else if you'd prefer."

"That's fine!" I was itching to dig into the pancakes. "Thank you so much!"

"Looks great." Josh already had a fork in his hand.

The pancakes were as delicious as they looked. Pillowy and comforting.

While we ate, Holmes arrived. "Josh! Glad they sprung you. How do you feel?"

"Guilty."

Holmes's grin faded.

"Guilty because I'm here soaking in the sunshine, breathing the mountain air, and eating a gourmet breakfast while Dana is in a concrete cell eating gruel."

"I mean this in the nicest way, Josh," said Holmes. "But if I were in your shoes, I wouldn't be saying I felt guilty. That's likely to be misinterpreted."

Josh smiled at him. "Good advice. It's great to see you, Holmes."

Amelia brought Holmes a stack of pancakes and a mug of coffee. She refilled my mug with tea, and Josh's with coffee.

When she left, Holmes tilted his head at me. "Any word on Shelley?"

"We found Shelley last night." I told them about the root cellar.

"Wow. How did we miss that when we were kids?" asked Holmes. "It would have made a great fort."

"It was probably grown over. It looks like it's been there for a very long time." I sipped my tea and watched as Josh finished every last crumb of the pancakes. "Josh, you said you'd like to bring this to an end. The easiest way to do that would be to tell us where the flash drive is."

Thirty

❧ ❧ ❧ ❧

He looked up at me with those clear blue eyes. "I don't know. I'm not sure there is one. Dana insists that she didn't steal anything."

"She also gave you a fake name and told you she was married to Mack Carrington. His name is Nate and they were never married." I sounded a bit harsh, but it was true.

"I don't know. I never saw a flash drive."

So much for that brilliant idea.

"So are the police going to set up a sting tonight?" asked Josh.

"One would think so. Dave wrecked his leg and spent the night at the hospital. I spoke to him this morning. He's coming back today, but the timing is terrible. Maybe Sergeant Hayward will handle it."

Holmes made a choking noise. "Not a chance. You know Dave will want to be in charge. Especially since Hayward has been making noises about taking over Dave's position."

"Do you have any suspects?" asked Josh.

I took a deep breath. "There's a nice lady staying with us named Judy Davis. I never imagined that she might be involved, but last night she wanted to know if I had received the envelope she shoved under my door."

Holmes nearly spewed his coffee. "No way!" He laughed aloud. "I've spent a lot of time with Judy and trust me, she's terrific. Besides, she's petite like you are. I can't see her strangling anyone."

"I hope you have better possibilities than that," said Josh.

"There's Nate. He has the most motive because he wants his flash drive back. He seems really nice, but he did lie to us about who he was. I guess he could have kidnapped Shelley and written ransom notes. But I can't see him murdering anyone."

"Holly," Holmes said sweetly, "*someone* killed two people. Two innocent people. It's really sweet of you to think everyone is so nice they couldn't have done the evil act, but *someone* did."

I gazed at Josh. I didn't want to come right out and say it, but I couldn't eliminate him. He could have murdered to save his beloved Dana.

I moved on. "And there are the Mellor brothers, Paul and Ted. They've been acting odd. Like they're afraid of being seen. And I did see them behind the church with a shovel."

Holmes leaned back against his chair and cradled his coffee mug in his hands. "I forgot about them. A friend of mine followed them around yesterday. He confirmed what you're saying. They dodged in and out of places and were always looking over their shoulders. He lost them when they went into the woods. He wondered if they had noticed him and were trying to shake him."

Josh brightened up. "Two guys? The shovel certainly sounds suspicious. And it would be a lot easier for two guys to cart a drugged woman around."

"Holmes, could we set up sort of a tag team to follow them? That way it wouldn't look like the same person all the time."

Holmes nodded eagerly. "Great idea, Holly! I'll set that up right now." He pulled out his phone.

I felt guilty about having them followed again. I was convinced that someone had been following me around and it had unnerved me to the point that I ran to Nate and Zelda for security.

"Now what's wrong?" asked Holmes.

"Do I show all my emotions that clearly?"

Holmes smiled at me. "Maybe I just know how to read you."

"It's nothing. I thought someone was following me. It's a creepy feeling."

"Maybe you should stick around the inn until we catch this person or persons," said Holmes.

"No one is going to harm me now. I'm the person who is supposed to deliver the flash drive tonight."

"We need Dave!" said Holmes. "You can't do this without the police on hand, waiting for him."

"We have a much bigger problem than that. We don't have the flash drive."

"Dana must have it." Holmes looked at Josh.

Josh threw his hands up in the air. "I never saw one. I swear."

"Here's what we'll do." I started stacking dishes to take them to the kitchen. "Josh, you stay here. Holmes, you go to work on the Davis house and set up your friends to tail Paul and Ted. I will check around town to see if I can find a flash drive that looks like the one Nate showed Dave and me. We could try to pass it off as the original. One of the pet stores might carry them. They're very cute."

Josh groaned. "What am I supposed to do?"

"Call me as soon as Dave shows up." I didn't wait for him to grouse more. I picked up the dishes and carried them into the kitchen, where I complimented Cook on his pancakes. After thanking Cook and Amelia, I made sure Oma was available to watch the inn.

I went up to my apartment to grab my purse and a shopping bag, so I would look legit. Before I left the inn, I called Dave to ask if he had checked the evidence room at the police station for the flash drive. He sounded groggy but was sufficiently alert to say he had looked but it wasn't there.

Trixie followed me out of the inn, but Twinkletoes settled in the sunshine on the front porch to sunbathe.

It would be easy enough to pretend I was still shopping for guests attending the Cat Fest. I suspected the paw-shaped flash drive was actually a cat's paw, but it had been my experience that most people didn't really differentiate between a cat's paw and a dog's paw. As long as it was the right shape and had pads on it, they assumed it was the paw of whichever animal they preferred. In reality, the biggest difference in paws, mostly useful for tracking, is that cat claws can be withdrawn. Most cat tracks don't show four little pierced dots. But dogs, who cannot withdraw their claws, will leave claw marks on surfaces.

Consequently, I browsed in stores that carried items for both dogs and cats, as well as specialty shops. Trixie happily tagged along, enjoying the treats she was offered.

My little shopping expedition worked to my advantage in one other respect. On the busy sidewalk, it was hard to tell if someone was following me. But I had the opportunity to pop in and out of stores and became convinced that someone was watching me.

I darted into the drugstore and picked up Trixie. Sure enough, someone walked by, craning his neck to see inside the plate-glass window.

Thirty-One

❈ ❈ ❈

But it wasn't the person I expected. Not Nate or one of the Mellor brothers. The pudgy man craning to see inside the store was none other than Sergeant Hayward.

Well! Two could play this game. Still holding Trixie, I left the drugstore and intentionally bumped into the sergeant by sideswiping him. "Oh! I am so sorry. My apologies, Sergeant."

I thought I saw a moment of unease pass over his face. "No problem. I'm fine."

"I'm so sorry. I had other things on my mind and wasn't watching where I was going. But you know, I'm glad that I ran into you." I smiled sweetly. "Pardon the pun. I think someone is following me!"

This man had better not play poker, because the look of apprehension on his face was priceless.

"I wouldn't worry about it too much. There are so many people shopping that it's probably just your imagination."

"I don't think so. I think it might be you."

He feigned a laugh, short and coarse. "I'm just out here doing my job. You know better than most that there has been some unpleasantness in Wagtail. And now your cousin is back in our midst and capable of committing another murder. I need to keep an eye on him."

"Isn't that what the ankle bracelet is for?"

He stared at me, his jaw muscles twitching. "Now see here, I intend to do my job. And I *will* nail him. It's just a matter of time. The only question is who his next victim will be. Let's hope it's not you."

I hoped I didn't show my unease at his words. "Quit stalking me or I will turn you in." I hurried off to the next store and watched the window, but he didn't even pass by.

As it turned out, I was so perturbed by Sergeant Hayward that I almost missed the flash drives at Purrfectly Meowvelous because they were so small. They were cute, though. White with little pink pad marks on them, they looked more like toys than anything that might contain passwords to millions of dollars. For a moment, I was struck by the sheer dumb luck of finding the exact same flash drive. But then I realized they were probably made by the hundreds of thousands in China and sold all over the world. They were inexpensive, so I bought several to add to our Cat Fest gift baskets.

On our way home, Trixie made a detour to her favorite ice cream place. She gazed at me with those sweet brown eyes and drummed her front paws in eager anticipation. How could I say no?

We went inside and I was shocked to find Nate there with Lucy and Lucy-the-dog.

No! What was Lucy doing with Nate? I should have told her about him. Thank goodness nothing had happened to her. My pulse raced. How would I get her away? What excuse could I use? "Hi!"

Both of the Lucys seemed very happy. Nate and Lucy, the person, were sitting at a table, eating ice cream sundaes. Lucy-the-dog sat on a chair and licked a scoop of dog ice cream that Lucy held still for her. White cream dripped off the dog's red muzzle.

Trixie placed her paws on Lucy-the-dog's chair. Her tail wagged wildly. Lucy-the-dog kept her temper, but she gave Trixie a little growl.

"Come join us," said Lucy.

"Thanks, we will." I bought a mini ice cream for Trixie and since I was there, I indulged in a cone of salted caramel ice cream.

Nate pulled up two chairs for us.

"Thanks!" We sat down to join them. "Looks like Lucy is feeling much better than on the day we found her."

"She has totally come out of her shell. It's really amazing." Lucy sounded perkier than she had since she arrived. "Nate says you can study to be an animal behaviorist. Did you know that? I'm going to look into that."

I smiled at Lucy. "That would be great! And so interesting."

"I could come live in Wagtail and work with animals who have behavioral problems. I wish we knew what happened to Lucy. She's such a happy dog now."

Nate grinned at her before he turned to me. "I went to visit Phoebe this morning."

I hadn't expected that. "How did it go?"

"Same old Phoebe. Even in an orange jumpsuit, she cannot bring herself to tell the truth."

"What did she say?"

"Aww, she denied taking the flash drive. I told her the

hotel cameras caught her. She won't be able to overcome that evidence. Even when I told her the French would try to extradite her, all she said was, "At least the food will be better."

"Can they do that?" asked Lucy, wide-eyed.

Nate tilted his head from side to side. "I'm not sure. If she committed the murders in Wagtail, then she'll have to serve her sentences for those first. A crime has to hit a certain level before the French will bother with extradition. Given the value of what's on the flash drive, I think they might."

He certainly spoke as if he was innocent. Or was he simply confident now that Phoebe/Dana was in jail awaiting trial on murders he had committed?

"My real concern is the flash drive. I don't know if the cops have it or if she hid it somewhere. And the really bad thing is that it could be anywhere. Paris, Turkey, Greece, all the places they went, or right here in Wagtail. My initial suspicion was that she would have brought it with her to the U.S. I still think that's most likely. It would be too dangerous to leave it in a place she might not be able to return to quickly. Phoebe is smart. She considers these things. She wouldn't have entrusted it to anyone."

"Not even to Josh?" asked Lucy.

"I don't think he has it," I said.

The dogs had finished their ice cream treats. They jumped to the floor and played, both tails wagging.

"He's coming around to the realization that Dana is actually Phoebe. He's worried about her. I honestly think that if he had the flash drive, he might give it up in exchange for Phoebe's safety."

"I'm sticking around for another couple of days. I've decided to give Phoebe one more shot at telling me, but this time, I'll offer her money. They say everyone has a price, right? I figure that she'll realize money in hand is a better bet than spending her life trying to break the passwords and possibly never getting a dime."

At that moment, Lucy-the-dog must have been trying to look in my shopping bag, because she knocked it over and the little animal-paw flash drives slid out of the bag and onto the floor.

Thirty-Two

❀ ❀ ❀

Lucy-the-dog took one in her mouth and ran around the ice cream parlor, teasing Trixie and trying to keep it away from her.

I would never forget Nate's face when he saw all the flash drives. At first he was surprised, and then his eyebrows furrowed in confusion, and finally his eyes met mine and I could see suspicion mingling with anger.

I kneeled on the floor and stuffed them back in the bag. Trying to make light of it, I said to Lucy-the-dog, "You're a curious little girl."

"What . . . I don't understand," said Nate.

I reminded myself that he could be the person who kidnapped Shelley. Or worse, the murderer. "The Cat Fest is coming up this weekend. They're so cute. I thought they would be a nice addition to our gift baskets." I hoped I had sounded breezy and not as flustered as I felt. I hadn't done anything wrong, but now that I thought about it, I could see how Nate might jump to a different conclusion. And worse than that, if he had written the notes, now he would know we were trying to pass off a look-alike flash drive that was blank.

"They're darling," Lucy exclaimed.

But the long, long moment of silence that followed was awkward and a little scary. I plucked one out of the bag and handed it to Lucy. "I'm glad you like them. Here's one for you. Maybe it will come in handy for schoolwork."

Nate continued to stare at me. I had the awful feeling that he was trying to gauge my involvement and intentions.

He rose to his feet. "Thanks for meeting with me, Lucy, and for bringing Lucy-the-dog. She landed with the right person."

And then he walked out.

"He's so nice, isn't he?" blathered Lucy.

My phone pealed, letting me know a text had come in. It was from Dave.

Meet me at the inn at 1PM?

I let him know I would be there. And then I would have to tell him that I had probably just blown the pickup for tonight, ruining all chances to catch the kidnapper and possibly the killer if it was Nate.

"It's almost lunchtime. Are you ready to head back to the inn?"

"Sure." Lucy stood up and placed the flash drive in her purse.

As we walked out of the ice cream parlor, Lucy said, "It must be nice living in the inn. I'm getting spoiled by having someone do all the cooking." And then she said, "Holly, how would you feel about Dad getting back to-gether with your mom?"

I nearly dropped my shopping bag. "What are you talking about?"

"It's just that they're together all the time. And Dad looks so happy. He's been a wreck ever since my mom left him."

I guessed I was the one who should be doing the wishful thinking since they were both my parents. But I was old enough to be far more realistic. "I wouldn't get my hopes up, Lucy. A week isn't very long in terms of matters of the heart. They're probably just remembering the good times."

"I don't know. I see the way they look at each other."

They did seem to be spending a lot of time together. "That's the problem with vacations. In a few days, you'll be back home in Florida, and everything will go back to normal."

She heaved a great sigh. "I hope not. Our normal was pretty sad."

As if fate meant to prove something to me, when we returned to the inn, my parents sat side by side on the sofa in the inn office. Lucy immediately told them all about seeing Nate and having ice cream and how she might study animal behavior.

Oma, Mom, and Dad listened, smiling at her youthful enthusiasm.

When they were through expressing their excitement over the possibility that she might become an animal behaviorist, Dad asked, "Any news on Shelley?"

"I spoke to Dave this morning. I think she'll be okay, except for the psychological trauma."

"I am shocked," said Oma. "How could anyone do something so horrible? Thank goodness you found her before she was killed. It is so barbaric. I shudder to imagine it. Our poor Shelley." Oma looked at her watch. "It is past time for lunch. You three go ahead and get a table. Holly, I need a word with you, please."

Mom, Dad, Lucy, and Lucy-the-dog departed together.

I knew something was up because Oma liked to take her lunch in the office.

"Close the door, Holly."

I did as she asked.

"Dave called me this morning. He will be bringing Shelley here instead of to her home. He does not wish for anyone to see her enter the inn. We have decided the best choice is to bring her in through the private kitchen and take her upstairs to your apartment. Dave, since he is not very mobile and must keep his leg up, will stay there with her. Two police officers will be acting like guests of the inn around the clock. I am very sorry to inconvenience you, but my apartment is already quite crowded with Josh and Margaret. If you wish to sleep in a guest room or perhaps at your mother's home, I would certainly understand."

"He thinks the kidnapper will come for her?" I asked, trying to follow this new development.

"Possibly. But only five of us will know that she is here. Dave, the two of us, Shelley, and Mr. Huckle, who can be trusted to be discreet and will bring her whatever she needs. They have police officers positioned in the woods to guard the root cellar, since that is the place her kidnapper would most likely go, either to check on her or to dope her up again. It is imperative that no one know she is here so that the kidnapper will proceed on the assumption she is still there. You are to meet Dave at one, exactly, and take Shelley up to your apartment via the back stairs. All right?"

"Absolutely, I'm happy to help."

She looked at her watch again. "Better get going. I'll cover for Zelda while she has lunch."

I nodded and called Trixie, who gladly romped through the main lobby, dispelling any thoughts of police on guard to anyone who might be watching. Just another happy dog in Wagtail. I eyed people as we walked through the inn, wondering which ones might be police. The dining tables were full, which wasn't terribly surprising. A lot of people liked our food and the ambiance.

I pushed open the door to the private kitchen. It was quiet and calm. Twinkletoes had taken refuge there and stretched when we entered. She wound around my ankles, mewing. I was pretty sure she was saying "Lunchtime. Food, please."

The magic refrigerator yielded something called Kitty Cod, Please and a larger bowl marked Doggone Good, which turned out to be beef chunks, chicken bits, and sardines mixed with macaroni. The name suited it because Trixie ate like she'd never seen food that good.

I made myself a turkey sandwich. While I was spreading mayonnaise, it dawned on me that Dave and Shelley probably hadn't eaten, so I made more sandwiches and warmed up a spring soup that had beans, carrots, and spinach in it. I checked the time. I still had a few minutes and carried a loaded tray upstairs to my apartment. I placed the soup on a burner to keep warm.

I returned to the kitchen and wanted to step outside to see if they were nearby yet, but I knew that was wrong. I couldn't afford to have it look as though I was waiting for someone. The clock over the stove made little clicking sounds as it ticked off the minutes. I had never noticed that before.

At two minutes past one, a man wearing a hoodie and using crutches, and a woman with a scarf pulled forward to hide most of her face, appeared at the door. I opened it for them and closed it as soon as Dave had hobbled inside.

Shelley threw her arms around me. She sobbed and I struggled not to join her. "I'm so glad you're all right," I whispered.

"Is Radar here? I owe him the world."

"He's not in the kitchen, but I'll try to sneak him up-stairs later on. Dave, are you going to be able to walk up two flights of stairs?"

"I'm not looking forward to it. But it's the only way. I shouldn't be seen here."

"Can I help, or do you need to do it on your own?"

"I can help him," said Shelley.

I gazed around. "Where is Duchess?"

"With my mom. Bringing her here was too risky. It would give away our location."

I opened the door to the stairs. Trixie and Twinkletoes raced ahead of them. I closed the door behind them in case anyone came into the private kitchen, then gathered some sodas as well as cheese and crackers to nosh on. At the last minute I grabbed a platter of chocolate chip cookies and, taking care to close the door behind me, followed them upstairs.

When I reached my dining room, Shelley was saying, "I can't believe my kidnapper hasn't been back to check on me."

Dave scowled. "All I can imagine is that he caught wind of the police presence out there last night."

I unloaded the sodas and food in my kitchen, which was open to the living room. "Are you saying he might have been camped out there or that he lived nearby and saw the police and rescue commotion?"

"That's entirely possible. Or he knew someone out that way who mentioned it to him."

"Maybe someone at the hospital unwittingly told him."

"Also possible. At this point, speculating why he hasn't returned isn't as important as being ready to catch him tonight."

This was the time I had been dreading. Having to tell Dave that Nate had seen the flash drives I bought. "Um,

Dave, should I lift your foot onto the ottoman so it will be elevated?"

"Would you?" he asked sweetly.

The cast on his leg was heavier than I expected but I managed to lift his leg. "Soup and sandwiches?"

"That would be great." Shelley stood up. "Let me help you."

"No need. It's all done." I pulled out some trays to make eating on the sofa more comfortable and set them up, then served the soup and brought in the sandwiches and sodas.

When they were eating, I sat near Dave. "I've been worried about what we can put in the bag of dog cookies since we don't have the flash drive. This morning, I went shopping and found the exact flash drive that Nate used." I took out the bag and plucked one from it.

"Those are cute!" said Shelley.

I laid it on Dave's tray. "They're a perfect match. On my way back, I treated Trixie to some ice cream and found Nate and Lucy there. Lucy's new dachshund sort of plunged into my shopping bag and the flash drives slid out of it."

Dave stopped eating. "You had a good idea, but it's a problem now. What did you tell him?"

"That I bought some for our guests who would be arriving for Cat Fest."

"Now if it's Nate who sent the notes, he'll suspect that the flash drive in the bag isn't the one he wants. That it's one of the new ones you bought today." Dave sighed.

"I'm really sorry. I set the bag on the floor and little Lucy just toppled it to get inside."

"There's nothing we can do about it now. Did you ever follow up with Judy Davis about the note?"

"No. I'll tackle that now." I left the two of them and hurried downstairs to Judy's room, with Twinkletoes and Trixie following me.

I knocked on Judy's door twice. She didn't respond. I texted Holmes to ask if Judy happened to be at the house he was building. He replied with a swift Yes.

I walked to the registration desk examining the face of each person I passed. Police? Friend? Or killer? My heart was pounding. I decided to take a golf cart. It wasn't a long walk, but I thought I could get away from someone faster in a golf cart than on foot. Not that the golf carts were particularly speedy, but they could go faster than I could run.

Dad happened to be standing in the registration lobby. "Where are you off to?"

I nabbed a golf cart key. "Over to the house Holmes is building. Want to come along?"

"Sure."

We walked out to the golf cart. Trixie and Twinkletoes hopped inside.

Dad shook his head. "I can't get over how your pets just go with you everywhere. They didn't even balk about getting into the golf cart."

I smiled. "They're used to it. Thanks for your help last night, Dad. I appreciated having you along."

"I was glad to be useful. Especially since Dave was on crutches. How he managed out there in the dark on uneven terrain is beyond me."

"He wrecked his leg again last night."

"I was afraid that might happen. Gotta give the guy a lot of credit. I don't know if I'd have held up as well as he did."

We pulled up in front of Judy's house.

"Wow. Nice!" Dad disembarked and studied the house.

It had a wide front porch and large windows that let in a lot of light. We walked to the front door. I knocked and opened the door at the same time. "Anyone home?"

"Back here," called Holmes.

Since my previous visit when Josh and Dana/Phoebe were hiding out there, drywall had gone up on some of the walls. It looked much more like a real house inside now. I could hear people working on it. We followed the sound of Holmes's voice to a large bathroom.

"How nice! You're my first guests!" Judy held tiles in her hands. "You're just in time to help me. I thought I wanted the bathrooms to be all white, but then Holmes showed me these beautiful glass tiles in turquoise shades."

"That's a tough choice. They're both lovely."

"Now I don't know what to do." Judy held up a turquoise tile and a white tile and studied them.

"Holmes, would you mind giving Dad a quick tour? Would that be okay, Judy?"

"Yes, of course!"

Judy propped the tiles up against the wall and focused on them. "I don't know. Do you think the white is too boring?"

"You can always buy turquoise towels and other accents."

"That's what I thought. But the turquoise tile is lovely. Holmes says we could use it as an accent if I think it would be overwhelming."

"Judy, last night you told me that you slipped a note under my door."

"Yes, I did. You do live upstairs on the third floor, right?"

"Yes. You had the right door." I didn't know quite how to broach this. "Can we talk about what the note said?"

She gave me an odd look. "How would I know? I didn't read it."

"Did you write it?"

"No. Wasn't it signed?" She lined up a few turquoise tiles.

"Where did you get the note?"

"In the registration lobby. No one else was there. I had Sassy and Patience with me on their leashes. You know how Sassy is. She jumped up on the registration desk and sent that envelope flying. I saw your name on it and thought I'd bring it up to you so it wouldn't get lost."

Judy tore herself away from the tiles. "Was that the wrong thing to do? I'm sorry if I erred."

"No. It was just fine. If I had been in your shoes, I probably would have done the same thing."

"That's a relief. Why are you asking me where I got it? Was it bad news?"

I nodded. "Yes, you could say that." I didn't think she was lying to me.

"I'm sorry that I was the bearer of bad news. I was only trying to be helpful."

"And you were. So which tile do you like better?"

"I'm thinking of using the white but having a horizontal band of turquoise in the shower."

"An excellent compromise. It won't overpower anything, and you can still add additional touches of turquoise if you like."

Holmes and Dad returned in time to hear what Judy had decided.

"Judy, this is a great place," said Dad. "I'm envious. I'd love to live in a house like this. I know you'll be very happy here."

"Thank you. Holmes gets all the credit." Judy smiled at him affectionately.

We thanked them and Holmes kissed me. Dad, Trixie, Twinkletoes, and I piled back into the golf cart and headed to the inn.

On the way, Dad said, "Holly, I believe I've been wrong about Holmes. Imagine being able to create something as spectacular as that house."

"Thanks, Dad. The better you get to know him, the more you'll like him."

He laughed. "That's what your mother told me."

Time ticked by slowly that day as we waited for nine o'clock to roll around. I busied myself by adding the flash drives to the baskets I had prepared.

Officer Dave made sure plenty of plainclothes police officers would be in the area and following me when I brought the flash drive to the bench as instructed. He even made sure I would be wearing a bulletproof vest. I thought that was probably unnecessary, but it gave me a small degree of comfort, so I agreed.

At seven o'clock, Dave, Shelley, Oma, Mr. Huckle, and I were in my apartment. I could see the fear in Oma's eyes.

"It's all right," I assured her. "I'm only dropping it off. I won't be there when he collects it."

"That's probably true, Liesel," said Dave.

Oma frowned at Dave. "Did you question Dana about the flash drive? We could avoid all of this if she would tell you."

"Of course we did. She's not exactly cooperative and she's a liar. I wouldn't rely on anything she said. Nate plans to offer her money, but I doubt that she'll budge."

"Ugh. My poor Holly. I do not like this at all. If she is not there, then how will you know who picked it up?" she asked.

"There will be plainclothes police officers standing by and watching. In addition, we placed a camera on Farm & Fork today before dawn. I will be monitoring it from here."

"Ach! This is terrible. Such an awful person. I hope he goes to prison for a long time."

Mr. Huckle handed Oma a cup of tea. "Here, Liesel, this will help calm your nerves."

On the off chance that the kidnapper wasn't Nate, we placed one of the new flash drives I had purchased in the bag of doggy treats. The kidnapper wouldn't know it was empty until he got to a computer. Of course, hopefully it would never get that far, because the police would arrest him on the spot

At eight forty-five, I left the inn wearing pull-on running shoes, black jeans, and a long-sleeve black cotton top. No jewelry that could be tugged. No scarf, jacket, or purse. A tracking device was sewn into my panties, just in case something went haywire. I carried the bag of dog cookies.

As always at that time of evening, visitors to Wagtail strolled along the sidewalks, stopping in stores, window shopping, and going out for dinner or drinks. I was nervous, but all the people milling around gave me a feeling of security. It might have been a false impression, but I didn't think anyone would be able to drug me and cart me off somewhere.

My heart pounded as I approached Farm & Fork.

Thirty-Three

* * * * *

No one sat on the bench. I knew a lot of police eyes were watching, but I didn't notice Nate or anyone else that I recognized hanging around. Holding my breath, I placed the cookie bag that contained a flash drive on the bench, turned around, and saw Sergeant Hayward watching me from only three feet away.

I was surprised to see him there. He wore his uniform as always. Had they not told him about the drop? Had they planted him to look normal? To protect all the people in the area?

My instructions had been to not interact with anyone. I walked away.

I was tempted to look back but thought I probably shouldn't. I merged into the crowds of people enjoying the night and strode home to the inn as fast as I could without attracting attention.

When I entered my apartment, Oma hugged me to her. "Liebchen, I am so glad you are safe. Dave has forbidden us from applauding or cheering, but we are very proud of you."

"Good job, Holly," said Dave.

Shelley and Mr. Huckle chimed in to praise me.

"It wasn't really any big deal." I shed the heavy vest, glad to have the weight off me. "Did anyone pick it up?"

"Not yet," said Dave. "Not yet." He grumbled, "What does he think he's doing?" He spoke into his phone. "Tell Hayward to get out of there!"

Dave, Shelley, and Mr. Huckle watched the camera monitor. I joined them. It was an excellent view. Even with all the people walking by the bench, it was high enough to see the bag clearly. And, unfortunately, to see a portly uniformed cop hanging around watching people.

Sergeant Hayward must have finally received the message that he needed to move on. He turned and walked out of the image, toward the Green.

For the next two hours the four of us watched the screen and munched on goodies that Mr. Huckle retrieved from the kitchen. Oma and Mr. Huckle finally begged off. Oma returned to her apartment and Mr. Huckle headed home.

Shelley, still tired from her ordeal, slipped off to bed in my guest room around midnight.

I fell asleep on the sofa and didn't wake until the first rays of sun crept into the sky.

Dave was still awake watching the monitor. The sidewalk was almost empty. A few early risers jogged by.

"I guess no one picked it up?"

"Only a Great Dane. His owner put it back."

"I can't believe this. That must mean it was Nate. He saw all the flash drives I bought when they fell out of the bag and knew I would be bringing a fake one." I shook my head, upset with myself. "After everything Dana-slash-Phoebe has done, I have to admit that I don't care for her at all. It breaks my heart that Josh is enamored by her. But now it looks like she might have been right all along. Not about everything, which makes it so confusing, but Nate was after her and I didn't believe her. If she just hadn't lied and run off and . . . we let her down."

Dave sucked in a big breath of air and let it out. "Not necessarily. It's a good thing this is on tape. At least it can be used in training classes to show how to bungle a drop. I have no idea why Hayward showed up. He clearly knew about the drop or he wouldn't have hung around watching."

"Dave, Hayward has been following me." I told him about my encounter with Hayward when I dodged into the drugstore. "And he's been hanging out at the inn a lot. Is it possible . . ." I didn't finish my sentence because it was so unlikely.

"That he's the murderer or the kidnapper?"

"It was stupid of me to think that."

"No. It wasn't." Dave looked at me with weary eyes. "I've been thinking about this all night. When did Hayward first show up here?"

"After Frank Burton was murdered and you were injured. He was angry because your team had already cleared the room and taken Frank's belongings."

Dave scratched his head. "I think that fits."

"I'm not following. Are you saying that Hayward murdered Frank?"

"I don't know. It's a possibility. Or he could have seen it as a means of getting the Wagtail job that he wants if he solves the case."

"Why would he follow me?"

Dave chuckled softly. "You and Trixie have a reputation for solving murders. He probably hoped that he would be able to piece it together based on what you were doing. Don't you see, Holly? He had access to all the police reports. He knew what we were planning. He might look like a tired older cop, but he's not dumb. He knew he wasn't supposed to be there last night. But he must not have known about the camera we installed."

"Or maybe he planned to pick up the package."

Dave's eyes met mine. "That would explain why he hovered around it until he received an order to leave the vicinity and he knew we were watching. He *couldn't* take it then."

"What now?" I asked.

The sound of a key in the door startled us. Mr. Huckle swung the door open and rolled a serving cart inside. "Good morning!"

He closed the door and whispered, "Did we catch our man?"

"I'm afraid not," said Dave.

"That's a shame. I had such high hopes. I brought Holly's usual request as you instructed."

"You need it, Dave. I'll shower and head downstairs for breakfast." I left them in my living room and got ready for the day.

I reappeared forty-five minutes later in a red-and-white floral wrap dress with three-quarter-length sleeves.

Shelley, wrapped in a fluffy white Sugar Maple Inn bathrobe, sat curled up on a chair. "I wish I could remember, Dave. All I know is that he came up behind me in my house. I remember him placing a cloth over my nose and mouth. I tried to scream and then I guess I passed out. The next thing I recall was waking up in the root cellar and drifting off again. It was too dark to see much in there, but I think I was alone."

I hugged her. "I'm so sorry that happened to you."

"I'm all right now. I'll be okay. But Carole won't be. Or Frank."

"I'm going downstairs for breakfast." I saw Dave starting to speak. "Don't worry. I won't say a word." Trixie and Twinkletoes sped out the door and down the stairs ahead of me. I walked outside with them for their potty break. While I waited, I heard voices. Men's voices. It was none of my business, of course, but I tried to make out what they were saying.

"We were doing so well and now this."

"Not all is lost yet."

"But what if the press finds out and there are cameras all over the place?"

"We can't let that stop us."

Where were they?

Suddenly, Paul Mellor's head popped up from behind a giant holly bush. His brother peeked over it, too. As soon as they noticed me, the two of them ducked again.

Thirty-Four

❁ ❁ ❁

Oma had drilled into Josh, Holmes, and me that guests came first, and we were always to be polite to them, no matter what odd thing they said or did. I still adhered to that rule. But I had had about enough of the peculiar Mellors.

"Hi!" I said cheerily. "Can I help you with something?"

Looking as if he felt rather sheepish, Paul emerged from his hiding spot, followed by his brother, Ted, who quickly said, "We were digging for worms."

"I see." I left it at that but met Paul's gaze straight on.

"You must think we're very odd," said Paul.

I crossed my arms. "A little."

"We're looking for the Andre Kowalska fortune." As soon as Paul spoke, Ted punched him in the arm.

"Oww!"

"Why don't you just paste it on a billboard?" said Ted.

"She won't say anything. Will you?" Paul asked.

"I don't know. I've never heard of this fortune."

"Now look what you've done. There is no fortune. Absolutely not," said Ted.

Paul elbowed him. "She's not stupid. She can look it up. I'm sorry if we've seemed kind of strange. Andre Kowalska buried a million dollars in gold somewhere. He left cryptic clues and we figured out that one of them leads to Wagtail Mountain."

"Shut up! Do you want her to be the one who finds it?" Ted rolled his eyes.

"There are hundreds of people looking for it, with TV crews following them. We got a head start when we realized it was on Wagtail Mountain. We peeled off from the crowd, so we're way ahead of everyone," Paul explained. "Which was why we didn't want you to let anyone know we were here. But we just saw Alicia and Don Michaelson, which means others won't be far behind and this place will be swarming with treasure hunters soon."

Ted threw up his arms. "Well, that's it. You have blown our chances. Why did I think you would be a good partner?" He brushed off his clothes. "My brother is a congenital liar. He makes up stories about hidden fortunes."

I couldn't help smiling. I pulled out my phone and Googled the Andre Kowalska fortune. Sure enough, loads of articles popped up. "The good news is that I really don't have time to look for a mysterious fortune. Don't worry, I'll keep your secret. I'll even wish you luck!"

Ted eyed me. "Do you know where there's a stone with an arrow carved on it that points north?"

"Really? Now *you're* handing her clues?" asked Paul.

"She said she's not interested," replied his brother.

I didn't have any idea. But I played along, mentally apologizing to Henry Wadsworth Longfellow for mangling his beautiful poem. "I shot an arrow into the air. It fell to earth near a hare."

As I walked away, I heard them arguing.

"Did you write that down?"

"Was that 'hair' like on your head or 'hare' like a bunny?"

"Where would a hair from someone's head be? Or is that some kind of euphemism for something else? A clue!"

I called Trixie and Twinkletoes and went to eat breakfast.

Oma, Dad, Ben, both Lucys, and Gingersnap were already there. I waved at Judy Davis, who was eating a stack of pancakes that looked like the ones Cook tried out on Holmes, Josh, and me the day before.

"Good morning." I slid into a chair. "I take it Aunt Margaret is watching over Josh?"

"They were up late last night, watching a silly movie and munching on popcorn. It reminded me of when he was a little boy." Oma smiled. "I never would have wished this situation on anyone, but perhaps this is a small ray of sunshine in our dark cloud. They are enjoying being together again."

"I've certainly enjoyed being here," said Ben. "Wagtail has a certain charm. I like the closeness of the people who live here. You don't get that much in the city."

"I'll second that." Dad sipped his coffee. "I don't know what I'll do when Lucy goes off to school next fall. I'll be rattling around in our house all by myself."

"Oh, Dad. You know I'll be home to visit all the time."

She said it with a sad smile, and I suspected she was thinking of her mother and how much she missed her. "You know, I could go to a school closer to home and live with you. It would save a lot of money."

"Oh no, you don't." Dad patted her hand. "I will not do that to you. You need to spread your sweet wings and fly without your old dad peering over your shoulder all the time. You're only young once, darlin', and I want you to take full advantage of it and explore the world."

Amelia arrived to take my order. "Sorry I'm so slow

this morning. Seems like a lot of people are checking out and trying to catch a morning flight. The specials today are the pancakes you tried yesterday, mushroom frittata, and French toast with mixed berries."

I knew I should opt for the frittata, but the French toast was too tempting. I ordered it, along with tuna for Twinkletoes and meatballs with scrambled eggs for Trixie.

When Amelia left, Dad said, "I'll be very sorry to leave tomorrow, Mom. Maybe I can come up here more often."

"Sure, you say that now." Lucy gave her father an unhappy look. "Once we're home, you'll be a workaholic again."

Dad nodded. "Maybe that's why your mother left me."

"I'll be back to represent Josh at his trial," said Ben. "I've often wondered if we shouldn't open a branch office up here."

I didn't want to encourage him. Besides, I was thinking that Josh might not need a lawyer soon if Sergeant Hayward turned out to be the murderer.

After breakfast, I dashed upstairs to my apartment to brush my teeth. Mr. Huckle, Shelley, and Dave were eating breakfast.

"Shelley, you're taller than I am, but you're welcome to anything in my closet that will fit you."

"Thanks, Holly."

"I'm sorry I can't stay. It's a busy morning downstairs." I brushed my teeth and left in a flash for the reception lobby.

I checked out early birds, called for Wagtail taxis, and forced myself to focus on the work at hand. Shadow brought luggage down to the lobby and Marina began cleaning vacated rooms and placing the gift baskets in them. Zelda arrived for her shift and took over the checking-out function. Everyone who worked at the inn was in high gear.

We had a slight lull in the afternoon before the new guests arrived to check in. I was covering for Zelda while she grabbed a bite to eat when a group of ladies arrived in a succession of Wagtail taxis for our afternoon tea.

They gabbed enthusiastically. One of them, a sweet-looking woman a little older than my mom, I thought, wore an eye-catching scarf in vivid shades of red with a zebra pouncing into the center. Her friends raved over it.

"It's a genuine Hermès!" she told them. "Brendan just flew in from Paris and brought it as a gift for me."

"He must be doing well, then," observed one of her friends. "They're very expensive."

"Has he gotten engaged to his girlfriend yet?" asked another.

The woman looked disappointed. "He hasn't said much about her. You know how sensitive our children can be when we pry about their romances. I'm under the impression that relationship might be over. He's picking me up here later. I'm hoping I can swing the conversation in that direction."

They started toward the main lobby when two words connected in my head. Brendan and Paris. There must be a lot of Brendans. That was a popular name.

Before I even gave it much thought, I called out, "Mrs. Hayward?"

The woman turned around. "Yes?"

I fumbled for something to say. "I thought that might be you. How is Brendan?"

"He's fine, thank you for asking."

"We certainly enjoyed having him here. Please give him our best and tell him we hope to see him again soon."

She stared at me. "Brendan was here? When did he stay with you?"

Uh-oh. "Earlier this week."

She brightened. "It must be another Brendan Hayward. My Brendan only flew in from France on Tuesday. Isn't that funny? What are the odds." She bustled off to join her friends.

What were the odds indeed.

Thirty-Five

I could hardly wait for Zelda to return from her break.

The minute she showed up, I tore upstairs to my apartment. Trixie and Twinkletoes raced alongside me.

I unlocked the door and let myself in. "Dave!"

He looked up from his laptop.

"It's the wrong Hayward. The killer is Brendan Hay-. ward, not his dad!" I told him about meeting Brendan's mother. "She thinks he only arrived from Paris on Tuesday, but we know he was here. He must have followed Frank Burton. Or figured out on his own that Josh and Dana would be coming here."

"Why would he want to kill Frank Burton?"

I sat down. I hadn't thought this through completely and thought aloud. "He stayed here at the inn while he murdered Frank and Carole. When he kidnapped Shelley, he went home to stay with his parents so he would have an alibi. His dad must have blabbed to him about the fake drop last night. That's why he didn't show up."

"That doesn't make sense. If he wanted an alibi, why wouldn't he have stayed with his parents when he murdered Frank and Carole?"

"Because he knew his parents would be watching him? He couldn't be out all night without them knowing?"

"Josh. If you're right, he'll be coming for Josh. Go get him and bring him here."

My heart thundered as I ran downstairs and along the corridor to Oma's apartment. Trixie and Twinkletoes kept up with me. I knocked on the door and tried to open it, but it was locked. "Josh, it's me, Holly. Open the door."

Maybe he wasn't there. He could be out on the terrace. But then I heard a bark. Radar! I knocked again. "Josh?"

I heard the latch clink open. Josh stared at me through a three-inch crack. He mouthed something at me and did that quirky thing with his head like he had when we were kids. Trixie pawed at the door. Radar barked again. I could hear someone whimpering.

Josh opened the door slowly, revealing Brendan Hayward behind him with one hand over Lucy's mouth and a knife in his other hand. My heart broke. "Let Lucy go. She has nothing to do with any of this. She's just a kid."

In a swift move, he released her and shoved her toward me. I caught Lucy in my arms and hugged her tight.

"You have lousy timing," said Brendan. "I didn't want to hurt you because of Holmes. He was always real nice to me."

"You don't have to hurt anyone. You can walk out right now. Did you know that your mom is downstairs having tea?"

"Mom? She said she was having tea with friends. I thought she meant at someone's house. Why doesn't anything work out for me?"

"You could leave right now, and we wouldn't stop you."

"He wants the flash drive," whispered Josh.

"I'll leave all right. But Josh is going with me. We're going to visit Roo. But now you had to walk in and mess everything up. Just like that Carole. I didn't want to kill her, either."

Either? That didn't sound good. "Why did you kill her?"

"She caught me coming in the night I murdered Frank. At first, I thought she bought my story about being on a date. But it weighed on me. It was sloppy. She would have ratted on me for sure. Just like you would. It was only a matter of time before she put it together."

Lucy let out a horrible wail and held me tighter.

I looked around the room for a weapon. Oma's doilies and embroidered pillows weren't any help. Pictures? A glass jar full of dog treats? My only chance was to keep him talking. If I was gone too long, maybe Dave would realize that something was wrong. "Why did you murder Frank? He seemed like a nice guy."

"It was me or him. I was trying to find Phoebe and kept seeing him. I realized that he was following them, too. So *I* followed *him*. We even flew back on the same plane. But he beat me to them and scared them off. I didn't need him anymore. Besides, if he caught them, he would have taken the flash drive and I wouldn't have anything for all my trouble. It was that Phoebe, or as some of you know her, Dana. What a number she was, eh, Josh?"

"What do you mean?" I asked.

"She used to be *my* girlfriend. She told me about Nate and how rich he was and how he had all this money that could only be accessed by the passwords on a flash drive. So the two of us, Phoebe and me, we cooked up a plan to get the flash drive. But Phoebe double-crossed me and stole the flash drive herself. Then she found this goon, Josh, and made him fly her all over the place. When I found out they were flying here, I knew it was my chance to catch up to Phoebe and get the flash drive from her."

"I see. You know, if the flash drive was on her, it would be at the police station now. Your dad could probably get it for you."

Brendan's eyes narrowed. "You're a slick one. I'm not falling for that. You two first."

Josh choked and started coughing.

I grabbed the jar of treats, clutched Lucy to me, hiding them, and we moved sideways as a unit. Brendan grabbed the collar on Josh's shirt. "Now real nice and quiet, we're all going to see Roo and you're going to give me the flash drive."

They shuffled behind us, out into the hallway and toward the curving stairs that led to the reception lobby.

In a tiny voice, Lucy asked, "Will he kill us?"

I whispered, "Hang tight onto handrail."

"Trixie, Radar, Lucy, come," I said softly. As soon as Brendan and Josh started down the stairs, I gave the dogs a sniff of the contents of the jar and threw the dog treats down the stairs by the handful. All three dogs scrambled heedlessly for the treats, getting underfoot. The noise attracted Gingersnap and Elvis, who immediately started up the stairs to take advantage of the treats that were raining down. Lucy and I held onto the handrail. Josh and Brendan tumbled forward. Josh managed to grab hold of the railing, but Brendan crashed all the way to the very bottom step and landed on his own knife.

Zelda and Lucy screamed. Shadow, Oma, and Mr. Huckle came running.

I was afraid Brendan could overpower us, but when he tried to move, he howled in pain.

While Shadow tied Brendan's hands behind his back with a leash, I called 911.

Thirty-Six

✿ ✿ ✿

The rescue squad was removing Brendan when Wagtail taxis pulled up with arriving guests.

Mr. Huckle rushed to sweep the remaining dog treats off the stairs. Shadow wiped up the blood. Oma ushered a shaken Lucy into the office while Zelda and I checked in the new arrivals and Shadow carried their luggage upstairs. I hoped that to the new arrivals, it simply looked like someone had an accident.

I took a minute to text Dave and Shelley about Brendan. They could come out of hiding now.

Dad, Lucy, and Mike would be leaving the next day. Oma wanted to take the whole family out to dinner, but Margaret, Ben, and Josh hadn't returned from Snowball yet. They hoped to have Josh's record cleared and his ankle monitor removed. And Josh hoped to spring Dana, whom he now called Phoebe.

We decided the best thing would be to order dinner when Aunt Margaret and the rest of them left Snowball. In the meantime, Shelley went home, and Dave, who was exhausted, headed for the police station in Snowball.

I tried to concentrate on work. Mom and Dad took Lucy and Lucy-the-dog out to a new dog bar where people could socialize while their dogs did the same. They hoped it would get her mind off the trauma she had gone through.

When five o'clock rolled around, I was glad for the lull in activity. The pet parade went on as usual. The guests went out to dinner as usual, and I settled on the terrace with a tall glass of iced tea. Trixie, Twinkletoes, and Radar roamed around.

I couldn't help looking across the lake. The inn skiff was still docked on that little pier. Maybe Shadow could borrow a boat and take me over there to retrieve it. A new tent had popped up exactly where Josh had pitched his tent. They had built a campfire and a black dog, probably a Labrador, sniffed around.

The door behind me opened. My family and a host of inn employees poured onto the terrace. Tables were rearranged and a buffet table was set up. Oma had ordered enough food for a hungry army from Hot Hog. Trixie wasn't the only one who loved that place.

To my surprise, Dave and Holmes showed up. And right after them, Aunt Margaret, Ben, Josh, and Dana, whom everyone was now calling by her real name, Phoebe. It dawned on me that the partly burned scrap of paper Trixie found in the smoldering campfire had probably had Phoebe's name on it. Frank had most likely discovered Dana's true identity.

I whispered to Ben, "What's Phoebe doing here?"

"Now that Brendan appears to be the killer, the police didn't have a reason to hold her."

"What about Nate's flash drive?" I asked Ben in a hushed voice.

He shrugged and whispered, "That's where it gets complicated. Phoebe committed the crime in France. So it's possible that the French could pursue the case and extradite her. There might be a means of pursuing her here in the U.S., but it's going to be complicated and not a sure thing. Nate had the right idea when he hired Frank. Eventually, Phoebe is going to go wherever she stashed it so she can retrieve it."

"She's free to leave town?"

"If she were smart, and I'm not so sure she is, she ought to stay out of France, and disappear quietly in the U.S."

Holmes interrupted to hug me. He held me tight, muttering all the appropriate things.

"I'm fine, I'm fine," I insisted. And I was fine.

He sat next to me at dinner, and thankfully, Dave slumped in the other seat next to me, forcing Ben farther away.

Naturally, the conversation turned to Brendan Hayward. He had suffered a spinal injury when he fell and, making matters worse, had fallen on his own knife, which severely injured his arm.

"They won't know the full extent of his spinal injury for a few days," said Dave. "The doctors are hopeful that he will be able to recover, but for now, he's unable to walk."

For a split second I felt sorry for Brendan, but then I remembered what he had done to Frank and Carole. They never had an opportunity to recover.

I was horrified. Poor Nate would never get his flash drive or his money back.

Lucy piped up to say that the day they arrived she had seen a boat coming across the lake to the inn's dock in the middle of the night. She hadn't given it much thought at the time. It had departed almost immediately.

Dad assured her it was probably someone fishing.

But that reminded me of the earring Twinkletoes had found. I looked at Phoebe, who sat at the next table. "Did you lose an earring?" I asked.

She gasped. "Did you find my snowman earring? I was crushed when I lost it. Honestly, it's so easy to lose things camping."

"Twinkletoes found it in the boat docked near your tent."

I could see the realization dawning on Josh's face. "That's how Radar got to the inn. You took him there."

Phoebe swiped her hand in the air. "He was fine. I had to do that to throw Brendan off our location."

"So it was Brendan you were running from the whole time?" I asked.

She looked as though she realized she had opened a can of worms. "I wasn't certain."

Dave massaged his forehead. "You don't have to lie, Phoebe. Brendan told us that you two hatched the plot together, but you double-crossed him and stole the flash drive on your own. You knew perfectly well that Brendan would come after you."

"Why couldn't you be honest with me?" asked Josh.

I expected Phoebe to answer him, but she turned to me and asked, "Could we go up to your apartment to get my earring? They're designer. Four figures!"

I was repulsed. She cared more about an earring than she did about Josh or Radar. It was clear that she had used Josh. I was glad that he had finally realized it. I certainly didn't trust her. Not even to go up to my apartment with me.

Josh must have sensed my reluctance. "You stay here, *Phoebe*." He nearly spat her name.

The two of us went inside and used the back stairs to my apartment. Josh opened the French doors to my terrace and walked out onto it, while I hurried into my bedroom to collect the earring.

I heard a creak as my walk-in closet door opened.

I held my breath and remained motionless as Phoebe entered the closet. Tiptoeing, I positioned myself so that I could see her.

Phoebe pulled out a small evening purse that I rarely used. She snapped it open and withdrew a white and pink flash drive in the shape of a paw.

I couldn't believe that it had been in my apartment all along. At least since the only other time she had been in my place, right before she took off, with Josh behind her.

When she left the closet, I confronted her. "Hand it over."

"I don't know what you're talking about."

"I think you do." Keeping my eyes on her, I yelled, "Josh!"

He ran to us.

"She didn't want her earring. Phoebe hid the flash drive in one of my purses. She just collected it."

Josh's mouth fell open. "You are worse than I imagined. I've been dealing with the reality of who you are, but this is inconceivable. Give Holly the flash drive."

She tried to bolt past Josh, but he blocked her and grabbed her wrist. "It's not in her hand, check her pockets."

She attempted to wrest loose, but I could see the slight bulge in her pocket and pulled it out. She stopped fighting Josh. In a sweet voice, she said, "I need to give it back to Nate."

I laughed aloud. "We're not that stupid. Here's your earring."

Phoebe glared at me. But the rest of the way down the stairs, she kissed up to Josh in her little-girl voice. I hoped she would leave Wagtail soon.

When I returned to the terrace, Holmes found me right away. "Everything okay?"

"It is now."

He wrapped his arm around me.

Poor Dave had fallen asleep.

Shelley was in the process of eating his dessert. "He finally asked me out."

"No kidding? When did that happen?"

"When we were in the hospital. He was so sweet. He stayed by my side until they made him go back to his room."

I gazed around. It had been a very long time since I was surrounded by family.

Oma and Lucy were laughing about something.

Josh and Phoebe were out on the lawn. I could hear her begging, but I was fairly certain that he was done with her.

My father placed his hand over my mother's. A look passed between them. One I remembered from my childhood, before their marriage fell apart. A look of tenderness and love.

But the truth was that they were all family to me. Mr. Huckle was like a wise uncle, Shelley was the sister I confided in, Zelda the fun cousin. At the Sugar Maple Inn, we were all family.

The next morning my phone rang. It was the wee hours, and the sky didn't yet show the first streaks of light. Casey whispered, "You better come down here."

I pulled on jeans and a top and tried not to wake Lucy, who was sleeping in my living room. We had shuffled family around to accommodate everyone. Trixie and Twinkletoes yawned but followed me down the stairs anyway. Two cops waited for me in the lobby. "Hi. Holly Miller. How can I help you?"

"We're here to arrest Phoebe Philips."

"But I thought you couldn't hold her?"

"We can now. We got word this morning that the French

have started extradition proceedings. She's a flight risk, so we're trying to get her before she leaves Wagtail."

I nodded. "I hope you have people stationed outside."

One of the cops nodded. "I tackled her after she jumped through that window. We know she's clever."

"Follow me. I'll get the master key."

One of the officers remained in the lobby and the other one walked down the hallway toward the registration lobby with me. Trixie and Twinkletoes ran ahead but stopped abruptly at one of the tall windows in the hallway. Both of them looked up.

Naturally, the officer and I looked up, too. Something dangled outside the building. It was just visible at the very top of the window.

The officer spoke into a radio. "Stevens, can you see something on the front of the building, west side?"

The radio squawked. "Eyes on the subject. Looks like she's coming right to us."

Shoe soles appeared at the top of the window next. Two officers were barely visible on the ground in the darkness.

Slowly, legs clad in jeans appeared, then a black T-shirt, and finally, Phoebe hung onto something with her hands over her head as she looked straight at us.

It might have been cruel of me, but she *had* caused a lot of trouble and gotten me up extremely early, so I waved at her and smiled. At that point, she planted her feet against the window and tried to climb back up, but she didn't have the strength to do it and fell to the ground, right at the feet of a cluster of police officers.

Trixie, Twinkletoes, and I joined the police outside. They handcuffed Dana, who bothered to throw a nasty look at me. As the police were taking her away, Cook and Amelia arrived, and the day officially began at the Sugar Maple Inn. As usual, Judy Davis was one of the first guests up and about. She joined Mr. Huckle and me at a table. Over

Cook's breakfast special, chocolate-filled French toast, I filled them in on everything that had happened.

Judy shook her head. "I can't believe that nice man, Brendan, was the killer. I sat right here and chatted with him over breakfast!"

"I'm very sorry about that."

"Don't be. You didn't know. And neither did I. He was so polite and sweet to my cats." A smile appeared on her face. "My husband is arriving today for the weekend. I can't wait to tell him the whole story!"

After breakfast, I texted Nate to ask if I could see him. He told me where he was staying, so Trixie, Twinkletoes, and I hopped on a golf cart and drove up the mountain. His rental home was two stories of glass. I rang the doorbell.

He opened the door. Luggage waited in the foyer.

"You're leaving?"

He shrugged. "I have to get back to work. I heard Phoebe is out of jail and that she was on the run from her boyfriend who wanted my flash drive."

"That about sums it up. Except that she was arrested again this morning and it looks like she will be extradited to France. I brought you something." I held the flash drive out to him.

"Ha ha," he said without mirth. "I don't think I'll be using those anymore. But thanks for the thought."

"I think this is the real one."

"Is this a joke?"

I shook my head.

He seized it and pulled a laptop out of his luggage. He plugged in the flash drive, did a little bit of typing, and files appeared on the screen. Nate turned around and hugged me. "I can't believe this. Where was it?"

"I'm embarrassed to admit that Phoebe hid it in my closet. It was there all along."

"I should give you a reward. How much is fair?"

"I don't want a reward. I just wanted to be sure it went back to its rightful owner."

One week later, Josh came running into the reception lobby. "What did you do?"

"I don't know what you're talking about."

"My company, Fly Me Home, just received a donation of a million dollars in your name for the rescue of cats and dogs. I'm to pick them up and bring them back to Wagtail for medical treatment and rehoming."

It took me a moment. At first I thought it must be a mistake, but then I realized that it was Nate's way of thanking me.

Recipes

❁ ❁ ❁

One of my dogs suffered from severe food allergies that did not allow him to eat commercial dog food. Consequently, I learned to cook for my dogs and have done so for many years. Consult your veterinarian if you want to switch your dog to home-cooked food. It's not as difficult as one might think. Keep in mind that, like children, dogs need a balanced diet, not just a hamburger. Any changes to your dog's diet should be made gradually so your dog's stomach can adjust.

Chocolate, alcohol, caffeine, fatty foods, grapes, raisins, macadamia nuts, onions and garlic, xylitol (also known as birch sugar), and unbaked dough can be toxic (and even deadly) to dogs. For more information about foods your dog can and cannot eat, consult the American Kennel Club website at https://www.akc.org/expert-advice/nutrition/human-foods-dogs-can-and-cant-eat/.

Do not feed your dog foods that have been seasoned. It's best to use plain food without additives or seasonings. Please read the labels carefully.

If you suspect your dog may have eaten something that will cause illness, call your veterinarian or the Animal Poison Control Center's 24-hour hotline at (888) 426-4435.

❧

Deviled Eggs

For people, NOT for dogs.

Makes 24 deviled eggs.
For a bigger crowd, double the quantity.

12 large eggs
½ cup mayonnaise
4 teaspoons Dijon or yellow mustard
Salt and pepper to taste
Paprika

Krista's note: There are an amazing number of slight variations in deviled egg recipes. I think this is largely because mustard varies greatly. I recommend using your favorite mustard because that will likely impart the flavor and amount of tang that you prefer. In my fridge right now, I have two jars of Dijon mustard. One is very mild and pleasant. The other one is so sharp that I would have to use a quarter of the amount of mustard in this recipe! So when making this, I recommend testing the flavor as you go. Also, buy your eggs in advance if you can. Older eggs peel better than fresh eggs.

Place the eggs in a pot in a single layer. Add water to one inch above the eggs. Bring the water to a boil. Remove the pot from the heat and cover. Let stand for 10–12 minutes. Meanwhile, fill a large bowl with water and ice cubes. When the 10–12 minutes are up, ladle the eggs into the icy water. When they have cooled, remove them and pat dry. You can do this step a day in advance if you like. Be sure to refrigerate the cooked eggs.

    Peel the eggs and slice each one in half. Remove the yolks and place them in a food processor, mixer, or blender (Note: You can mix the ingredients by hand with a fork. However, I much prefer the silky results from a high-speed blending device.) Add 1/4 cup mayonnaise and 2 teaspoons mustard and combine. Taste. Add the remaining 1/4 cup mayonnaise and 2 teaspoons mustard (or reduce or increase to your taste), salt, and pepper. Mix well. Place in an icing bag with a large round or open star icing tip. Fill the egg whites with the egg yolk mixture. Sprinkle with paprika.

🐾

Nell's Bellinis

NOT for dogs.

1 mango
3 ripe peaches
1 bottle sparkling wine

Peel the mango and the peaches and remove the pits. Place the fruit in a food processor or powerful blender and purée. Spoon the purée into champagne flutes about ⅓ full. Fill with sparkling wine.

🐾

Crostini with Prosciutto and Salmon

NOT for dogs.

This is a recipe you can have fun with.
Keep it simple and use flavors that you like.
There are no rules!

1 loaf ciabatta bread or baguette

Extra virgin olive oil
Goat cheese
Prosciutto
Honey
Chopped parsley
Freshly ground black pepper
Ricotta cheese or cream cheese
Smoked salmon
Fresh dill (optional)

Preheat the oven to 375°F. Line a baking sheet with parchment paper. Slice the bread. Brush each slice with olive oil on both sides. Bake 8–10 minutes. Remove from the oven and top with your favorites.

For prosciutto:

Spread goat cheese on the bread. Top with prosciutto. Drizzle with a little bit of honey and garnish with a sprinkle of chopped parsley and a twist of freshly ground black pepper.

For salmon:

Spread ricotta or cream cheese on the bread. Top with sliced smoked salmon. Garnish with a sprig of fresh dill or a twist of freshly ground black pepper.

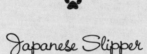

Japanese Slipper

NOT for dogs.

Midori
Cointreau
Fresh lemon juice
Honeydew melon slices (optional)

Place equal amounts of Midori, Cointreau, and fresh lemon juice into a shaker filled with ice. Shake and pour into a cocktail or martini glass. Garnish with a small slice of honeydew melon (if using).

Spring Salad with Maple-Balsamic Vinaigrette

NOT for dogs.

Asparagus spears
Extra virgin olive oil
Garlic powder
Salt and pepper
Mixed spring greens
Walnuts
Red onion
Apple or pear

Preheat oven to 400°F. Wash the asparagus and snap off the tough bottom ends. Line a baking sheet with aluminum foil and spread the asparagus spears on it. Drizzle with olive oil. Sprinkle with garlic powder, salt, and pepper. Using your hands, roll the asparagus back and forth lightly to spread the seasonings. Roast 15–20 minutes, depending on the thickness of the asparagus.

Place the mixed spring greens in a large salad bowl. Slice the asparagus into bite-size pieces. Chop the walnuts and scatter them over the salad. Slice the onion into rings and add them to the salad. Peel the apple or pear, remove the core, and cut into bite-size chunks. Toss the salad with Maple-Balsamic Vinaigrette.

Maple-Balsamic Vinaigrette

⅓ cup extra virgin olive oil
⅓ cup balsamic vinegar
2 tablespoons maple syrup
2 tablespoons Dijon mustard
Salt and pepper to taste

Combine all the ingredients in a small bowl and whisk together.

Ocean Delight

For dogs.

1 cup spinach leaves
2 carrots
1 cup (cooked) plain quinoa
2 cups (cooked) macaroni
1 pound fresh cod

Place the spinach in a small pot with 1 cup water and cook over medium heat until limp. Peel the carrots and slice them into rounds. Place the carrots in a pot with enough water to cover them and cook until tender. Prepare the quinoa and macaroni according to the package directions.

Preheat oven to 400°F. Line a baking sheet with parchment paper. Place the cod on the parchment paper and roast it for 20 minutes.

Break the cod into small flakes, removing any bones, and place it in a bowl. Chop the cooked spinach and add it to the fish. Add the carrots, one cup of cooked quinoa, and two cups of cooked macaroni. Add ½ cup water and mix everything together. Be sure it's not too hot! Serve at room temperature.

Peanut Butter–Apple Dog Treats

Makes about 40 cookies.

To be used as treats only. They are not a meal.

Do not use peanut butter that contains **xylitol**. It is deadly to dogs.

Please remember that peanut butter is rich, so don't give your dog too many!

½ cup peanut butter (check the label and do
   NOT** use if it contains* **xylitol)*
1 large egg
½ cup whole-grain rolled oats
½ cup all-purpose flour
1 cup peeled, diced apple
   (about 1 medium apple)

Preheat oven to 350°F. Line a baking sheet with parchment paper.

Place the peanut butter and the egg in a mixing bowl. Mix thoroughly. Add the rolled oats and flour and mix. Add the diced apple and mix one last time. Scoop a little bit of the dough into your hands and roll it into a 1-inch ball. Place it on the parchment paper and flatten to about ¼-inch thick. Repeat with the remaining dough.

Bake for 15–18 minutes. The cookies should be crunchy. Store the cooled cookies in the refrigerator. You can also freeze them, with parchment paper between layers. Be sure to let them thaw before serving.

Acknowledgments

I feel incredibly lucky to have written nine books about Wagtail and for that, I owe heartfelt thanks to my readers. I am overjoyed that you continue to love Wagtail, Holly, Oma, Trixie, and Twinkletoes, and that you come back for more!

Special thanks go to my editor, Michelle Vega, who is always so kind and enthusiastic. I must mention the artist of my covers, Mary Ann Lasher, who gave Twinkletoes such a wonderful expression on this cover.

Although writing is a solitary endeavor, I know that my circle of friends is only an email away. Some days I feel like they're right here with me. Thank you for always being there, Ginger Bolton, Allison Brook, Laurie Cass, Peg Cochran, Kaye George, and Daryl Wood Gerber.

My dear friends Susan Erba, Betsy Strickland, and Amy Wheeler are wonderful and haven't tired yet of sending me ideas for books and strange things they find on the Internet.

I cannot omit my agent, Jessica Faust, who encourages me every step of the way, even when I have new ideas. She's simply the best!

I will add one more person without naming him. I was contacted by a gentleman who asked if I could use his wife's name as a character's name. He has to be the most thoughtful husband ever! Of course, I have never met her, so the character is solely the product of my imagination to fit the story. I hope they will both be pleased.

Ready to find
your next great read?

Let us help.

Visit prh.com/nextread

Penguin
Random
House